THE RESURRECTION
of REY PESCADOR

THE RESURRECTION
of REY PESCADOR

ALFRED CEDENO

THE GENIUS BRIGADE
PUBLISHING COMPANY

THE GENIUS BRIGADE PUBLISHING COMPANY

The Resurrection of Rey Pescador

Copyright © 2016 by Alfred Cedeno

ISBN-10: 1519295480

ISBN-13: 978-1519295484

Scripture used from KJV Bible.

Printed in the United States of America

First Edition: July 2014
14   1 2   1 11 0   9   8   7   6   5   4   3   2 1

TO:

Marta, my wife

A special thanks to the original brigade of geniuses who built this world with me: Lane, Jarrett, Drew, Jon, and Kolby. Gentlemen, this universe is ours until our metal hearts stop ticking.

As kingfishers catch fire, dragonflies dráw fláme;
As tumbled over rim in roundy wells
Stones ring; like each tucked string tells, each hung bell's Bow swung finds
tongue to fling out broad its name;
Each mortal thing does one thing and the same:

GERARD MANLEY HOPKINS

I've heard of pious men
And I've heard of dirty fiends
But you don't often hear
Of us ones in between.

I've heard of creatures
Who eat their babies;
I wonder if they stop
To think about the taste.

SPENCER KRUG
"Us Ones In Between

PROLOGUE

21 June 2037
Pescador Palace Hotel and Lodge
26 N. Main Street
Lone Pine, California

Dear Rebecca,

Sid Cutler has stopped my heart three times. I always hoped he'd finish the job.

Maybe that isn't how I should start a letter, but after being polite and cautious to you for a lifetime, I'm ready to tell you the truth.

The first time Cutler stopped my heart was that most ordinary of procedures just after my birth. The second was on a bridge in Chicago—we'll get to that later—and the third was to silence me from telling you Rey's story—a story that neither Sid Cutler nor I ever wanted told. It's probably the only thing we agree on.

Rebecca, each sentence I write is evidence of my serendipitous survival: my heart still ticks and ticks. It's evidence that there is a battle over my life and the stories I know.

More importantly, it's evidence that I'm sorry.

Certainly you remember Cutler's third attempt on my life better than me. It was July of 2021, the evening after we drove Christian to a Church in Portage Park where a white bus that said "North Side Bible Chapel" would take him to a summer camp in Wisconsin. Do you remember how he walked quietly—with that classic Pescador swagger—to his seat on the bus where he glanced at us only briefly through the half window? His tanned, long face, red on his cheeks from too much time in the Chicago Park District pools, glowed; his lips curled into a half smile; and his dark eyes, like those of his father, signaled with absurd arrogance that this was a journey fate had destined.

You cried a little as the white bus left our vision. All of the mothers cried. But I had seen that look on another face. I couldn't cry because I already know how that story ends.

There we were; you and I alone in the Hyde Park house. We drank red wine on the green couch in the front room and laughed about the past. Even the house told stories, reminding us of the time I pushed Rey from the porch to the front room, courtesy of the window.

A heat wave rested on the city. The Chianti roasted our blood.

You cried about Christian "growing up too fast" and worried about him sleeping in a boiling cabin 100 miles north. So I told you about Rey and me during our childhood summers, about how I never had air-conditioning, and how I slept on the ground to stay cool. Of course, when Rey was over, he never let me sleep—there were tales to be told, he would always say. You looked at me that night. You were sad. "David," you said. "There still are."

I knew the story you wanted to hear, but first I told the wild stories of Rey's youth: rickshaw races down Michigan Avenue, gambling with billionaires, live TV pranks, pseudo-scientific attempts to time travel, to teleport, or to make someone fall in love with someone else. I am not sure if you believed those stories. The world of the Genius Brigade was fantastic: filled with chivalry, pipe organs, and sacraments; and equally robot fights and rocket ships. But whether you believed them or not, I knew that you still loved the idea of Rey Pescador in all of his anachronistic beauty.

You placed your head on my shoulder.

I loosened my collar and breathed deeply to smell your hair.

You pulled your legs onto the couch cushion.

I rested my feet on the coffee table.

You folded your hands out of my reach.

I loosened my collar more. I thought of finally taking it off. Then in the middle of my stories you asked about Rey's resurrection, about the journey to the mountain. You wanted me to paint a picture of the landscape, the beauty of the granite, to tell you about this mountain so far away from everything you've known.

I tried to change the subject. I had never told this story before. But there, close enough to smell your shampoo, I couldn't say no, so I stalled in silence.

You sat up and looked at me, with your bright eyes and long, slender face pleading that I tell you everything.

"Well, I don't really want to," I started. "I never have, but it's hard to say no. Where do I start?"

I'll never forget your response. "Where should you start? At the bottom of the mountain, of course."

"All right, here it goes, but I have to warn you it's not short."

"Then run to the corner and get another bottle of wine. We're out."

How could I disagree? It would certainly help lubricate my memory.

It wasn't any cooler outside. The city of Chicago sang to the tune of cicadas and three million ticking hearts. I never thought I'd miss that noise, but I do now.

It must have been a sight: David Rosario, middle-aged pseudo-celebrity priest, almost sprinting past the bungalows, around a corner to a convenient store in full clerical collar on a Saturday night. I imagined people wondering why I ran. Hopefully, they couldn't tell that it was for a woman. But it's hard to imagine men running for many other things.

In the store a few kids surveyed the chocolate at the counter. Chocolate was a good idea. Chocolate, wine, and stories of Rey: just what every woman wanted. The clerk greeted me as buddy, like he always did. I passed my customary bargain wine for something worthy of a tall tale. It was eerie. I swear the lights flickered, but admittedly the rest of this memory is surreal and dubious.

Lights flickered; a man in a white fedora opened the door; and sirens boomed through the humid air.

It felt like the old days when terror warnings shouted that death was near to any who didn't seek shelter. I even waited for the deafening announcement throughout the city. ATTENTION: Everyone report to the nearest heart kit and plug your hearts in now. But I knew there were no more terrorists.

I paid in haste, and ran back to the house. At the bottom of the steps, between the maple and oak trees, in the full heat of summer, I collected my breath and listened to the steady machine inside of me. It was four steps up the porch. I stopped on the third, symbolically remembering that first time you visited my home. I looked into the window. You should have closed the blinds. Anyone could see you, well, anyone who was standing on the third step looking in the window.

Your legs were right angles on the couch. You were asleep. I've never wanted to be with you so badly. The whole sky was pressing down on me. I guess it technically always was, but the wine exposed gravity's influence. I'm sure in that very moment thousands of pounds of air were pressing on me and making sure that I remained outside while you slept on the couch. I fought it with all my might. Studying your legs under the blanket, I found the nerve I never had and climbed the final step. I imagined touching your ankle and moving my hand upward. Still asleep you would stir.

The world spun faster than I could stabilize. I stumbled then collected myself.

A car slowed in the street behind me. Someone was watching. I turned to see a black Cadillac drive away. It could not be him, I thought. It must be just another black car in a big city. With all my strength, I pushed myself toward the door and collapsed.

Immediately, my chest was silent.

Silent.

My heart had stopped.

How long was it before you pushed the door open to a sea of blood and wine? For me it was ages staring at the roof of the porch, not noticing the cobwebs or seeing the neighbors run to my aid. In fact, I saw nothing for a long time. Nothing but the face of Sid Cutler, the spherical genius who created my robotic heart. I blamed him for keeping me outside of the house. I still do. He did this. I tried to shout that he was silencing me from telling you about Rey, but I feared it would end my life. Also, I couldn't speak.

Fear Sid, I remembered the advice from a lifetime before. Fear Sid.

Kneeling beside me on the chipping paint of the porch, you pulled off my collar and unbuttoned my shirt. I had always wanted you to do that, but in a different context, I guess. At the top of my scar, you peeled away the patch for the outlet and shouted to a passerby to call an ambulance and get a heart kit. Of course, we had no heart kit. Muffled voices shouted, "Father David!" and "Plug him in already."

Did the world keep spinning too fast? Ages passed again, and all I saw was you. I heard nothing. You were there looking into my eyes. All I saw was your gray blue irises, you hair curling toward me.

God, just let me live. It was certainly the first time I had prayed that. Be careful what you pray for, I guess. I promised to myself that I would tell you the story once I woke up. I would find and kill Sid Cutler. I would marry you.

Of course, it was a lie that I had told myself. All men of inaction tell lies to themselves. The problem with people like me who remain in the recesses of the mind is not that we hate the physical. It is that we love it too much to act on it.

I blacked out.

When I awoke, I was mute in a hospital bed again. You were there in the harsh fluorescent light. You hugged me. Your breath warmed my neck even more. But all I could feel was surprising lightness of my mortality. I am mortal. It was a relief. I will die regardless of how efficient each ounce of metal in my chest is.

Finally noticing you, I concluded that in this mortal life I deserved some mortal sin. I promised to myself again to love you in a way that Rey never did. Rey loved the idea of you: the girl from the neighborhood—the simple, beautiful girl, who could ground him to something real. But I could love more than the idea. I could love the person, the body, the face, hair, and voice. I could love you. But before I could defrock myself, I fell into a morphine sleep and awoke in an empty room. You know the rest of that story.

Rebecca, now that I am back here, at the mountain again, alone, I will write to you all of the words that I couldn't speak about Rey and L.J. and me. I will write them as Rey would. I will include colors and details and archetypes and femme fatales galore. I'll throw in robot fights and trips to hell if I can. After all, Rey was fantastic.

As I've been planning to commence this journey again, I wasn't sure exactly where to start until I remembered your advice in Chicago.

So now I know to start in Lake Michigan, AD 2000, with a woman and a drink.

I am writing these letters in hopes that you forgive us, Rey and me, and in hopes that you will join me here soon.

I will start, right here, right now, in the water at the bottom of the proverbial mountain, of course.

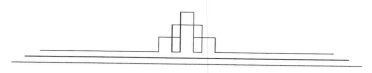

REY'S ORIGINAL SIN MYTH

CH 1

AUGUST 2000

Lub-Dub-Lub-Dub
Tick-Tick-Tick

The penultimate human heart was still beating on a 20-million-dollar yacht, under the half-buttoned oxford of Rey Pescador who was still very alive. Lub-dub.

His heart could attest. Lub-dub.

He was my cousin, my enemy, my best friend, and as I think about him now, decades later, he was the only real man that I have ever met. I can imagine it—lub-dub—the rhythm of his human heart, that ancient, meat technology. I sense its unsteady pulse. Lub-Dub. And I wonder if it still moves to that syncopated beat.

Rey watched the water steal the light of the moon, absorbing it into its black abyss. All one body, it crested and dipped simultaneously again and again: a million different waves. At its crests, it showed the string of light from the moon. In its valleys, Rey only saw darkness.

A single beam reflected the moon and separated the lake into two: east and west, left and right. Lub-dub. To his left the skyline of Chicago dimly glowed through the haze of about fifty nautical miles and billions of molecules of water and air. To his right sat the dunes that were, in his mind, at least, the foundation of Michigan and The East. Here he was free: able to swim to either shore or simply sink into the ship's great room where women and men danced to celebrate his human heart (although, they certainly knew nothing of his heart at this point). They only knew that he was the new king of the spoken word, the written word, and any other type of word. They knew that it was the biggest

13

party the Midwest had seen in a year, and that Sid Cutler had personally invited them.

If only I was there. If I was there and knew the significance of that water, I would have acted as priest and tied Rey to the ship's mast—metaphorically, at least. The splinters would have drained his blood: a small sacrifice to appease God's wrath. He would have died then and there without countless sins and stories.

If I had filled his ears with wax, he would have survived. If I had placed pins in his eyes, he would not have seen her and would have never dived into those moonlit waves. If I had never taught him to swim, he would be here, on this planet, now.

But I wasn't there. I wasn't invited.

Rey Pescador was perched on a rail on the starboard side of a yacht filled with loosened bow ties and short dresses, each bought and paid for—not necessarily directly—by that fat orb Sid Cutler. Earlier that month, Rey sat in a leather office chair in some anteroom amidst Cutler's vast Chicago headquarters, watching harried assistants and managers and executives skitter from room to room holding sheets of paper. Fifty floors in the sky, the sun shone through a magnificent window, which the workers ignored in their movement of paper. The corporation puzzled Rey as much as cell division had in Freshman Biology class a few years prior, and the business itself seemed a type of organ or system with each cell moving with preternatural purpose. The 18-year-old up-and-coming superstar already believed these people were innately less important than him because they sold out for a corporate life. Now he believed that he was the enzyme catalyzing all of their movement. Just before he put pen to paper to approve his first book for publication, the enormous mogul sauntered passed the glass and eclipsed the light from the window. Surprised to see Rey, he turned from the executive with whom he was speaking and approached the poet.

"So you're back from your travels to our southern neighbors? Have you brought me anything?" Cutler asked.

"A book to publish. It's called *Nepenthe Incantations at the Fountain of Youth.*"

"I knew you had the gift, kid. I'm proud of you. We need to celebrate. Listen, Don, get in here," Cutler shouted to the executive outside the doorway who was now speaking on a phone.

"Don, get Rey the keys to Mona Lisa. I want him to use her this fall."

"What is Mona Lisa?" Rey asked.

"My yacht on Lake Michigan. I want you to have a taste of your future, Rey. You couldn't matter more to this organization."

"I don't know what to say."

"You better always know what to say, that's why I'm paying you. Now, listen, call Don and have him set up a release party on the yacht. I'll come. And tell Don to bring the new singer. He'll know who I'm talking about."

"Thanks again, Mr. Cutler."

"Call me Sid."

"Thanks, Sid."

Now, the day that Rey's first book, *Nepenthe Incantations at the Fountain of Youth* was released, Cutler threw Rey the first A-list party of his life, and for the first time in his life Rey shied away from the crowd. Maybe he wasn't comfortable yet with praise, though I kind of doubt that. Either way, he was alone on the deck for a while until the sublime intonations of the singer's voice pulled him increasingly closer to the dance floor: close enough to see the dresses twist in the artificial light. The flesh of his heart contracted harder at the sound and the sight until he looked at the water of the lake one last time before determining he might have to enter the part in triumph. That voice, he never stopped talking about it, was deep and jazzy. He saw his face on the brass rail in front of him. His hair was short then. He was thin. His body still vibrant, but his face the exact face that you remember from when you met him ten years later.

He stepped toward the dance floor, but the song ended. The singer stopped. So Rey left the trance and returned to the brass rail and the lake

The singer's feet, gently as a bird's song, pressed heels against the teak behind him. In his mind she had flown from some pantheon and landed on that deck at that moment to make him a man—or something absurd like that. "Mr. Pescador," she sang. He loved the way she sang his name like that. Mr. Pescador. He wasn't sure that anyone had called him that before.

"Call me Rey."

"Well, Mr. Pescador, you should be dancing. It's your party. People might think you are rude."

"I don't dance much."

"What are you looking at?"

"The water, the waves, the island."

"How far do you think it is?" she asked.

"Well, from my experience, which is more extensive than most my age, islands are usually farther than you think. Some sort of optical illusion or something."

"Do you think you could swim there?"

"Yes."

They looked at the water, until Rey realized that he could look at the singer. He could forget everything else and look at her body against the waves and wind and moonlight. He could look at her face, at her dress. She was now leaning against the brass rail. Her arm just inches from his. "Before our swim, let's have a drink," she said. "Try this."

"I have a drink already."

"Not this type."

"I've really had enough. Too much maybe."

He still watched the light in the water. She moved closer. Her breath warmed the back of his neck. Her arm reached around him with a wine glass filled with burgundy liquid.

"Drink," she said. He faced her. She wore white. A white dress; the cotton shook in the breeze. It rose. It fell. It moved to heaven.

"What type of wine is that?"

"It isn't wine. It is whisky. Lilac Whiskey."

"What does it taste like?"

She kissed him. It was a lovely liqueur.

While it is almost impossible for me to believe Rey's coyness in his version of this story, the fact that he insisted it, makes me certain that it must be true. He disclosed to me months later that while he had looked at the water a tangible loneliness had gripped him. He could only think about a woman he had met two months before, who had inspired his book of poems. Though he had no intention of seeing her again, he felt that his melancholy would somehow honor her. Yet, the singer extracted his malaise: the idea of her voice, her lightness of step, and her claim about swimming to the island appealed to his mythical sensibility. The air of summer had changed with the leaves. This woman gained his attention once and for all with a single sentence.

"Well, I'm swimming to that damn island," she said.

She took off her shoes and handed them to Rey, then sat on the railing facing him. She pulled him close to her with her legs. In that moment he loved everything that she represented. He loved her face. Over the course of the next decade he would never forget her face or her voice. But most of all the scent of Lilac Whiskey on her breath captivated him.

She laughed then stood on the railing. She was thinner than he first thought; maybe too thin for his taste. Her legs were as soft as her voice. She stood, lifted her arms into the sky, and then jumped backwards, gracefully emerging into the water, first arms, then head, then chest, then legs. Her shoes in his hands, he stared into the darkness. Moonlight reflected over all of the water, but he only saw that single straight line on the waves from which she emerged again. Intoxicated by the night, he climbed the railing and took off his shoes. She called to him.

"Are you going to follow me, or what?"

"The only thing that could stop me is if I was tied to this ship."

"Well, I don't see anyone ready to do that. Not here. Not now."

He watched her in the water. In the rise and fall of waves, the white dress clung the surface. She opened the bottle and drank. She sang "Mr. Pescador, Mr. Pescador" over and over until he flew from the ship into Lake Michigan. He swam twenty feet below her and saw the void of light that her body left.

Each time Rey told me this story, he called her something different, but my favorite was when he said, "She was a dark circle, a string of primordial proteins." Rey called himself lightning suspended between earth and sky, suspended by the poles of gravity, and the moon.

The electrons of a wet, white dress broke his stasis. As he

rose, he opened his mouth and drank. He swam to the surface. He reached the bottle: it was empty. It sunk. He kissed her and tasted the vapors of the Lilac Whiskey.

Its flavor never left his mind.

THE KILL SWITCH

CH **2**

At 20 years old Sid Cutler had given Rey Pescador a yacht, a muse, a book, a publicist, and fame beyond belief. All he ever gave me was a bottle of Lilac Whiskey and a tin heart (all right it probably isn't tin, but I'm no metallurgist).   The worst part of my metal heart is the kill switch, both the switch itself and the name. I understand that the history of kill switches throughout technologies made "kill switch" a logical choice for any switch that turns something off, but when the Robotic Heart Campaign [RHC] introduced the idea of a kill switch, you would think people would have reacted more vehemently considering what exactly it was killing. I guess with the fear of the SCR epidemic and the prospect that the largest generation America had ever known would be forced to live on circuit boards for decades, the reality of a formal or informal kill switch made the transition to the RHC's kill switch natural. But still, the name should have been changed. That's the problem with placing scientists in charge of language.

On my worst days, when I forget why I am telling you these stories, or when I have no hope that you will come here with me, or that Christian will learn how to live with this machine in him any better than I did, all I can think about is the kill switch and the simplicity of hitching a ride to Lone Pine Medical Center and asking an ER nurse to plug me in to end my stay.

I won't do it, I promise.

I don't want to hurt you like that again. Also, I have one final plan to make it home. But I will get to all of that.

Last night I slept in the hotel. As much as I like roughing it in the backcountry, I can't resist a night of luxury while I write and wait. This morning as I made coffee, I regained the hope of death and resurrection. My fingers became numb, and I thought the ticking had stopped. I thought the rhythm I heard was merely the coffee pot dripping. The slow drip mirrors my artificial heart. One-two, one-two, tick-tick, tick-tick. They say that our natural hearts said lub-dub or tun-tun en Espanol or something like that. What an absurd sound, soft around the edges, deep burgundy and vulnerable. Flesh and blood hearts, rotten to the core, cursed. Lord have mercy. And now, steel and blood coincide from birth to 150 years at least. Lord have mercy.

These organic hearts, were they flesh like the meat at the deli, like a bull's heart, so broad and real, so vulnerable to bullets or spears or knives? Were they edible after roasted over a stake in the deepest equatorial jungle? I suppose people just thought an artificial heart was more efficient. I can drink my coffee all day and never worry about my blood pressure, my heart beating too much or too hard or too fast. But I can't die unless I cut back the scar tissue, plug in a chord, and enter "run.uninstall.exe." Suicide is the only way to heaven: a Catholic priest's ultimate catch-22.

Rey told me that before the RHC humans had fight or flight responses, and when nervous their heart would beat more quickly. He said he felt it daily, even when talking with beautiful women. I used to look at you in the café and never worry about the arteries expanding to the point where my pores opened. I spoke without fear that my sympathetic response would reveal my secret love for you. But even with these modern conveniences, I sometimes wonder—what if. What if, I could hear the lub-dub of my own heart once, it could lull me to sleep, something that the tick-tick, tick-tick of RHC titanium could never do.

Why do I care so much about these robotic hearts? People have asked me, and I rant about theology and the body and mortality, maybe about heaven. But really, it is more about Rey than anything. You probably suspected that I envied him. I have at times, but I never envied the one night stands and fame and fortune—at least, I didn't envy them as much as his heart. Writing it down sounds absurd, but well, I guess it is. The first vivid memory of my childhood was meeting Rey Pescador and learning about his heart. It changed what would have otherwise been a normal life. That sort of catalyzing power is something to envy.

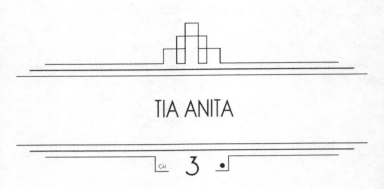

TIA ANITA

CH 3

OCTOBER 1981

In Irish Chicago, October leaves fall and cover the alleys and front steps and grass until all you can see is yellow and orange and golden brown. Do you remember it? Those fall days as a child when we South Side kids helped our parents rake the leaves in giant piles and ached nostalgically for an agrarian life that neither our parents nor we knew, nor ever would. We lived there just a few blocks from your childhood home, among your kin whom my father—enlightened as he was—called "potato eaters." That is to say that relatively early on I was the brown kid at a white and red parochial school who, according to some, was ruining the church and the neighborhood.

I don't like to talk about it, and I certainly don't blame you or your generation. After all, Rebecca, you saved me literally and figuratively. I only mention all this because it is partly why I clung to the absurdity of the Genius Brigade.

Our old bungalow was blocks away from St. Xavier's campus. When I turned six, my mother let me ride my bike past the Presbyterian Church and through the neighborhood to the university. I road fast through the campus grass dodging trees and students until I found the only body of water around. A small hill accelerated me to Lake Marion, and by the time I hit the bottom, it felt like I was going one hundred miles an hour. I miss the rides.

I was cruising around the lake that morning collecting leaves for a school project. My first grade teacher, Sister Patrice,

22

expected us to be "scholars in the long tradition of Catholic greats." She said that to her first grade class almost daily. I bought it. She once made me stand on a desk and state, "I am a mighty Catholic thinker: I stand on the shoulders of saints and giants." That day, I was a child with life ahead of me, believing that statement, believing that I could create something powerful. I guess I still do.

I rode my bike around the lagoon at least a dozen times surveying the trees for a leaf that was truly extraordinary. I don't know what I expected to find, but the maples and oak and ash of my neighborhood seemed unfit for the one Holy Church of the Almighty Creator of the Universe. My final lap for the day, I noticed something in the water. Originally, I thought it was a leaf: a leaf as brilliant orange as a dreamsicle that withstood the toxic water of the lagoon. But as I drifted closer, I saw that it was another bottom-feeding carp. There were dozens there. They terrified me, to tell you the truth. Then, in a moment of uncharacteristic imbalance, I drifted too close to the water and fell into the dirty lagoon. I climbed out quickly, though retrieving my bike was no small feat.

Ashamed to go home, I waited in the warmest spot of the sun worried that some carp disease had slimed its way onto me. What if it was a virus that rusted my heart, or a parasite that lodged itself in my brain and made its home until it took over my thinking completely and made me say horrible things in class. Reveling in my paranoia, I worried that I was so worried.

As the air cooled, my mother's car passed the park and turned toward the church. She stopped at the four way stop three houses down and turned left to the alley. I jumped on my bike to meet her. If I could make it into my room and change before she arrived, I could delay her discovery of my exploits. I could bike another day.

She pulled into the driveway next to the garage that was filled with garbage and toys and an old Jeep that only started once during my childhood. I parked my bike, and as I glanced at my mom to determine her mood, I realized that she was not alone in the car. Tia Anita sat in the passenger's seat. Neither opened her door.

My clothes were still wet, certainly wet enough for my mother to detect my mischief, but Anita was my favorite aunt. It was worth getting caught to greet her right away. Standing in the driveway under the autumn sun, her tinged red, olive cheeks betrayed her tears. Tia Anita smiled at me. She had the same angular nose as my mother. The same dark brown hair that twisted as it fell. I did not see the baby in the backseat, but he was there. Rey Pescador was there fully alive: flesh, blood, and soul sleeping in the back of a 1980 Chevy Malibu wagon. My mother unrolled the window slightly and told me to go inside to my room.

I would have argued if her voice had permitted anything but obedience. It didn't. Without a word I ran to my room as fast as I could, impressed with my ability to hit every step with such speed on the way upstairs. My twin bed was soon covered with leaves. My walls were covered with White Sox posters; it was an attic converted to a bedroom. The ceiling sloped enough that even as a six-year-old my head hit the lowest point of the ceiling. The door was opened a crack, so I could hear the conversation. I thumbed the wet leaves from my pockets onto the bed to create an illusion of disinterest in the conversation downstairs, until it was clear that no one was coming to check on me for a while.

Anita's voice bounced against the old hardwood floors into the walls and back out to my room. I pushed the leaves away, slowly exited my bed, and walked to the top of the stairs. From there, I heard my father speak. It's hard to describe, but it's as if he spoke from the back of his throat when he was angry or sad, and I could never tell which was which. He seldom yelled. Rather, he got quieter. It was his way of taking the darkness, the weakness of his anger, and rendering it powerless. As a kid, I guess I thought that he didn't want to hurt my feelings.

He begged Anita to stop crying. I feared looking down the stairs, but my curiosity lifted me off the bed. Alone in the hallway, all I could see was a maple stairway and beige drywall that twisted the cacophony of tears and syllables to a fiction real enough for my childish mind to comprehend.

My father paced steadily.

My mother bounced syllables against the wall.

Anita cried.

In this memory I feel Spanish. I feel that distant language in the room. How do I change that conversation to English? I guess I have to, so here is my translation. "What's his name?" my mother asked.

"Rey," Anita said. "Rey Pescador."

"Rey Pescador? Like the bird?" My mother added. My father was silent for a long time.

"Yeah, I named him after his father."

"Where is the father?"

"I don't know."

"But his name is Rey Pescador. We can find him."

"I don't know his name. I mean, I guess I named him after..."

"Shit, Anita. What is wrong with you? Give him our name, at least. He even looks like a Rosario."

She stayed silent, but my mother continued the barrage.

"Where did you meet him?"

"Does it matter? He's gone!"

"No. I guess not." Now she was silent for a moment before more calmly asking, "Will he try to find him?"

"He never knew I was pregnant."

"Dammit, Anita."

My mother's responses were less than helpful. She began to cry. What transpired after that embarrassed me. Anita confronted my mother on her sanctimony, her "grieving," and then catalogued my mother's shortcomings as a sister, daughter, and Catholic. It was a barrage. My mother fought back. I feared they would physically fight. I imagined my mother who seemed so frail compared to Anita, the taller, stronger, prettier sister. The argument continued, something about family honor, something about sin, and ultimately, something about whores. At this point, Anita finally took off her jacket. Then my little mother cursed Anita and the father and everything else she could think of. It was hard to imagine Anita's olive face, or my father's stoicism under his scholar's beard.

My father shouted, "Maldito sea!" which silenced everyone. That line I remember distinctly. Outside of the post-tear sniffles, the room was heavy with silence.

Then I heard the cry of the baby. Anita rocked him. She sang to him. My father broke the stalemate asking, "Are you going to keep him?" My mother would have asked, "Do you expect us to watch him?" But my father had more tact and empathy. He actually stroked his beard. He also would have happily raised my new cousin.

"No," Anita said after a long pause.

"Is that why you showed up here? To pass off your..." My mother started, but Anita responded too quickly.

"I was never going to ask you to raise him."

Another awkward pause.

Then I erupted. I sneezed, in the hallway. My eavesdropping was no longer secret. Anita climbed the stairs and kneeled on the third step from the top to hug me. My parents' embarrassment was clear. Anita hugged me for what seemed like a long time. The scent of her perfume, mixed with sweat from the argument and cigarettes from the drive, still haunt my memory.

"David," she said. "This is your baby cousin, Rey. You are going to be very important to him."

I nodded and stared at the sleeping child. Having no other cousins, brothers, or sisters, newborn Rey was a unique creature to me. Anita continued, "He is a very special baby. I love him with my whole life. But I am not going to be able to raise him myself."

She explained to me, as a proxy for my parents, the origin legend of Rey Pescador, his fantastic birth, and how the Virgin Mary told her he was special, and how he would be raised in a small orphanage just down the street that the monks ran, and how he would fight against evil and hear God like Samuel. My parents probably thought she invented the story for me, a young boy, but I'm convinced that she believed it.

I had already met the monks down the street whom she said would raise Rey. We had eaten at that surreal urban monastery a dozen times. My father taught at St. Xavier's and often prayed and researched with the brothers, most of whom were affiliated with the college on some level, faculty or staff. I had never heard of the orphanage there. I think Rey was one of maybe four or five kids who ever stayed at the monastery and about a third of his life, he lived with us. But in that moment, nothing seemed strange about Anita's plan. I had heard of Hannah and Samuel and stories of orphans. I didn't realize that living moms didn't give their sons to the church in 1981. I didn't realize that children weren't "special" in the way I thought Anita meant after reading books of kids overcoming great obstacles. I thought, of course, this is how it works.

So in my childish foolishness, the next part didn't surprise me at all. My mother shrieked while changing Rey's clothes and said, "My God, where is his scar?" Anita said, "He has no scar. I would never put one of those machines in him," I didn't realize the significance or danger of Rey's human heart to our family. Perhaps Anita really had the vision she claimed during labor, that vision of the Virgin Mary in the midst of the mountains. Or perhaps she thought it was the only chance that he would be able to keep his human heart through childhood. Either way, I sensed that Anita would kill to keep Rey's secret from being known.

I didn't need any warning to stay silent on this matter. I was young and maybe delusional, but I knew that this was a journey worthy of Sister Jean Patrice's highest hopes: a calling from God. So when they told me, "David, you must not tell anyone about your baby cousin's heart," I nodded my head up and down over and over. And I did it, I kept Rey's secret safe, at least until it wasn't a secret anymore.

ROYGBIV

CH 4 •

JULY 1993

Rey spent most of the summer of 1993 under water avoiding the wrath of the gods of war and weather. In his mind he was a knight or monk or wandering angel of a deity who slept galaxies away.

He was twelve. Who says that?

A southerly front of heat, no doubt the work of Ares and Poseidon, forced the kids from the projects to the pool in our neighborhood. Usually, the black and Mexican kids wouldn't even cross Western Avenue, but when the Chicago Park District closed pools and beaches due to funds and bacteria, respectively, those of the darker hue migrated into the white neighborhoods, where the pools were curiously clean. There was some violence and much police presence, but overall it was fun, and it took the pressure off of Rey and me, who for summers before had been the only brown people in Mt. Greenwood.

The heatwave turned the city into a skillet, and my dad said that it was only a matter of time before someone's brains got scrambled. He was prophetic, many times over. It was the most violent summer the city had seen. The violence stayed east of Western Avenue until July 10th when, despite Rey's belief that God would always keep him from danger, the violence erupted in our own pool.

Rey actually believed he could stop the violence. He believed he was called to be some post-modern knight errant. Some monk

28

had read Rey all of these legends and chivalric romances and foolishly told him about the hero's cycle, though I suspect he would have figured it out on his own. Don't let the loveable celebrity façade fool you, despite his serious gaps in education and lack of formal training, Rey was a literary prodigy. I have spent a lifetime studying, at times in near isolation, but I can never understand fiction in the way that Rey did as a child. He consumed adventure books, verbalizing that they were "the leaves a caterpillar eats to learn to fly." He said that at ten and internalized every word of every story believing that a single person, a single child even, could do something in the world. He was a weird kid. He lived a weird life. That being said, on this particular summer, on this particular day, he put his books aside and was seeking a vision of something sublime in the aquatic, concrete box of a park district swimming pool.

He dove as he always did from the high-dive to the very bottom of the deep end and sat and thought. He sat there and waited and waited. The lifeguards had stopped looking for Rey a year or two before. He did this daily. He sat there at the bottom of the pool for a minute or even two; then when his fleshy heart demanded oxygen, he swam to the surface. He always wore a black tank top. No one understood why, except for me. Maybe that is why I always came to the pool with him, to make sure that he never took off his shirt and exposed himself as odd in this world of uniformly scarred children. Among the adults, the scars were all different. Some were thicker; others were disturbingly long—evidence that early RHC surgeries lacked the uniformity of the surgeries from the late 80s and on. But everyone had a scar—except Rey. The prospect of Rey being caught terrified me from the moment I learned of Rey's secret. I worried late at night. I'm kind of embarrassed to admit, but I even developed an ulcer in fourth grade and told the doctor it was because my mother made stuffed peppers too often, but she and I knew that I was concerned about Rey.

Rey spent that late Friday afternoon searching for the colors of the spectrum in the water. He stared up at the people diving. He always wore goggles but often removed them distrusting their perspective and came home with crimson eyes. He was a weird kid. He saw their eyes close and all the pieces of air that clung to their clothing become bubbles that rose to the top. The summer day camps had left, but most parents weren't home yet. So more and more kids flocked to the pool, sensing the violence that had been baking for weeks.

I wasn't always with Rey during these journeys, but he had told me about everything (several times in fact, that's no surprise, I'm sure). In fact, that day I had taken my car to get its emissions checked. Then I went home and napped before grabbing a copy of Dante's *Inferno* and *Pride and Prejudice* and heading to the pool. I was almost a senior in high school. It was summer reading. I chose *Pride and Prejudice* to impress this blond lifeguard whom I thought I loved. She may have been more impressed if I actually talked with her. By my count, Rey was on his second dive when the air changed.

The word is an alarm: FIGHT. Though it never needs to be said. Every electron changes as Ares breathes on the arena, which was in this case a park district pool. Rey couldn't sense any of that. He was underwater. He watched the waves slowly becoming still as every kid exited the pool. He assumed it was a lightning warning or adult swim or something like that, so he stayed and stared at the sky. For a moment he thought he saw the full spectrum of colors. He thought he saw something beautiful in the direct line between the falling sun and the pool: the initial traces of indigo, orange, and violet, but his vision was interrupted.

The spectrum vanished as the two bodies in black and red swim trunks shattered the glassy water above Rey. The water turned red. Rey swam to the top between the two bleeding shells, but a third plunged into the water and hit him hard.

He briefly lost consciousness.

The blood engulfed him. He could hardly see. He needed to breathe. His heart gasped for air amidst the red. Just two feet away he saw a green flash: the rhythm of electrons kept steady pace even outside the shell of a human. It was Gus Alvarez's Robotic Heart cut from his body. Gus was a victim of a brutal senseless style of gang murder that was in vogue: you'd take a knife and slice it through the yellow layers of skin and scar tissue to the metal heart.

Rey held the flashing heart and tried to save its owner by pulling him to the surface. But the corpse was too heavy, and Rey had been underwater for nearly two minutes at this point.

His vision blackened. He reached the surface and touched the red paint on the concrete that warned against running. He passed out.

When they dragged Rey from the pool, the lifeguards ran for the RHC Heart Kit that had jump started a dozen kids' hearts that summer already. I was terrified. I knew the secret of Rey's heart and knew that this could kill him. Or if they noticed that he had no scar, or if I protested, they would bring him straight to the hospital to implant that loathed tin pump into him. While he lay on the concrete, I tried something that I had seen in old movies dozens of times. I began pushing on his chest, then pounding, then pushing again. I didn't know how to do it, but I continued to try. Behind me was a massive crowd of kids. Not one looked my direction; they all stared at the corpse now fished out of the water. Nevertheless, I felt like every eye in the South Side of Chicago was looking at me. I tried again. I opened his mouth to let him breathe. After a minute that may have been hours, a lifeguard pushed me away. He asked what the hell I was doing. I picked Rey up and slung him over my shoulder. He coughed. He spewed out chlorine and blood. He breathed. We ran home, so they couldn't question us. Rey stopped swimming for a while after that.

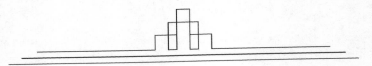

GOD'S GIFT TO WOMEN

CH 5 •

JUNE 1998

Before writing about Rey's next episode of youthful greatness, I want to remind you of his third and final *Time* cover, in September of 2008. It featured him in silver, yellow, and black wrapping paper with a ribbon on top of his head. The corresponding article suggested that Rey requested these colors for their "leonine associations." Though, as the article also suggested, Rey was not sensate during the time of the interview because he was "under the influence, or inspired as he might say, by his muse." The article didn't explain what it or Rey meant by this, and despite my near encyclopedic knowledge of Rey's mythology (maybe more fittingly, neuroses), I don't know what that meant unless Rey was drunk on Lilac Whiskey or something.

In this absurd, muse-inspired image, Rey looked like a giant, handsome bumblebee. His hands were not wrapped, but all but a few finger tips were hidden by the large card that covered neck and face under his eyes. It read: TO WOMEN, from GOD! The article was titled, "God's Gift to Women: The Rise of the King of Poetry." To her credit, the author covered more than Rey's favorite restaurants or beers or exotic date locations; she claimed that Rey represented the return of masculinity to a post-feminist society.

This claim was bogus and offensive.

I bring this up now because Rey commenced his journey to the cover of *Time* and the forefront of women's—and quite a lot of men's—sexual desires when he was seventeen. Though, even at his most vain and depraved, Rey never longed to be a sex symbol. You have to remember where he grew up: in near silence, surrounded by stained glass and prayers without the love of mother or father, but he had the fantastic reality of literature to comfort him and show him exactly how and why love was essential.

I am getting ahead of myself.

You were probably too young to completely remember the social significance of poetry in 1998 to the city of Chicago, but I'm sure you remember some of it. Even your elementary school must have explored some of the more family-friendly poets: Collin Krug, or CuRLE, or any of the Nichola sisters. When poetry stormed Chicago the hearts of the city clicked with appreciation. For a while the gang shootings even seemed to diminish. Poetry brought hope. The violence, the fear, the ennui all were cured in the trochaic, the iambic, and the sublime. Poets became celebrities. Critics were kings. Rey was soon to be the crowned prince.

Rey woke to the sound of AM sports talk radio as he had for his three years of high school. It was June 21st, his junior year had just ended, and the city was celebrating the solstice with its biggest poetry slam ever. Poetry had grown from the bars and lounges to theaters. Poets were local celebrities. The Solstice Slam was at the Aries Theater (it's amazing to think how much bigger the venues would get). Tickets were nearly impossible to find.

It was 8:00 AM, and the monks well into their morning duties. Rey slid out of bed, brushed his teeth, and shook his head, so his hair would stand up just right: not quite an afro, not quite a Mohawk, and not quite anything else. He approved of his face in the mirror. He had a goatee at the time and short sideburns. The small chapel on the second floor, just below his room, welcomed him as it did every morning. The open stained glass had no screen, and flies joined his morning prayer. In the middle of the room, in the middle of the year, he lay prostrate and divined that the Almighty Creator of the Universe ought to conquer his foes in today's verse competition by speaking audibly into his ears a poem so profound that the room would fall silent in awe then roar in celebration.

So Rey Pescador climbed out the stained glass window onto the oak tree; it was his favorite exit, which he usually used only if he needed to sneak out after curfew. Today, even though he could have walked out the front door without anyone noticing, he exited in a style of drama befitting a prophet of God. He sat on the tree branch for a while, listening to the cars and buses and birds. Then he dropped to the branch below and shifted to the other side of the tree, where he could reach the light pole on which he slid to the ground. He wore basketball shoes, navy blue shorts that fell just below his knees, and a yellow T-Shirt, just another kid from the city. His hair announced his arrival on the bus. He bounced to the 'L' transfer.

Later Rey told me, "David, that summer sun fed my swagger. God sent it to fuel my meteoric rise. Then, David, things got interesting."

Rey's version of his entrance to the theater is too absurd for even me to tell: the out of body experience, the teleportation to the stage, the flash of light and the fragrance of incense. Even Rey doesn't claim that story was all true. I wasn't there, but I think it's most likely that he just walked in the service entrance confidently, as if he belonged. When people saw his face they believed that, yes, this kid must belong here.

He walked on the stage after a performer finished. Right after, before the MC could announce the next performer. Holding the microphone like he was the voice box of the Creator of All Things, he shouted, "We're gonna try something that my boy Icarus did a few years back. Are you all ready for some sunshine?"

In the history of the world, no one had ever held the second syllable of the final word of that sentence as long.

In this crowd, in this theater, Rey had already lost the respect of every critic and judge and everyone with a degree in English. Yet, the room erupted. The truth is, most people fit none of those categories, but everyone knows the work of the muse when they see it. Watching Rey nearly elevate above Aries stage, the women who ran Bronzeville determined that yes, they were ready for some sunshine, and they were more than ready for Rey Pescador.

"All right ladies and gentlemen, get ready to fly on the wings of King Fisher. Rey Pescador is in *this* house."

The problem that arose at this particular juncture was that Rey did not have a poem to perform. He was, after all, a prophet on a singular journey to restore peace and justice and beauty to the city. Things like composition and revision might only hinder the voice of God. For a moment, Rey saw the whole crowd that sat under the modern auditorium. He felt no spontaneous overflow of emotion, other than that of fear. He knew he won the crowd's largest and most vital demographic: black women, and yet he knew he would lose everyone if he did not produce something with rhythm and rhyme in the next few seconds. Before he could speak with the confidence that was already brewing in his delusional mind, he saw a fat white cannonball man sitting in the third row, next to the most beautiful girl he had ever seen in his life.

She had blue eyes and dark brown hair. Fascinated by the combination, Rey felt enveloped by the fantastic reality that she was waiting on his every word. Surely, Rey had seen the combination of brown and blue before, but the colors of that face triggered something that sparked each synapse in Rey's mind and fired the only heart in the room to beat uncontrollably. He caught his breath and spoke into the microphone.

"All right, let's see what we can do here." He looked at the girl. "The material that I brought isn't fitting for such a beautiful crowd, so I'm going to try something that hasn't been perfected since my buddy Bill Shakespeare walked the earth. All right, it's game time." He extended his arms as far as he could, parallel to the ground, and raised his chin toward the catwalk. Then he shouted,

MUUUUUUUSSSSE! MUUUUUUUSE
Sing through me and tell me the tale

Still looking at the sky:

What's that? I guess the muse, well, she's still backstage with that last poet. But it don't matter. She'll come around, but I don't need her.

I don't need no muse,
Cause she's everybody's shorty.
I'm Rey Pescador
I make that sun shine.
I'll make that moon rise.
I'll make those words leave my tongue
Like that raven flies.
You see I got this heart,
And now I've got my start.
Don't tread up on me,
Or you might break apart.
I'm the king of the fishers
'Cause the fisher king,
Feels the broad shoulder wounds
Of this city's streets.

I'll heal those gunshot scars
I'll find those stolen cars
'Cause I see the fog like cats' feet
Come rollin' in on 24s
     'Til 22s stop that beat.

    NOW LISTEN
    LISTEN!

Right here in a Chicago Park District pool, they stabbed Gus Alvarez
    I saw his heart blink green and green and green.
    Then it blinked blank.

And I saw his blood beat red and red, and red filled that water
That floated over me,
So don't tell me, that this is just poetry because I can still see him.
You can still see him through the chlorine. You can see his brown,
tanned

Mexican chest cut open by a gang-bangers blade.
He's here now, cause in my heart you can see all these
Dead kids come back to life.

And we can fly on the wings of the king of poetry. We can fly until
the sun burns the lead out of our eyes and we say, man that Icarus must have
just been a bum.

Then without a split-second hesitation, he put the microphone back on the stand then threw both microphone and stand into the air with the incredible force of a future, minor league baseball sensation. It rattled around the catwalk and fell down with a thud. He ripped the cord out of the ground and in two swift loops tied it around his waist, then dove into the crowd. His goal of course was to travel about thirty feet and land directly in front of the beautiful girl, kiss her, then take her hand and escape the room, marry her and live happily ever after.

But he missed his target by about two feet, landing directly on the Cannonball's stomach. He bounced off. Few saw. The crowd was getting to its feet applauding and trying to get close enough to touch the young poet. This gave enough distraction to keep most people from seeing Rey's humiliation.

The Cannonball Man backhanded him and knocked him to the ground at his feet. Rey stood up ready to fight, but the man grabbed Rey's shoulder in a mock fatherly posture, pressing his enormous thumb into the meat just behind Rey's collar bone, sending a shiver of pain and submission through Rey who stood straight and looked the enormous man, who was surprisingly only as tall as Rey, in the eye.

With his right hand, the fat man reached into his pocket and pulled out an envelope. In the middle it said:

Alfred Cedeno

The Prince of Poetry, *Rey Pescador*

The only words the man spoke were, "Get back to me whenever you'd like." When he turned, he eclipsed the girl, whom Rey had not forgotten. He tried to reach her, but he couldn't move past the fat man or the now overwhelming crowd.

The rest of the day was a blur for Rey Pescador. It was the first time he got drunk; the first time he graced the cover of the *Sun Times* and *Tribune* that heralded "The King has Come" and "Rey Pescador Takes Flight" respectively. Yet among all of the revelry, Rey felt both empty without the blue-eyed girl and saddened for her that she missed out on the gift that was Rey Pescador.

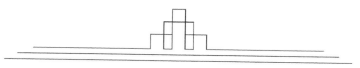

THE PUERTO RICAN PROUST

6

MAY 1999

The school year began six weeks after Rey's poetry fame began and ended six weeks early for Rey Pescador, the newly crowned Prince of Poetry. I doubt he ever told you about his expulsion, Rebecca. He remained deeply embarrassed by it his whole life. If Rey saw his plunge after the singer into the water of Lake Michigan as his initial descent into darkness, then the expulsion was the announcement to put on his seatbelt, because the descent must begin soon.

On a sunny, but still too cool Monday in May, Rey started his final week at the massive all boys Catholic high school by strutting into the main entrance. He surveyed his kingdom of backpacks and high fives. He was pleased.

Greeting the 3000 boys who rushed into the building was a gaggle of newspaper reporters from the school's monthly paper, *The Standard*. Harried, they tried to distribute a newspaper to each boy. Half the papers usually landed on the ground ten feet in, but this time, most of the boys still held the periodical in hand and read as they walked the hallway.

One especially sheepish reporter, shuffled to Rey and placed a paper in his hand. The boy said something like, "It's an honor" and scurried away. Rey glanced at the paper and learned that the source of the commotion was a source more worthy than any other: Rey Pescador.

The front-page story chronicled the fledgling poet's rise to citywide celebrity. Any adult reader would, no doubt, recognize the juvenile prose filled with worship of the school's favorite student. Little did they know, major journals would soon offer equally hyperbolic praise for this young man of letters.

Among other absurdities, the feature stated, "Rey is the second coming of James Joyce. He's the Puerto Rican Proust, whose verse is only overshadowed by the poetry of his 400 meter dash." Evidently everything from Rey's strange childhood to his incredible abs was newsworthy. That is to say that in the underground gay community of Brother Rice, Rey was a god of sorts. In the aboveground athletic, macho all-male school, Rey was a man among boys. The once silent freshman, who lived with monks; who wept more than once in literature class; who remained nearly silent, yet confident, for two years, had emerged his junior year as a mythological figure, equal in resolve to any of the saints or heroes these boys had studied in their lives.

I can imagine Fr. Wasilewski seeking a way to discredit the student celebrity. Though Rey had never broken any significant rules, his singular arrogance could and must be an illustration that pride comes before the fall. For this reason, when Fr. Wasilewski walked into the sacristy on a Friday afternoon, just after school had recessed for the weekend, and discovered Rey Pescador, poet extraordinaire and school sacristan, in a very soon-to-be carnal embrace with the girl whose curious blue eyes and dark hair had inspired Rey months before at the Aries Theater, the elderly Priest determined that he would destroy Rey Pescador's reputation.

First, the old man wielded a processional cross like a lance and lunged toward the startled youths. Irina, the girl whom Rey believed he loved, ran out the door while Wasilewski, still sacrilegiously armed, threatened the young poet with the sharp metallic symbol of forgiveness. Rey wasn't sure what the proper response would be. He could have grabbed another cross to take arms, or he could repent, or he could just dodge the cross and knock the old man over. Later in his life, he might have grabbed a manuterges and used it as a red cape to a bull, but now all he could think of was how to keep from being kicked out of school. Yes, that had to be the plan.

Hoping that sincere repentance would save him, Rey fell to his knees. He wept. Fr. Wasilewski could have no idea how much he had lost. Nor could he understand how weak Rey felt to want something as badly as he wanted Irina in that moment.

Understanding the significance of catching the most popular student in the school in what he thought was the ultimate sin, Fr. Wasilewski delayed the inevitable. "Rey Pescador!" He shouted, "Report to my office first period on Monday morning prepared to explain your actions to the clergy and school board." He left. Rey stumbled out, drunk on communion wine, wondering where Irina had flown.

Rey determined to find her. He had to see her again. He had to smell, and taste, and feel her. He walked south on Pulaski surveying potholes filled with asphalt and neighborhood watch signs and streetlamp after streetlamp hoping to regain some vision of beauty—of Irina. He said he never thought she'd leave his mind. Then he remembered the last place he had seen her: the sacristy filled with ambos, and burges, and corporals, and dozens of other hand carved items. Each of these items carried mystical and liturgical purposes; he wanted that for himself. He went back to school.

He was obsessed with those holy items.

They were as beautiful as anything he had seen in the city. As beautiful as anything he had seen, since he had been almost nowhere else.

He almost envied the inanimate objects: what would it be like to wait and wait stationary like that until it was time for such a specific purpose?

While reflecting, Rey remembered Irina and couldn't quite synthesize how enjoying someone so beautiful who longed for him too could be so sinful. He longed for beauty and passion, yet all he could see were apartment buildings, bungalows, strip malls, and gas stations.

So he went to the monastery and slept amongst the icons and drywall until he woke.

He imagined Irina climbing into his bed. He imagined telling her to leave to save him from expulsion; that would be something to show his virtue to the board.

He imagined her staying.

After waking up hung-over and depressed, he saw the orange light of the setting sun scatter through his room. He reread the letter on his bedside table, which the obese man from the poetry slam handed him before Irina slipped from the auditorium, only to find him in the sacristy months later. It was a wild story, a wild coincidence.

No one would believe it. No one would see him as a victim. It was a bad excuse: some girl just showed up while he was folding the liturgical cloths. No one would believe Rey's current theory that an obese businessman—the internationally famous Sidney Alfonse Cutler—would send a girl to Rey Pescador so he would get expelled and achieve his destiny in poetry and rap sooner. They certainly wouldn't believe that Cutler would offer a virtually no limit credit card and the requirement that Rey travel the world and write on his dime, or that Rey would have waited ten months already to explore this option. I doubt some of it myself, but Sid was interested in Rey's talent, and until this moment he had turned Sid down to be a normal high school superstar.

Monday morning Rey walked the six blocks from the monastery to the school—the heart of Irish Catholic Chicago—as penitentially as any teen ever had. He had even cut his hair so as to prove that he at least wanted to respect the men in the hearing. He refused to have my father, the brothers, or any other leader in the community speak on his behalf. Of course they found out, but when my dad visited him, he just said that he deserved whatever Fr. Wasilewski decided. He never doubted that he was destined to greatness. Therefore, he would be forgiven, graduate, go to Notre Dame and continue the trajectory to become a great poet in the tradition of Dante, Dryden, Cardenal, Chaucer, and Pope (though his list was longer and grander).

The principal's conference was not only full of board members, but also student leaders and the newspaper staff. Rey asked politely if he could confess and plead for forgiveness without such a crowd. His plea was denied.

Father Wasilewski began, "Rey Pescador, were you in the sacristy committing a mortal sin with a young woman this past Friday, May 7th?"

Rey tried to determine two things: the first was if his liaison had yet reached mortal sin status; the second was how he could answer the question without sounding arrogant. What was a mortal sin these days? He wondered. He knew he had messed up, so he just started speaking, "Well Father, I don't think it was a mortal sin yet, but I mean, I was planning to continue sinning. What I mean to say is that I confess that I sinned big time, and that if you hadn't walked in, I probably would have committed what would certainly be considered a mortal sin."

Fr. Wasilewski stood with all the force and authority of a shepherd who would now send out this sheep and pronounced, "You are hereby expelled from Brother Rice High School. You may no longer attend any school in the Diocese of Chicago. If you wish to transfer your credits to another educational institution, be advised that your current semester's progress will not transfer. And, well," he looked rather dramatically at the crowd, "May God have mercy on your eternal soul."

He really said that.

The room was silent. Rey knew of nothing else to do but push his chair back, stand up, and exit through the middle of the room.

He would never grace the halls of Brother Rice High School again. He would never race for the state championship in the 400M dash. He would never again lean back in his desk knowing he possessed the most brilliant answer to the question and knowing that the teacher would call on him soon. He also sensed that he would never see Irina again. For a moment he considered the possibilities of his life as an orphan dropout. He saw his potential future: waking up at eleven after delivering pizzas for a few years, then take the GED, and spend a few years hung-over taking buses to a city college where he'd cynically ignore the professors and remember how great he used to be.

But Rey decided that wouldn't be the way his story would go. A student reporter asked him what he'd do next. Rey replied coolly, as always, "I will perform penance."

"What penance do you think you should be doing after this type of thing?" the reporter mumbled; it was clear Rey's response had been unexpected.

"The best penance is living well. It is finding beauty and truth."

"Isn't that revenge?"

"What?"

"The best revenge is living well. Right?"

"No more questions."

The newspaper staff and student groups followed him, but he would answer no more questions nor acknowledge the school ever again. He was on a mission of beauty and truth, after all. They continued to follow him, trying to interpret his heroic expression for a while. But he didn't see any of them. All he saw was the May light, the concrete, the perfect sky, blue enough to make him determined to find eyes that type of blue and walnut hair to complete the act that got him expelled.

The first business that he could find was a convenience store. His followers now left behind, he began his new journey alone at the far reaches of society. He strutted into the liquor section, grabbed a bottle of whiskey and approached the counter. The clerk was just a few years older than Rey and had probably met him before. Rey knew the kid wouldn't card him or give him a hard time. After he paid, Rey asked, "Do you have any cups around here?"

"Uh, I don't think so."

"No matter, we'll drink it out of the bottle. What's your name?"

"Sean," the clerk said.

"Of course it is," Rey said. "Sean, my friend, I am going to make a phone call, and then you and I are going to get hammered. Do you understand that?"

"Hell yeah."

"I knew you would, my friend."

Rey reached into his left pocket, grabbed the embossed business card, dialed the number, and waited for about six rings.

"This is Sidney," the heavily breathing man answered.

"Mr. Cutler, this is Rey Pescador."

"Rey, it's about damn time."

"It is. I'm in. How does this work?"

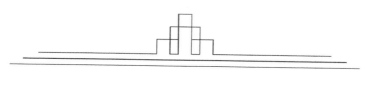

NEPENTHE INCANTATIONS AT THE FOUNTAIN OF YOUTH

7

AUGUST 2000

Sid Cutler catapulted Rey across the world to explore the sublime. Rey flew to South America on "the wings of poetry" (yeah it hurts to write it as much as it hurts to read, but that is what he said).

And you, Rebecca, were beginning classes at St. Mary's. Did you enter the world of adults ready to conquer the world, or did you think you were just another girl from the South Side at the college where South Side Irish girls like you go?

All I know is that you never entered a room like another girl from the South Side—at least not any other one I've met.

The best way I can describe it is this. Imagine the surreal reality of a PTA meeting dispersing. All the cool moms trek to some nondescript chain restaurant for drinks and dessert. One gets lost on the way and walks into the dim bar and grill smiling more than the rest. You don't notice at first how beautiful she is. You also don't notice how understated her clothes and shoes are. But she is anything but simple. She laughs the loudest, and when someone gets the wrong side with her meal, she asks to see a manager. Everyone else wants to ignore it. She solves the problem, while becoming friends with both the manager and the server.

During dinner, she befriends the most annoying woman and somehow manages to have that woman and her most loathed enemies trust her. She is like a social super hero.

I probably didn't explain it right, and you might be rolling your eyes, but I promised to tell the truth. As Rey would say, it was all true. I imagine that even as a freshman, you had those powers. You probably walked into each class more prepared, capable, and unknowing of those traits than any other student. I love you for that.

To summarize and return to the past: Rey was flying, you were lovely and learning. All the while, I was trying to find meaning in a metal world.

I had just finished my first graduate program at Chapel Hill and taken a position teaching an Intro to Bioethics course. My southern, simple life was almost over (though I didn't know it yet). But for a few more months, I would maintain the steady simplicity of an academic life.

Mondays and Thursdays I lectured. Tuesdays were laundry day. Fridays I graded. Every morning started the same. I would wake on the twin bed in my rented English basement bedroom in a gorgeous colonial house. Among the wealth and beauty of that town I lived as sparsely as I could. My walls were bare. Only books, a cot, and a chair signaled life to my rare guest. But I was not a hermit. I traversed across campus each morning. All day Wednesday, I wandered hoping that some gorgeous undergrad would recognize me from class and ask me to coffee to explain all of the mysteries of the world. Of course, at 26, I knew every mystery there was.

Amid the southern belles and hills I felt homesick. While I recognized its beauty, I never felt comfortable in a place still rippled by ancient tectonic action. The hills were not for me. Chicago's alphabetical streets in such a neat grid, and its women bundled in black coats for four months a year led me to apply to jobs at Northwestern, University of Chicago, and even UIC. Daily I checked my campus mail. No job offers arrived. However, I had been receiving something better for about six months, letters from the adventures of Rey Pescador.

They generally started the same way: HOLA COUSIN, or HOLA PRIMO, or HOLA CUZ. Then he'd rattle off 200 word sentences with allusions to every Greek myth he could remember, which I guess was pretty much every Greek myth. There was always an absurd chase after a beautiful Latina. Often there was a debacle involving mistaken identities. For a few months, I wondered if he was just transcribing telenovelas. He wasn't. They were all true, just ask him.

But of all the bizarre stories, only one was truly dubious. He also sent a video with it as if he wanted to corroborate his success at this medieval quest. Almost completely forgetting about poetry, his journeys from Chile to Mexico and now to Las Isla de Encanta, made Rey believe that he was another Latino in the line of the greatest European explorers; however, unlike those who traveled before, De Leon, Coronado, De Soto, Cortes, and the other infamous servants of God and gold.

Only Rey served neither God nor gold on this trip: his was a quest of leisure and hallucination.

I laughed when I opened the manila envelope and saw scrawled in red felt-tip pen the title, *Nepenthe Incantations at the Fountain of Youth*. It made sense that Rey's imagination and need for immortality would lead him to think of himself as more than another 19-year-old sowing his wild oats. I believed it was fiction, and a fantastic melodramatic fiction. I expected no other kind from Rey. I expected the typical stories of serenading ladies, while their body-building boyfriends napped and line upon line about how his hair was growing back and how he could now grow a decent beard. Most of his letters were just that.

I never expected him to take over the world of art and entertainment. My expectations, though logically contrived, underestimated America's desire for the mythopoetic, the cliché, the beautiful and absurd. This specific quixotic, "true" story featured a love interest named Aldonza, for God's sake. The one man who had an aging heart struck a chord with the billions who could only wish to wish to want to find the Fountain of Youth's strange elixir. Thus, it was this letter to me that sparked Rey's first great literary triumph.

Leaving the college post office without my usual jaunt to the coffee shop, I returned to my hermitage to view Rey's video: inconstant sepia pixels showed a man standing in the middle of an inner-city plaza. It was clearly a city square in Latin America. 200 years earlier the women walked around such promenades to draw the eyes of the men from their porches, churches, and games. Now there were no women to draw Rey's eyes from the middle of the park. Rey had obviously doctored the film. The sepia style proved that. I was surprised that he took the effort. He usually never touched technology: he feared it like it was an angry god.

Distorted audio popped and cracked. In his corresponding letter, Rey wrote that they were gun shots although they may have simply been the hooves of the emaciated horses that ran the cocaine addicts to their next fix. Rey's face entered the picture. A man screamed behind him, "turn the damn camera off." The 19-year-old, soon-to-be celebrity spoke to the camera, "I have spent all of my years looking for beauty and truth, and love. Today, I am told, my journey will end. There is a man in this city who has a charm to cure memory, to erase pain, and to instill youth again, a youth that will never age."

The video turns to snow at this point. For a moment, at least. A man in a white tuxedo flashes on the screen. A dead lapel rose. A bird feeder. An ocean gently pushing the ocean to the earth.

That was it. That was Rey Pescador's first adventure in film. It was virtually worthless, yet if you ever asked Rey about it, he would have told you it was *Citizen Kane* and the *The Godfather* combined.

The folder also carried Rey's explanation of his most famous journey in his almost unreadable prose. I spent a fair amount of time editing it before it became the introduction to his first book. The most famous writer in history couldn't use Standard English spelling or use punctuation if his life depended on it, which he claims it once did in Tijuana.

Here is the revised letter.

Rosario,

Blessings cousin. I must start with the truth of the story. I am sorry that I do not have a more traditional update. But God has gifted me with something that prior only angels tasted.

Crippled by Helios' yellow ray, I sing to the north wind.

Aldonza, she is beautiful, cousin.

How did I get here? How did I? Cousin, it pains me to say that the muse or the Virgin Mary it was not. Rather, L.J. Brovault, my newest acquaintance and friend of my benefactor, Sidney Alfonse Cutler, informed me at a party in Memphis that the Fountain of Youth would bubble one last time this century. L.J. is a 12-year-old Ph.D in the Spirited Sciences. Though I doubted this prepubescent genius, I listened to his absurd claim because I had been searching the continent for months for a new experience, a new poem, and a new face of solace worthy of calling my muse and had learned that only in the most absurd stories can truth lie.

So when Brovault handed me a "bonafide" map, I took the first train to Miami, then a boat (that's a whole other story) and was in San Juan by the morning.

That was only two days ago.

Aldonza, she ignored me last night. With burgundy fingernails, she brushed my arm, and I—the fool of fools—left that San Juan Casino in search of everything that has ever made a man search.

They say Menelaus recruited men with promises of glory, pride, and camaraderie, but his soldiers killed for the same reason as him: to see Helen freed from captors bathing in the wine-dark sea.

And so I followed her, Aldonza that is (not Helen), onto the beach. I breathed poetry, but burgundy-nailed Aldonza skipped away, around the hotel through the dark alleyway on a neon lit street.

A plane filled with packages flew just overhead. Its engines roared.

"Marry me!" I cried. She laughed, "You aim too high." Turning her back she danced across the cobblestone street and disappeared behind one of San Juan's thousand rod-iron doors. I jumped across the street and landed outside her apartment. The façade was blue. They were row houses, but the neighbors on left and right had fronts of red and yellow respectively. It was a beautiful street. I flew up to her balcony. Romeo approached Juliet: cliché approached beautiful cliché—I needed no legs, no arms, only wings.

I knocked on the door.

I breathed the summer night.

The saltwater in the air healed an ancient wound.

Next to me was a birdcage. A mostly black fowl, with a triangular tuft of silver hair on his crest, like a dying king, peered through his brass bars at me. Aldonza moved the curtain back, but the screen door remained closed.

I spoke first, "What's his name?"

"Did you seriously climb up on my balcony to ask my bird's name?"

"Yes."

"I should call the police. Leave, Rey."

"If you were going to do that, you would have done that already. What is your bird's name?"

"Coco."

"He looks tired."

"Well, he's old and you woke him up."

"How old?"

"Does it matter?

"I've heard they live quite long."

"He is almost 100-years-old. Now leave, Rey."

"Leave with me."

"Where?"

"I don't care. Anywhere. China, Russia, Singapore, Tanzania. Wherever you'd like. What is the one place you've always wanted to be?"

"I don't know. Listen, Rey I have work tomorrow."

"Work? You must be kidding? I am offering you my heart."

"Is that all you have to offer? Something freely given at birth?"

"What else would you want?"

"Something more valuable."

"Money?"

She slapped me on the face. I laughed. What else could I do?

"Wait, you don't get it. I misspoke. I can offer you everything and anything, my heart, my soul, my body, my quest, and this rose." With a slight of hand I produced the rose I had been waiting to give her.

"A rose? That's even more fleeting than love. You aren't helping your case. And your body? Well, a man's body is not hard to find."

"Depends on the body." I moved in close to kiss her, but she turned her head again.

"What is this *quest?*"

"Tomorrow, I will find the fountain of youth."

She laughed, as if I was joking. But oh, things changed. She moved near me close enough to kiss. Her lips grazed mine.

Then incandescent light shone from behind her.

"Leave, Rey!" she said in a hushed shout rushing inside. I heard a man's voice in the apartment. I thought about fighting him for her honor, but I had to focus on my quest. She had distracted me enough.

City lights scattered stars and the moon hid behind a cloud. Having nowhere to go, I waited on the balcony and sang quietly to the bird until I fell asleep.

I have never slept like that. I hope I do again.

By noon, I was in Lozia at the center of town. Water moistened the grass under my feet. In the plaza an old man with an Amerindian face stood. His face was sand. He spoke quickly, not delayed by the customary rules of grammar and personal space. I could smell him. Garlic and fish. Nine fingers held a shovel. He marked the spot. "Friend," he said, "you must dig."

The shovel unearthed a rocky surface.

One foot deep.

Two feet deep.

Then three and four and five. Do you realize what it's like to dig a hole like that with my condition?

My eyes were now below the surface. Then my eyebrows and forehead and scalp. Only the highest point of my hair protruded out of the hole when I saw it.

David, I can't describe this in prose. I promise I will write a book of poems trying to capture the beauty of this moment.

The water wasn't just water. It was so clear. I mean it shone, but not like special effects in a film. It was just so perfect and beautiful. Shit, I don't know how to say it in prose.

I knelt in the heat. My sweat mixed with the ancient liquid. Kneeling, I crossed myself, wet my hands, and washed my face. I washed it again and again.

It smelt of honey.

The tropical sun looked down on me and burned coffee into my skin. I shouted "El Fuente de la Juventud!" The old man looked at me and laughed. "Would you like some water?"

"Friend, I am not thirsty."

"Do you know what this is?"

"I am not thirsty, friend. It is for you. You are the only one who needs this."

"That can't be true."

"Why else do you think you are the one who found it? Where is everyone else?"

In that hole I saw a specter, David. I swear it wasn't just the Caribbean sun, but even if it was, what the hell difference does it make. I saw my mother. Not just a photo of her like I'd seen at your house growing up. I saw her. I fell in the mud, and she was there hovering above me. She told me not to drink. She told me death comes to all men. She vanished, and I saw the old man looking into the earth at me.

"What the hell are you looking at?" I shouted. But he just smiled and laughed. Realizing how much he knew, I shouted at him again, "Can it heal wounds? Can it inspire poetry? Can it bring the dead back to life?" He laughed again and again. He looked at me thumbing the shovel. The remnants of his missing finger revealed the outline of a tattoo. He said nothing.

I took the rose from my pocket.

I dipped it in the water.

Then I realized I didn't need to ask him those questions. The answer was no. I was the only one who wanted this. It was only for me. If the dead could return, I would have never found it.

Of course, no life returned. I filled my water bottle with the precious liquid and climbed out of the hole. I lay on my back with my knees bent and feet hanging in the hole.

I prayed to Mary asking her to bring life back. I touched the rose; a pedal broke and fell to the ground without any hope of new life. The old man saw my sadness. He handed me a bottle of wine. "Drink this, it's nepenthe. To forget is better than to relive."

I had never heard of nepenthe. I drank about half of the bottle: the pink liquid ministered to my heart and mind. I saw more things that I can't describe in prose, but don't worry, the poems are coming. I sat there for a long time under the August sun. When I came to, the hole was just dirt. There was no water. There was no mud.

What drove thousands to search for centuries was now just more moisture in the Caribbean air.

I breathed it in deeply, but I'm sure at that point it had been dispersed into a million molecules all around. There were about four ounces left in my water bottle. So I left. It was two hours of hitchhiking and public transportation before I was back in San Juan at Aldonza's apartment. I still had not determined if I would drink any of the sweet liquid.

I climbed the balcony. I knocked on the door, but she only looked through the blinds and said that her boyfriend would kill me if he found me.

The sun set. The ocean rose toward the blue moon. On it men sailed and swooned and drank and created life and beauty. The only thing between the ocean and the eternal elixir were centuries-old apartments, a casino, restored cobblestone, a water bottle, and my hand.

Coco sang in the cage next to me. "Brother," I said looking at his silver feathers, "you deserve it more than me." I poured it in his cup. He drank the water. His feathers darkened. His eyes shown. But I never took a sip.

I just drank that sweet nepenthe and hoped Aldonza's boyfriend would not return before I was sober enough to climb down.

It was all true,
Reymundo X. Pescador

When I first finished the letter, all I could do was laugh, not at the story, but at Rey's signature. Maybe he was trying out noms de plume, but his name was not Reymundo, and he had no middle initial. Later this concerned him. He said he wanted to make sure that I didn't think the story was fiction because he signed a pen name. I told him that I knew he only ever spoke the truth. That seemed to assure him.

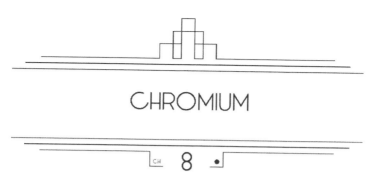

CHROMIUM

CH 8 •

I'm not sure what type of story you expected when you opened the first page of this letter, well letters, well I'll call it what it is, this book. I hope you enjoy it. I hope you believe me. Most of all, I hope you forgive my idiocy, board a plane, and fly to me.

I love you Rebecca. Six weeks ago, when I tried to take my life, I hadn't forgotten that. I just forgot what love was. And I hope that by the end of this story you understand my love in some vital way.

Perhaps you expected Rey's story to be something more complex, something darker. Maybe you thought that Rey's childhood was plagued with abuse, suffering, or failure so as to spur him to medicate his pain with fame. Maybe you thought Rey was innocent, a victim of circumstance. Or you may have thought of him as incurably and sympathetically flawed. If so, I hope you are relieved. Perhaps you expected something more commonplace. You probably thought I wouldn't believe the image Rey painted of Rey. If so, I hope you are thrilled.

I wonder what these stories have changed about how you see me: David Rosario the conscientious student; the reluctant priest, the man of inaction; David the older cousin who both saves and follows his should-be brother. Has this version of David as refugee spurred sympathy?

Overall, I hope that this vision reveals what you above all people have always seen from life—something beautiful from our world.

It's hard to believe that these stories happened thirty years ago. It seems so much longer. But I guess it was another life, another reality, a fantasy.

After all, we both know that when Rey left, the world changed forever.

I've been trying to figure it out for these decades, and the closest I can come is this. Soon, I'll get to the details around this moment, but in Time Square, he once composed a poem, freestyle where he said:

> "Capture my history in
> cathartic electrons, in this moment
> of brilliance. A flash of light:
>
> a million humans illuminate
> the ultimate soul in electric light."

To me, Rey was a flash of electronic light. Every moment of his life we saw it, and now the electric light has vanished, and we're left with something unnamable, something even more synthetic.

Our world is passionless. Without sex or crime or angst or even violence.

Despite the anguish over my artificial heart, I recognize that the monotony that Cutler brought led to a surprising peace in the city, which is inherently good. Certainly, something gleams within the fog of industry and entertainment.

I guess what I'm fumbling around saying is that even without Rey there is still hope, I think— there is still beauty in this world, even if it has been melted in a dozen laboratories and wrapped in painted chromium.

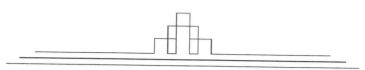

ROBOT BLOOD PART 1

CH 9 .

APRIL 2007

Rey said the Atlantic was cool that April day, not Lake Michigan in April cold, but colder than he'd expected.

We're now almost seven years from the publication of *Nepenthe Incantations at the Fountain of Youth* and its infamous launch party where Rey vanished from a boat and appeared later on an island, alone.

I know I'm skipping much of Rey's fame, but you know much of those years already, and well, there is much too much to say about all of that and plenty of others who have said it—especially the Bard from the Barrio himself.

Being a college student much of that time, I assume that half of your friends had Rey Pescador posters festooned throughout their dorm rooms. Did your professors rave about him in class, like my colleagues did? Did you know anyone with his iconic signature as a tattoo? Did you know anyone without that tattoo might be a better question?

While Rey got famous, I continued my journey toward becoming what I've always wanted to be and what I've always been, an academic.

A few months after Rey's boat party, I was accepted to the University of Chicago's Ph. D. in Spiritual Sciences and Theology. Once I finished my courses, I started "researching" with Rey and his brilliant friends as they traveled the world. He seemed to want me around. But in April of 2007 I was not around when he met the only friend he'd ever say was closer than me.

It was in between a month of successful HBO shoots for his new mini-series and his European Tour of Farse (his first satirical tour of the arts, which promised to provide American humor to Europe in a way those old world folks hadn't seen since Twain), that Rey decided to take a Mediterranean holiday that would now reach its pinnacle, literally, as a new adventure would begin.

Cyprus, Montenegro, Southern Spain and now Gibraltar welcomed him as a young King of the arts ought to be welcomed: girls swooned, women chased, and men, well, they did the same thing but tried to hide it. Rey left the crowds and found a famous rock on which to rest.

On the European side of the strait, Rey reclined on the table formed by a limestone overhang, successfully hidden from the adoring fans, the relentless media, and the demands of any of Cutler's talent agents who managed Rey's career. Currently they were discussing his agenda. Two options arose:

1-Rey could swim the strait—a feat that had become much easier, and ironically, even less common since the artificial heart; though Cutler must have known that Rey would not benefit from the stamina it provided. He may have been the only one outside of our family who knew.

2-Rey could take a sexy photoshoot in St. Michael's cave.

Rey was always a both/and type of guy, and knew that photos must be taken, but ultimately, the day would end with him in the water of the strait, regardless of what his handlers thought.

He sat about 100 feet down from the pinnacle of the Rock of Gibraltar. Throwing a rock into the water, he watched it disappear immediately. He threw another and another until there were none left within arm's reach. Unable to write, or at least not wanting to exert the energy to summon the muse, he leaned on his left elbow and sketched a picture of himself in his journal. He was not a skilled illustrator, but his natural perfectionism ensured that he noticed flaws on the paper and corrected them quickly. He used the eraser more than the graphite, and after years of sketching an unchanging face, he had learned to create his likeness on paper.

The image was his profile: a slightly sloping forehead leading to honorable, deep brown eyebrows that narrowed as they quickly approached his temples, a non-distinct nose, with dots for stubble, an above-average sized lower lip, and a perfectly square chin that reached slightly farther than most initially noticed. All of these details, he captured. He included dark brown hair in a ponytail—though he never wore his hair in a ponytail—and black wayfarer sunglasses.

When he finished erasing and redrawing, he thought of composing a poem, but he couldn't locate the muse. He told me first he needed to see her, and then he could call out like a madman. I think most people thought it was an act. Maybe it was, but if it was, it was an act that he kept consistent even when he was alone. Rey had written little since his second book. Compared to every other best-seller, he seldom wrote, but when he did he wrote perfectly in bouts of mania that left critics and fans in tears or laughter. The dozen or so poems or songs he composed in a weekend were enough to inspire the artists and producers and media around him to build something truly beautiful.

He had achieved what he wanted from the moment he left Brother Rice High School: total and complete fame. He could walk onto any street, on either side of the strait and have a crowd of people gather.

And now Rey was alone.

His solace did not signify him begrudging his fame or desiring to be normal, like those celebrities who say they only wish they could go to Disneyland without anyone noticing. Rather it was an opportunity for him to let the undying love directed toward him sink into his mind like any number of stones falling through salt water.

A Barbary macaque jumped onto Rey's limestone ledge. He chattered at Rey. Then Rey at him. Rey lifted his hands above his head, established dominance, and invited the monkey to sit at his side. They chattered for a while. Rey tried to instruct him to throw rocks into the water. The monkey tried to instruct Rey how to scratch himself.

Someone slinked down the precarious path toward Rey and the monkey's mesa. Rey couldn't determine who it was for a while, but finally he saw Tito, one of his assistants (technically an agent for a major talent company in the Cutler group) maneuvering himself slowly toward Rey.

I'm sure his real name wasn't Tito. He looked more like a Thomas or Steve or Chad. But Tito is all Rey ever called him, and he certainly never introduced himself to me. Waiting for the agent to reach Rey and interrupt his musing with what could only be an obnoxious schedule update, Rey stared at the talent agent, lit a cigarette, opened his journal, and donned a creative pose to feign discipline. The truth is that Rey had not summoned the muse and would never reread anything that came from his pen in such a vulgar state.

While Rey posed, waiting for the obnoxious man to speak, he realized that at the pinnacle of the gray rock, two comically opposite brooding characters had arrived and directed their glare at him in matching sunglasses: Sid Cutler and L.J. Brovault.

At this point I only knew three things about L.J. The first was that he earned his Ph. D. famously at 11 years old. The second is that just before receiving his Ph. D., he met Rey, who was 18 at the time and told him about the fountain of youth. The third is that for the last year or so, people predicted he would do for science what Rey did for poetry.

When Rey saw L.J. on top of the cliff, L.J. was 17-years-old, six feet tall and about 120 lbs. Even with his sunglasses he appeared to be squinting.   Tito, despite several near tragedies on the journey, finally reached his target; his bald head reflected the yellow light that bounced off rock, cloud, and water. Rey concluded that the only propitious response would be to ignore the bald businessman as long as possible. After several traditional attempts to begin a conversation with the celebrity whom, at this time was only interested in teaching a monkey to throw rocks submarine style, like a Japanese pitcher, Rey finally responded, "Tito, you're in my light, brother, I am working hard here. I pay your salary. Could you have some respect?" "Sorry, Rey, but you have to go up there. Lawrence says it is urgent."

Rey lay on his back and looked upward at the foils standing at the stop of the cliff. "L.J., why don't you come down here and meet Carl? Carl is the monkey. Wait, Tito, your name isn't Carl, is it?"

"No, it's …"

"Perfect! This is great, L.J. New monkey with a great name and Tito even approves. Thanks a ton, Tito. I'm pumped, now get down here, L.J."

The sixteen-year-old pint-sized prodigy turned to the half-ton billionaire next to him. I'm sure that he was afraid to invite Sid Cutler down the rocky path, knowing that Cutler could not make his way down such a complex surface. The usually socially-awkward child prodigy chose well by asking Cutler's permission without extending invitation. Cutler responded superciliously, "I'm not your father. Do whatever the hell you want."

"Don't worry about the kid, Sid," Rey shouted up the cliff. "He's in good hands. I'll take him home. Believe me, he'll be more productive if he has some fun every once in a while."

"I have plenty of fun," L.J. barked.

"Bring some rocks, L.J."

"Why?"

"I've thrown all of mine."

"What? What do you mean?"

"Little stones, bring some."

"Why?"

"Just do it."

L.J. descended as Rey continued to admire both the likeness of his own profile and his ability to create such an uncanny image. Then for a moment he paused to admire the image itself. The pair hadn't seen each other since Rey lost five hundred thousand dollars to L.J. in the Ironic Rickshaw Derby in Brooklyn.

"What's up little man?" Rey said addressing the pale kid, who wore a brown Brooks Brothers suit that he purchased almost two years before. Since then, the little genius's arrogance had blossomed, and the deep brown faded from his tweed jacket. His arms grew, almost as much as his cockiness, which left him with a discolored short jacket that might have smelled if L.J. ever left air-conditioning or lifted anything other than a stylus. That being said, in the world of Brooklyn rickshaw racing, the kid was a god, and his jacket was his scepter. Just a month before this liaison with Rey, he attended the first "Little Man in a Brown Suit" film festival, in which mostly Columbia and NYU film students created documentaries, animated films, and even a zombie genre flick about the kid who everyone just knew would be the first to time travel.

L.J. didn't respond to Rey for a long time.

"What's up little man? You bring the rocks?"

"Don't call me that. And no, I did not."

"Why not? What are we going to throw?"

"Throw where?"

"Into the damn waves."

"Why would we do that?"

"Because, young scholar," Rey donned a mock-heroic tone, "we are men, human men, and that is what men do."

"Throw rocks?"

"We create beauty and movement. You're a freakin' physicist and expert in religious bullshit or something. You should know."

"I know that we have more important things to discuss."

"What could be more important than watching a spontaneous decision of the mind, not even the mind, of the arm, the spinal nerves, send a piece of the earth that rested in one spot, baking in the sun since the great flood for all we know, into the ocean and see the water envelope it and continue its path, changed only slightly by the foreign body that entered it and is now forever changed?"

"It's a strait."

"What are you talking about?"

"What the hell are you talking about, Rey? I come down here to discuss something important and present a golden opportunity to you, and you talk about throwing rocks into the damn ocean. Well, it's not an ocean: it's a strait and probably the most famous strait in the world."

"Watch the language little man. I don't want your mom to get pissed at me."

"My mom is dead."

"Mine too. Sorry."

"She is?"

"Well, I think so, maybe."

"Sorry."

The men sat in silence. Then Rey stared L.J. in the eyes for a long time.

62

"You know that I would have thrown anyone else in the water, any other man, at least."

"I know."

"You know that I tolerated that, not because you are 10-years-old or something, but because you are my friend."

"I know. I'm seventeen."

"I know. All right, so what is the plan?"

"The plan is this: I have triangulated the location of the world's first poem. It's the perfect opportunity for both of us, and it is in a tongue that I can translate with the proper research. You can help me make it sound poetic and all, and we can present it. I think it's worth another national book award and Nobel for you and me respectively."

"You know that is the second dumbest idea you've presented me with."

"I know."

"Well, I'm in, but only under one condition."

"What's that?"

"You go up there and get some damn throwing rocks."

"Fine, but you'll have to teach me. I've never thrown anything before."

"Neither has Carl. Actually, he's probably thrown some shit before, but well, I don't think that counts."

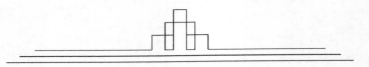

ROBOT BLOOD PART 2

JULY 2007

While Rey and L.J. threw rocks, I wandered the Vatican library, a mystic searching for enlightenment.

I drank coffee and wine from morning until morning, seldom sleeping more than three or four hours. I read. I wrote. I fell in love.

Brenda, my research assistant, flew from Chicago to work with me. She was engaged to be married, but during the day I became more and more desperately infatuated with her. At night, I replaced her with the Italian beauties who dragged me home from nightclubs and bars. After all, I was the fair-skinned cousin of Rey Pescador: the cousin equal in passion and hope and anything-but-equal in swagger, wealth, or confidence. Both the beauty of the Vatican and the touch of a dozen strange women promised the infinite and delivered ennui.

When I feared the summer would only continue in this cycle of self-hatred, L.J. Brovault rescued me with a single text message: POET REY PESCADOR URGENTLY REQUIRES YOUR COMPANY IN ETHIOPIA.

Thirty-six hours later, I lay under a tree, five miles outside a small Ethiopian village wearing the traditional garb of a Coptic catechist, swatting mosquitos off my hands, and hoping that the adventure would end before it started. Ten yards away Rey said, "This ought to attract some attention," and took off his white Oxford, tied it around his waist, and prepared to hail a passerby.

"No one knows you out here," I said. Neither celebrity

responded.

L.J. still worked on the car: he had been cursing Soviets and their engineering for the better part of an hour.

"Do we really want to be found?" I asked.

"Of course we do. We need to make it to St. George's. That is where the vision will be," Rey said.

"Of course. The vision will be there tonight. I almost forgot."

"And why wouldn't you want to be found?" Rey asked me.

"Rey, I know you've basically copyrighted optimism, but you must realize that we are lost in a hell-hole with bands of soldiers who have been killing from youth hoping to find a way to survive. And I'm walking around with a couple of multi-millionaire Americans with loads of cash and diamonds on them."

"I have virtually no cash on me."

"Rey, your monkey is wearing a gold medallion."

"Carl, has no cash on him. And that medallion is only 14K gold."

"Whatever."

"David, my albums and books sell great in sub-Saharan Africa, especially in Ethiopia. These people have been housing the Ark of the Covenant for like two freaking millennia or something. Give them some respect."

"I could be in Italy with the most beautiful women."

"Shut up, David."

We slept in view of the hills that were our destination, first in the old diesel and then right on the road when it became too hot. The bugs overcame us, so we sweated in the back in the diesel again. Just before dawn, I awoke and climbed a small Wanza tree to watch the sun rise and avoid the gnats that hovered about four feet off the ground. It was beautiful. As a kid watching Hollywood movies, I always thought the sun was bigger in Africa. Of course, I knew it wasn't actually bigger, but I figured it was some sort of phenomena that made it seem bigger than any other place on the planet. I don't know if it was or not, but it was a beautiful morning. I still wore the catechist robe. Rey had traded my clothes for it, thinking it was the garb of a priest and would help us. I don't know why he thought a Mexican man in

Ethiopian Orthodox vestments, who spoke no Amharic and had no cultural understanding of the people, would convince people that the celebrities who traveled their sacred sites were to be respected. Actually, I think he was smarter than that and mostly wanted to create a spectacle and piss me off. Even though I was a lay person at that point and not even pious, despite my academic interests in faith, Rey called me Father Rosario when he was drunk and I was tipsy.

Despite the initial annoyance at the robe, I embraced it as I watched the sun rise over the valley. I imagined myself as an original Christian, in the cradle of humanity. I imagined the awe they must have felt when they first heard of a man who walked out of a tomb and flew into heaven. I imagined the power they felt eating the body and blood of God incarnate and the hope they felt when someone told them of theosis. So I prayed there for the first time in a long time. I wished there was a real priest to hear my confession. I can't say I heard God or had a vision, but I can say there was something infinitely beautiful about the sunrise.

The boys woke up. I jumped out of the tree. We ditched the car and its provisions. Our cell phones had died without making a single rescue call. Now the sun was hot.

Far down the gravel road, we saw a car.

The sun illuminated each stone. Each stone heated the air.

It was only 9:00. We danced in joy as it drove closer and closer to us.

Not only did it pass us, but it found a puddle in the middle of the ground spraying filthy water all over Brovault. He cursed, threw his phone at the car that bounced down the mud road.

"Dang! My phone is going to be ruined."

"Nice throw. You are getting better," said Rey.

"What is a cab doing here anyway? And a puddle? I thought this was the dry season. I thought this country didn't see rain for like six months a year."

"I don't know. You're the scientist."

"I'm not a freaking meteorologist."

"Didn't the rainy season just end when we were in Kinshasa?"

"That's like 500 miles away."

"What difference does it make?"

"You are so ignorant."

"Shut up," I yelled. "The car is coming back." But L.J. was too worked up to stop. He continued cursing everyone and everything, but especially Africa and cabs and puddles and, "God forsaken places with cabs and puddles like New York City." He always said it like that, "New York City," like it was the most otherworldly place on earth.

He certainly traveled a lot, but that was always with Cutler or a handler. It wasn't until this year when he began gambling and racing in the rickshaw circuits that he ever left the convention centers or hotels. And even with that, it certainly was clear that until this trip with Rey, the strange little genius had never been outside for more than three hours in a day.

In the old Datsun L.J. continued his belligerence against the cab driver and everyone else in the world. After no more than a quarter mile, the driver pulled over, pointed a revolver at us, and ordered us to leave in surprisingly clear Italian that Rey and I understood enough to move quickly. L.J. understood no romance languages or the international language of firearms and had to be dragged from the vehicle by Rey and me. We weren't robbed, which was the initial concern, but things were looking bad for the boys and me. I think the guy just didn't want to hear another word from L.J. Brovault. I can't blame him too much for that.

We walked back to the broken vehicle. Noon passed. L.J. continued to work on the diesel. He was now sure that he could fix it. He had ripped off the hood and hovered in the bright sunlight over the engine. His back was beet red. "If only Dr. Knapps was here," he said.

"Who is Dr. Knapps? Your mechanic?" I asked.

"No, he's my cat."

More hours of heat. I feared dying out there. I was a weak academic, even more weak than I am now.

Finally, the engine roared to life. We lumbered to Lalibela, checked in to our hotel a day late, watched the summer Olympics on satellite T.V., and ate Pizza Hut for dinner. L.J. roared whenever America won a trophy. His enthusiasm charged Rey, and before we knew it, it was a regular expatriate celebration. We ran around the hotel singing the Star Spangled Banner in the fading daylight. The street kids danced with us and a ten-year-old named Eli told Rey that now was the time to see St. George's, in the vesper light.

He whispered to Rey a plan.

We fired up the diesel. Rey made me pray a blessing over it. I reminded him that I wasn't a priest. He just said, "Clothes make the man."

L.J. and I rode in the back seat. Carl, Rey, and Eli took the front. Rey raced like he was in a Brooklyn rickshaw through the winding streets back into the country. We approached a silo, where Rey and the boy ran to meet what appeared to be the boy's father. Rey gave the man his watch and all the cash on him, and then Eli and Rey entered the silo and returned with ropes and a small hang glider.

As darkness fell over the valley, we reached St. George's. Then with our final 10,000 dollars, Rey bribed the guards to leave. I'm sure they didn't need 10,000 dollars, but it's pretty cool to bribe someone with that much money.

I'm not sure if you have ever seen a picture of St. George's: the monolithic church was a giant cross carved into the Ethiopian hills hundreds of years ago. That is to say ancient artists and workmen carved all but a forty foot cross-shaped building from the mountain. I don't know if I've ever seen anything from that world that was so remarkable. How many people had sojourned across Ethiopia for the last 800 years to worship in this place? While Dante wrote and Columbus sailed and Shakespeare watched mediocre actors recite his brilliant verse, people worshiped in this giant cross. I wonder if it ever seemed normal to them to walk into the cliff like that. Was it as routine for them as going to the ATM or grocery store?

Rey tied a rope to his waist.

Eli tied the other end to the diesel.

Rey grabbed the hang-glider and ran faster than anyone outside of the Olympic village could and jumped off the hill from which St. George's had been carved.

Rey leapt and sailed over the church. It really wasn't that far across, and with his speed and a hang-glider, he flew well beyond his landing zone. So he tried again, only this time he started from farther back. I asked him why he wouldn't just run more slowly and not risk falling. He just laughed at me and began his launch.

Rey danced on top of St. George's. We decided to take a more traditional approach. After creating a series of redundancies to make sure we would not fall, we climbed upside down pulling with our hands and hanging with our legs over the gap to the cross. Carl climbed to his father first, then L.J. and Eli. I was last and charged to bring the provisions: wine, sunflower seeds, seltzer water, Doritos, and a few loaves of bread. Once I crossed, Rey cut the rope.

"Why the hell did you do that?"

Rey didn't seem to understand the question and shouted to the sky something about Icarus and Aldonza.

We feasted on the ancient, holy site. We slept on the roof, on the cross of Jesus Christ. Rey must have woken just before I did at the first light of dawn. When I opened my eyes and sat up to survey the majesty, Rey had just launched himself off the church and into the pale blue morning. A gust of wind pushed him upward for a moment before he fell silently to the continent below.

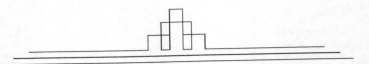

ROBOT BLOOD PART 3

CH 11

AUGUST 1, 2007

After gliding off St. George's, Rey bounced down the continent, dragging L.J. and me with him. We were pinballs vulnerable to gravity and every neon obstacle as we approached what could be certain death or a well-timed strike by a flipper culminating in more vainglory as we rose and fell to earth again.

During August we stayed in a villa in Fish Hoek, South Africa. We surfed, fished, and drank. The journey had already provided countless tales from Rey and a series of poems and published articles, most notably: "U.S. Swagbassador to Africa," "*CARL<3!*," and "The Genius Brigade." For the sake of brevity, the end of the journey is most important. You have to get to the end of this journey.

One morning when I was conveniently asleep, Rey and L.J. escaped the villa to the mountains. There in first rays of the sun, Rey placed a chisel to the wall of the famous and ancient Peers Cave.

L.J. chanted in Latin; Rey called to God for help, after all this was a vital stage in his quixotic mission from God.

With one strike the chisel cracked the wall in a perfect 8.5 by 11-inch pattern. Rey carefully removed the cracked rock, and pulled from the wall a tablet upon which the world's first poem had been written. There it waited for someone worthy to read it for over 15,000 years.

I guess I should have mentioned earlier that I believe nothing in this dubious account, but it is fun, and Rey and L.J.s elaborate work to prove its veracity was endearing.

A strong wind blew southeast that morning. That much I have verified and appears to be rare in August, perhaps a miracle in itself.

I can't, however, verify the "God's honest truth of the story" that Rey told me dozens of times about his battle.

The force with which Rey dislodged the tablet—that had rested within that ancient wall for so many millennia that it appeared to be part of the wall itself— unleashed a cloud of dust throughout the cave, covering both men before escaping into that temperate August winter. The southeasterly wind, usually prominent in the summer months, called the Cape Doctor, descended upon the peninsula. The dust escaped to the Indian Ocean. The Cape Doctor threw it far into the ocean.

Rey and L.J. climbed out of the cave to the top of the rocks. Rey thanked God, and L.J. praised the Cape Doctor. The dust scattered far over the ocean dissipating until its contents were unidentifiable to any animal who may be seeking the ancient poem, that is any animal, but the second most poetic creature: the albatross.

Seventy miles offshore, Lord Magnon sensed something (I hate saying his name, but Rey always insisted that I refer to him by his rightful name, which of course, Rey invented but claimed it came to him in a vision). The bird breathed the dissipated molecules and knew that the poem his kin had protected for millennia had been unearthed. That most poetic of fowl dove into the water, captured a fish for energy before turning north to battle that other poetic bird, Rey Pescador, for a tablet so precious either creature would die to protect it.

The albatross approached the beach. He could certainly see three miles inshore where Rey danced and L.J. translated the ancient text.

L.J. transcribed the text directly onto his arm to have a clear and legitimate copy in case anything unforeseen should happen as the geniuses descended the mountain. They brought no paper or camera by which to document their work. It was a common trope in Rey's adventures. Despite being constantly surrounded by paparazzi, none of Rey's wildest stories seemed to be documented.

When L.J. finished, Rey grabbed the tablet and held it above his head for a final time. The furious Cape Doctor blew. The tablet elevated from Rey's hands. The Cape Doctor tried to shatter the poem onto the rocky earth, but the noble and powerful Lord Magnon had other plans. The great fowl snatched the tablet with its incredible beak. He landed with delicate authority on a rock about fifteen feet from Rey and L.J.

Rey had not spent his life on a mission as God's greatest poet to fail his quest like this. He ran across the rocky surface and jumped to the massive bird's perch. He landed, somersaulted, and tackled the bird.

Lord Magnon pecked Rey in the right eye with his beak. Rey crumpled to the ground. Then the bird unfolded its massive wings. He grabbed the poem with his beak, and began to take flight. Seeing double, Rey had a fifty-percent chance to catch the bird and save the poem. He chose right, of course. Rey held his right foot and commanded him into submission.

The bird landed before really taking flight. It dropped the poem and sat on it. Rey determined to kill his opponent. He knew the bird would prefer to die after failing in this calling. Rey pulled his knife out of its sheath (he never traveled in places like this without a knife). Lord Magnon bowed its head. Then Rey remembered Coleridge's masterpiece.

He could not kill this creature.

He could not let it live without the poem.

So Rey picked up the tablet, gave it to Lord Magnon, and watched the bird fly toward the ocean propelled by the incredible wind.

Rey and L.J. walked back to town. They rushed to the villa. I was reading Wordsworth and drinking coffee when Rey burst through the door, L.J. a dozen feet behind.

Out of breath, Rey looked at me and smiled, with his eternal smile. I closed Wordsworth. It was story time.

"David, you'll never believe what happened."

Perhaps that was the only true sentence Rey told anyone that day.

ROBOT BLOOD PART 4

CH 12

AUGUST 2007

15,000 years after humans first entered Peer's Cave to escape the sky's wrath, Rey and L.J. famously carved a rectangular hole in the cave. One week later, I followed Rey up the dunes to the ancient shelter in the temperate beauty of a South African winter night for this battle that was not-so-creatively titled "The L.J. Brovault Fight of the Millennium."

To celebrate two months of epic encounters in Africa, L.J. staged what he believed would be the greatest fight in history. He could only sell 200 tickets, because of the cave's size, so he sold them to the 200 richest, most depraved gamblers he could find. It's incredible how much people will spend to watch people fight in an ancient arena.

Those 200 people were now sitting on 200 steel chairs, watching two men whose steel hearts furiously pumped blood to limbs in hopes to concuss a human brain.

L.J. found it delicious.

After the welter-weights finished the opening fight, L.J. strolled into the circle to regale his patrons with long-winded cantor, "Welcome, friends. Welcome! Of all the moments in all the days, in all the months, in all..."

The inebriated crowd endured a seemingly unending rhapsodic speech from the man they hoped (and expected with good reason) would soon owe each of them thousands.

"Let's get this fight going!" he said as he pushed aside a dozen men in charcoal suits to reach his elevated throne.

Each heart clicked with Cutlerian precision, except for Rey's organic heart that throbbed as he spotted a woman in a red dress. It is a myth that the color red attracted Rey—though plenty of women had dyed their hair crimson after receiving backstage passes to see Rey Pescador, and blogs claimed that these women had better success attracting Rey than the others. But it wasn't the color that mattered— it was the confidence with which a woman in a red dress moved that triggered something chemical in his heart. At least, that's what Rey said.

Hair, dress, hat, blouse, etc. mean less to a man than how they make waves of pheromones and light dance before approaching the essential recesses in the occipital lobe. Rey reached the red woman, placed his hand just under her shoulder blades, on the valley of skin between fabric hills, and whispered something absurd. She feigned surprise at his black eye. "How did you get that?" she asked, allowing Rey to walk her outside of the cave to see the very place that he conquered the bird.

The fight began. I turned to the circle and consumed the violence.

The bodies observing became a single organism: it swayed and jumped. It chanted in bloodlust.

It gasped. I couldn't see the fighters from my vantage point. I only saw the circle of men swell and shrink with each punch. A fighter hit the ground shaking the cave floor.

Dark liquid shot on two cave walls. Awe, delight, horror. Brovault screamed, "No! He's dead!"

I rushed to the poor, dying soul. I don't know how I expected to save him. You know the extent of my medical training. Regardless of my incompetence, the wall of bodies instinctually let me enter, then I saw that there was no human fighter in the center, only a mangled humanoid robot, a tin shell, over a steel, robotic, heart. It wasn't a boxing match at all. It was a robot fight.

I almost started to laugh, but Brovault dove on the crushed pop can of a creature in hysteria screaming what I presumed was its name.

I placed my arm around Brovault's shoulder and spoke quietly, hoping not to embarrass him or let him embarrass himself anymore, "Listen, L.J. you're losing it buddy. It's a machine.

Maybe you lost some cash, but you look like a lunatic."

He reached into the artificial organs and covered his hands with the black oil. He stripped off his shirt and smeared it on his chest.

"Seriously, dude, you've lost it. Let's get back to the hotel."

"He was intelligent," Brovault confessed to me, then again he said it too loudly, "He was intelligent."

The crowd was mute. Firelight illuminated panoramic mourning on the sober faces. Their sadness pissed me off beyond belief.

"Listen, you pieces of shit!" I shouted. "You think you are no different from this machine because you have the same heart. Because this thing is coded with a human genome and synthetic blood, you think it is your brother or something?" I laughed again. "You think that. I, however, do not. I've spent my entire theological career exploring the implications of the RHC and the implications of the possibility of intelligent machines."

My passion was not winning the crowd. No one wanted a lecture, so I decided to act, just one time.

In a fit of mania I hoisted the remains of the beaten athlete from the ground. The other bot had dismembered this AI creature, so I only needed to shoulder the weight of his split torso and head. He was smaller and lighter than I imagined, about my height and weight. There was something beautiful in his engineering. His creator took great care to ensure he was perfectly designed to kill. From his titanium and carbon-fiber alloy to his Kevlar joints, he was a work of art with a specific purpose.

I raised the robot to my face: the torch-lit chromium projected the grotesque image of my face on a metallic frame with an open chest; my RHC organ blinked green and bled. In the flicker of flames, the crowd erupted behind me. Pandemonium invaded my cerebellum; the rhythm of their chants invaded my stomach. My heart clicked one with theirs. I guess it always was, but I felt it in that moment. My being dispersed into that single organism bent on violence and hate.

I lifted the robot above my head.

I thrashed the corpse to the ground.

I turned to the victorious bot behind me; I engaged him in

battle.

"I too have a metal heart. Fight me!"

Its eyes and ears and radar perceived. Fortunately, for me, Rey had returned to the cave after hearing the roar. His focus— momentarily distracted from the dress by the crowd's elation— shifted to me. He ran into the arena to save me from the automaton. As it lifted its metal fist to my throat, Rey slapped the artificially intelligent being on the back, "Who the hell let this guy drink?" He laughed trying to evoke emotion in a being that was less intelligent than L.J. would have let on. "I mean, you'd crush him." My eyes were still locked with the creature. My posture still beckoned violence, which was all its circuits could comprehend, but Rey managed to place himself in front of the robot, cutting off its ability to see me.

Clear from its field of vision, the tension lifted. My limbs were still connected to my body. After Rey made a few jokes attempting to ease the machine's anger, he sobered and looked at me. "Dude, that machine is going to kill you. Let's get the hell out of here."

Brovault started taking bets against me, which I still think is proof that I would have won. Rey and I scurried out of the cave. A red dress covering white legs fluttered after us.

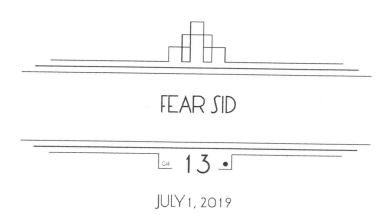

FEAR SID

JULY 1, 2019

In Africa the Genius Brigade was born. Rey owned the world. L.J. became a household name. I followed my cousin to the edge of civilization and nearly died.

Of course, once again I'm glossing over most of the stories, and some of the important people, but the only ones I ever cared about were Rey and L.J. and, well, I have to admit Carl. He was seriously a cool monkey. I'm concerned that I'm also missing the stifling presence of the member who created the Genius Brigade, who sent us to Africa and back to the United States. He's haunted me for decades, but during those years, we didn't know how evil he was. We didn't notice how he loomed over everyone, and in everyone, but Rey.

I'm not fearful anymore; I'm ready to tell you who Sid Cutler really is.

During the heart-breaking summer of 2021, two weeks before I collapsed on the front porch, in the abnormal heat, you went to Oak Street Beach with Christian. It was after Sunday mass and lunch. I was writing in my study. Do you remember the homily that I gave that morning? You probably don't. I mean, it was one message sixteen years ago. I remember this one, though. I remember you and Christian sitting there, in the front row with about fifty other parishioners. I brought it with me here to California—the homily that is. I just reread it. Not my best work.

I brought a lot of things here. I don't want you to think that I am living in squalor carving these stories on rocks and having

77

some grad student type and deliver them to you. Certainly, I've been more comfortable, but the town is luxurious now compared to how it was when Rey and I first traveled here. It's filled with the esoteric type of crowd that would come to the place where Rey was resurrected. They remind me of the stories that I've forgotten, and when I'm alone I review all of my notes and journals from the last sixty years. I have everything I wrote while I traveled with Rey. A dozen Pescador biographers can't even approach the knowledge I have on my cousin. I wrote down virtually everything he said to me. And he told me virtually every thought he had.

Anyway, let's get back to Sid Cutler and my homily. As I mentioned, the homily itself was not the most artful, but the topic was important: the problem of evil. I explained that, though he was no longer popular in contemporary religious conversation, we must not forget that the devil still exists. Afterward, while you and Christian went to the beach to enjoy the mania of a holiday in Chicago, I stayed home as usual, and read and sucked in the air-conditioning wondering if I should have joined you at the beach. If I was Christian's father and your husband, rather than merely the surrogate for a better man, would I have gone, or would I have sat there in my study believing I had better work to do? I should have gone to the beach with you. I'm sorry for that. I should have been a better father to Christian. I'm sorry for that too.

That evening when you put Christian to sleep, I listened to you two from my study. I heard you pray. Did anyone else in the world have that type of faith anymore? Then I heard Christian's twelve-year-old voice ask, "What does the devil look like? I need to know."

"Why do you *need* to know, honey?"

"Well, think about it. I mean, seriously, what if this guy tried to hurt us?"

"He can't hurt us."

"Because of Uncle David?"

"Not really. Uncle David is a good man, but more importantly the devil can't hurt us because of this man." You pointed at the crucifix around your neck. You took it off and gave it to Christian.

"Can I have it?"

"Yes. Yes, you can. It was your father's. It should be yours now."

You continued to talk. Shit, Rebecca, of all the conversations I've ever heard that one scared me the most. I physically shuddered when Christian asked about the devil.

Fear Sid.

That was the saying. It was the one command I had always followed. Even as a grown man, under my Chicago Bears fleece in July, I froze in fear. You see, I've wanted to tell you this for decades, but knew you would think I was insane. I figure at this point, if you trust me still, after the whole fountain of youth story, then this is just another part of a whacky life.

Here is the truth.

I have seen the devil a hundred times. I've talked with him. I've smelled his cologne as he lumbered by me. I've flown in his jet. I've sat in his office. And not only that, you've seen him too. He was at your wedding. He was there watching the sacrament. Shit. One more thing, Christian already knew what he looked like. He had seen the devil almost daily. He was on a poster in the den room with his father and two other men: that infamous newspaper photo; however, a *Tribune* cover could never show his likeness. He hates everyone. Every tick of my heart he accuses me of my great sins, of every sin there was.

The truth is that Sid Cutler is the devil.

This is not some metaphor cooked up by my fantastic poet cousin. This is the God's honest truth.

But I have stopped fearing him. The thing is this, Sid Cutler thought that reminding me of my sins would bring me down. He thought it would ruin me. But what Sid Cutler didn't understand is that the memory of my sins was my great strength. It allowed me to see the need of grace. If Cutler knew that, he would have ceased to accuse me altogether. God knows he tried everything else.

So while you were talking with Christian in his room that night, I almost pushed the orange and blue fleece blanket off my lap to warn him about Sidney's fat pink face and gregarious laugh, about how he always conned someone into following him with the same tactic. First, he made you want something more than anything in the world. Then he made you think it was wrong to want it. Then he gave you what you desired, so you felt like you were damned already, so you might as well keep going. Then he would take it away and make you truly damn yourself to get it back. But I didn't leave my office. I just rocked in my chair and read my book.

After all, I didn't need to tell Christian about him. Why should I? Sidney never won a battle against us and never would. We had grace, and if there is one thing Sidney never understood, it was grace.

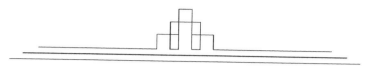

THE FALL OF FAME

FALL 2007

What could be more iconic than that photograph turned poster that graced Christian's wall and the walls of every poetry, sports, rap, or science fan who admired, but would never pursue enigmatic fame? And let's be honest, who didn't fit those criteria in 2007?

I remember when the reporter asked for just one photo and Cutler told the men and boy to huddle up. It was just outside Riley's Steakhouse as the sun was beginning to set. The vesper light illuminated four men with their characteristic features: Rey's smile on his ageless face, Cutler's sweat and the smoke of his cigar shrouding his clammy, sun-burnt skin, Riley's blank gaze with eyes focused just below the camera's lens, and L.J. Brovault's sixteen-year-old frame uncomfortable under the right-wing of Cutler. The headline simply read, "SID CUTLER'S BRIGADE OF GENIUSES."

It was the image of the year, but it certainly wasn't the only moment that stood out.

While I won't claim to own a traveling in time machine like L.J. famously claimed, I do have some other images of that year to whet your memory:

Rey Pescador walks out of a St. Rita's Catholic Church in Chicago. A paparazzo snaps a shot. Rey, who was in the church to

81

use the bathroom and is still extraordinarily drunk, pukes in the bushes. Paparazzo catches moment, but it looks like he is bowing in reverence (the guy made puking while drunk into an art form). Later that day, Rey signs a deal, quite ironically, as a Catholic abstinence spokesman. "I just like to give back to the teens," he says in his interview, before saying, "I mean take away, I mean,

shit." The diocese of Chicago only used the first part of the quotation.

A fighting robot lies in a ring inert. The imprint of a human fist reveals that this is not a technical problem: no need to call customer support. Out of focus between the robot and euphoric fans, Edwin Riley's left arm proclaims victory in the only legal human vs. bot world championship we would ever see.

A magazine ad captures Brovault lying in the center of three piles of books in a University of Chicago library. One of his famous notebooks sits on his chest with a series of equations on the paper, but only one equation is legible: RHC = Life. The caption of the ad says, "The most important equation of my life is a no brainer. Register your heart for upgrades today."

Surrounded by his brigade of geniuses, who are all wearing Scottish kilts—including Rey, which is quite the sight—Sid Cutler cuts the ribbon for a new golf course in Death Valley. A semi-permeable dome keeps the air a modest 65-80 degrees, depending on the season. It is his most glorious excess.

Rey Pescador announces that he is both the spokesman for Reebok and Adidas and that the two companies are merging. He celebrates by wearing a shoe from each brand while he answers questions from reporters regarding his National Book Award and Spanish Language National Book Award for his book *This Primal*

Life and its Spanish translation, respectively. I watch it live. I am angry. I wrote the Spanish version and half of the English. Rey does not thank his translator, rather he says, "The language is just in my blood, amigo."

The fall of 2007 began and ended full of images like that. The Fall of Fame, that is what we called it, though I can't remember if that was a pop culture phrase or a GB phrase. Either way, during that season excess defined my cousin and his closest friends. Even Carl gained a reputation as the platonic form of monkey stoners, which he probably was.

Rey and the crew visited dozens of colleges selling books and rap albums, giving lectures, reading poetry, and partying with girls all over the East Coast and Midwest. The image of Rey that permeated the national conscious was a man sleeping in bedrooms of women all over the U.S. while he reveled in the poetry of his own charm.

That depiction of Rey isn't entirely untrue.

He was a Lothario par excellence, but I think even at his worst he was more than that. He didn't only chase women and tout his swag; you would have just as good a chance finding Rey in the library or chapel or jotting in a notebook about the meaning of life in a small brewery just off campus without any intentions of getting laid.

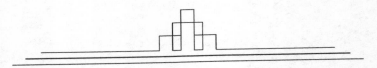

A DAMNED MYSTERY

CH 15 •

FALL 2007

That's where I found him: in a small brewery drinking an amber ale when he was supposed to be at a photo shoot and Cutler's cronies swore they were done "working in these conditions" with Rey Pescador. They weren't. The College Tour ground to a halt.

Rey glanced out the window in Bloomington Indiana at leaves the color of his beer, jotting down his thoughts, hoping to be acknowledged but not interrupted.

I sat down. Neither of us said a word, except for me when I ordered a stout.

Rey was writing, but mostly we sipped beer and watched each person who walked by admire the celebrity, not sure how to respond to his greatness. Rey often analyzed every person around him. Anyone wearing tweed would be a professor, or probably a professor. Any beautiful woman must be an English major and must be talking about his poetry. But this time he said nothing for about twenty minutes until he started to gesture toward the two women sitting at the table directly south of us, at the front of the restaurant.

"Do you think they're talking about me?" he said too loudly for my comfort.

"You're sitting right here, they can hear you."

"I have to piss. Tell me if they say anything about me."

Rey went to the bathroom.

I had a mission now, to eavesdrop. I probably would have anyway, not because they were attractive, but because I always eavesdrop at restaurants. The girl whose back was toward us was blond and in her mid-twenties. The other was probably thirty with hard dark brown hair. She was lovely. That is all I remember about their features, though I'm sure Rey could have written an epic poem on them.

Though I scoffed at his vanity, I was certain they would start whispering once the poet left the room about how amazing he was and how much they wanted him. I mean, he was freaking Rey Pescador, and this was 2007. Another reason for my suspicion was that at the time, and probably now, I knew nothing about women and was tainted by Rey's view of them. Here is what I remember of their conversation.

"I haven't been saving as much money as I want to lately," the blonde one said.

"I hardly save anything. You'd be depressed to see my bank account. I shouldn't even have a bank account."

"All these adult expenses are getting to me. I mean, I don't even have kids, and I still live with my parents, I should be able to save more, but my car broke down, and I have to pay for grad school applications. And my parents made me pay my dog's surgery bills to teach me responsibility."

"Well, it only gets worse. Save what you can now, and try to get a high paying job in literary criticism or something."

"I don't know, I think I want to go into sales."

"An idealist."

"Have you tried the Tolstoy Panini? It has pesto."

"Yeah, it's good."

Rey would have described his trip back from the bathroom as an attempt to garner the devotion of the fairer sex. Sometimes I forget what a misogynistic bastard he could be. His attempt was futile. The women noticed his strut and just rolled their eyes after he passed their field of vision. So it was thus proven: women could resist Rey's charm, and relatively easily, I might add. Rey sat, smiled at me like a thirteen-year-old boy certain that he had just changed some girl's life with a love note, and took another sip of the beer.

He stared out at the sunlight for a while.

"David, can I tell you something?" he asked.

"Of course."

"I think I'm depressed."

"Seriously, you're the happiest person I've ever met."

"Maybe depressed isn't the right word."

"It might be. But depression, true depression, often leads to inactivity. I mean a depressed person has trouble getting out of bed and finds no joy in his favorite things."

"Yeah, that isn't quite it. I guess I feel aimless. I'm not a kid anymore."

"I know you aren't."

"But I act like one."

"I know you do."

"And on top of that, let's be honest, this isn't exactly the life I wanted when I was a kid."

"It kind of was, wasn't it?"

"I mean, I wanted to be famous, but I wanted to do something great, not just get drunk with beautiful women every night."

"Life is hard."

"I'm serious, I don't want to keep doing this."

"Then settle down. Become a monk like you said you would be in high school."

"I didn't want to be a monk. I wanted to be a saint like Francis with the freaking stigmata or one of those guys who killed a dragon. Being a writer is fine if I'm Shakespeare and Cervantes rolled into one, but I prefer to be the type of saint that cripples a regime and is badass enough to have parents name their kids after him for a millennia."

"Well, your current trajectory isn't exactly sainthood, but you may have some kids named after you. Some might even be your own."

"That's not really the point. I'm not sure what is though. Unless, well, I think I figured it out, David. Yeah, I figured it out."

"What did you figure?"

He took a long drink of amber ale. He looked past the women to the window and the Midwest sun.

"As far as I can tell, I'm not depressed, but I heard something once, something so beautiful that I was convinced it was God telling me that my life mattered, that I could do something great, and now that voice has faded. It's like I can't hear what I'm listening for. I'm obsessively searching, and you know what? I can't hear it with all this noise around."

"So what are you going to do?"

"I am going to keep writing. But once my current contractual requirements are finished, I'm through with public fame until I hear the voice I'm looking for."

"That's not at all what I thought you were saying."

"I'm a damn mystery."

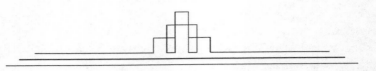

SHAKESPEARE X CERVANTES = REY PESCADOR

FALL 2007

The night we drank beer in Bloomington, he locked himself in his hotel room and refused to exit. I drove back to Chicago. A telegram from Rey was waiting when I arrived. I swear no one used telegrams like Rey; though I'm not sure he ever mastered it as an art form.

David, thank you for the advice STOP You are right STOP I need to become more famous STOP I am committed to ditching my current image and working enough to become Shakespeare and Cervantes in one STOP beautiful brown package STOP

Rey flew to L.A. to fulfill his contractual obligations.

Rey wrote the literature of all time that fall. That fact you certainly know.

Fueled by his success, he proclaimed to the world just how great he was during the season premiere of the live HBO series, *Genius Circus*.

I watched it live with Brenda, my research assistant, her sister, and Brenda's fiancé. There in the apartment that Brenda and Tom—or Brian or Chuck whatever his name was—shared, I had to endure three dehumanizing conversations:

1-Brenda's compliments of me and my role as Rey's adviser. It was obviously a surprise, blind, double date, and I was paired with the wrong person.

2-Tom/Brian/Chuck's contemptuous tone toward Brenda— he ultimately exited with a door slam.

3-Rey Pescador's absurd interview with some poor wannabe

journalist.

I think the interviewer's name was Bridget Murphy or something absurd. She was very Irish looking, of course, and she took her first serious job seriously despite being hired because of the myth that red attracted Rey "The Bull" Pescador. I shouldn't have brought this up. It's hard not to go on a fifty-page tangent, but I guess the Brenda era gets me angry. We'll get to that.

Rey sat next to Bridget, flirting and waxing eloquently about Africa and Europe and "good 'ole American diners with the best waitresses around." Ms. Murphy played along as the red-haired, long legged interviewer by asking a few softball questions about Rey's skin treatment and hair care.

Then she shocked the genius who was fully intoxicated on her legs and his greatness by asking, "Some have said that there would never be a moment when the popular and the artistic combine. Rey, we know you are popular, but last month several important professors, including Kerr at Stanford, said that your writing is not truly 'artistic,' or at least not high art. How would you respond to his criticism?"

Ignoring the second part of the question, Rey addressed the first, "But why can't they? Why can't beauty be entertaining? Why can't art matter to a regular American dude? I think it's just because there have only been a few great artists-scholars in history. A few great geniuses: Shakespeare, Cervantes, Twain, Plato, etc. Each at their own time, or at least within their own countries locked away, working and showering the people with the beauty of their words. Shakespeare and Twain were popular. But I mean, think about it. Holy shit... Can I say that?" She nodded. "Then HOLY SHIT what if all of these men were writing, speaking, and inventing in one room at the same time? The fame... the power; that's what we're seeing."

"Are you comparing the popularity of The Genius Brigade with the brilliance of these great thinkers?"

"Hell yeah!" Rey cried out. The crowd erupted. "Hell yeah; even the Bard himself never had two billion tune in for an HBO special."

Neither had Rey Pescador. This type of fact checking, however, was never explored by the equally infatuated media.

The audience forgot standard decorum as Rey stood on top of the coffee table and stripped off his oxford (though he kept his undershirt on), did a front flip, and Brovault jumped down from the rafters to a microphone and gave a scintillating lecture on the possibility of a rose.

A stage hand stealthily handed Shannon another note card. Disgusted both with the wording and content, but wanting a job, she read the final question, "Rey and L.J., you have given us so much already, but I am told that you have even more to give. Is it true that you have a new book coming out that will be greater than any of your previous works, a book that is both primal and academic?"

Rey looked at L.J., who was supposed to speak, but he simply stared into Bridget's eyes. Usually, L.J. ignored women but something about Bridget stunned him.

"I'll answer that one sweet-heart," Rey replied. "The rumors are true. This summer we participated in tom-foolery on both sides of the Atlantic. We have trekked deep into Africa and found the world's first poem. The journey was a near-disaster, one crew member died, another contracted rabies, and several syphilis. I even saved Brovault's life on the way. After contracting malaria, I lost about fifteen pounds, and no bros, I do not recommend that as a weight-loss routine. But all jokes aside, we have compiled the information and created a documentary film, a book of poems, and an academic volume on the experience.

"Thank you Rey, thank you L.J."

The Nielsen ratings proved that no one had grown tired of the Genius Brigade, but the numbers were still a fraction of the number of two billion viewers that Rey claimed. No one noticed; no one took notes; no one was sober; no major news outlets contended Pescador's outlandish claims. In fact, *The Christian Science Monitor* read: "He's delivered everything that he claims, beauty and truth, truth and beauty. All of these he's given to the masses and I'm pretty sure he's responsible (both directly and indirectly) to more children being born this year than any chick flick in the history of cinema. And for that, he is a life-giver as well as a scholar."

No one even cared that less than a decade earlier genius Rey

Pescador had been expelled from school and was drinking in a South Side Seven Eleven wondering how to get his GED. No one noticed that of the Genius Brigade only L.J. Brovault and I had attended college, and I wasn't technically a member. Also, the handsome amateur boxer Edwin Riley whom *Time* Magazine called "Fists of Genius Riley," wasn't even a scholar, let alone a genius. Riley had dumb luck, the eye of Cutler, and happened to beat Rey in a street fight outside Little Italy just before literally punching the lights out of a robot: genius was a world away. No one noticed. No one cared.

No one cared except for me, still pissed that Rey didn't thank me for the National Book Award and still determining whether I should make a move on Brenda's sister or hope that Tom/Brian/Chuck would never come back.

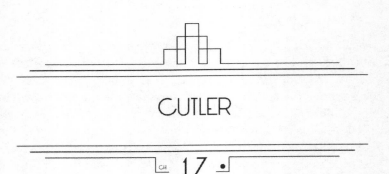

CUTLER

FEBRUARY 2008

When his office door opened, Sid Cutler engulfed Rey Pescador with a grand paternal hug. The two laughed about something. Rey looked at me and said, "You remember David." Sid nodded in my direction, saying, "David."

Rey and I sat in armchairs looking at Sid from his throne behind his mahogany desk.

Sid smiled. He chuckled a little bit.

"I am very happy you two are here. We are going to do amazing work together this year," he said and leaned over to shake Rey's hand, but Sid Cutler never shook my hand.

I have, however, imagined the sensation.

Unless you've met him I doubt you can imagine Sid Cutler: he sweats, always; he has the yellow and pink hue of a newborn baby; his handshake, I imagine, is textbook—firm, but not too firm, almost forgiving considering its potential energy (if anything about him can forgive).

He could surely burst a football in his fist.

He looks his victim in the eye during the 2.3 second embrace. It's just long enough to know that, yes, he can crush any hand, and no, he will not crush this hand at this moment. Not only does he look you in the eye, but in the very pupil and maybe beyond: to all the rods and cones that trigger color and light and emotion.

The glistening sweat on his spherical face made him at times almost jovial. Like a great stage actor, he opened his mouth wide when he spoke. Also, like a great actor, he was clearly acting. The thing is that only cynical audience members would notice, and they could never convince anyone else that he was unconvincing.

Despite observing all of this over the years, I still trusted him during that meeting. I wanted his approval.

Rey approached the planet that is Sid Cutler for orbit, shook his hand. Both men sat. Cutler did not look my direction until he was seated. He never reached his hand out. He did, however, speak to me, "David, you know I'm Mr. Cutler, and this is my assistant Cassandra," he motioned toward the woman who was entering the room from a second door behind Sid's desk.

"Hi Cassandra," I said uncomfortably. "Thank you for having me here, Mr. Cutler."

"Well, your cousin can be pretty convincing," Sid said.

"My charm is allegedly legendary," Rey added.

Cassandra filled three glasses with pink liquid. Sid cast a vision for the next year, the wealth and fame of Rey and his brigade. We all drank Lilac Whiskey. Sidney coughed and cleared his throat over and over again. Cassandra broke crab legs and fed the meat to the corpulent executive.

"Let me tell you something, David. I enjoy crab legs," Sidney said. "But I cannot stand the feeling of crushing them. Cassandra has a firm grip and was originally hired for this very purpose. She makes more than most people, has benefits, and was hired merely to crush crab legs. Now, David, you are here in my office hoping that I change your life?"

"This kid can write philosophy and theology like it's nobody's business. He's at UC pulling mid six figures or something, but my goodness, Sid if you read these ideas," Rey began.

"I've heard your pitch, Rey; I want to hear from David.'"

"Yes sir, well I've written several things that might be interesting, but the thing I'm really hoping you like is my dissertation." I waited for him to speak. He shivered. His jaw shifted to my right and muttered something unintelligible.

"Forgive me, David," he said. "I suffer from neck spasms. Rey is used to them, I'm sure."

"I'm sorry to hear that," I said.

"Cassandra is good at keeping me relatively loose, but these long days can be painful," Sid added.

"Well, I will try not to take up too much of your time." He looked at me, but did not respond.

I started to explain my dissertation, but a moment in, he jerked again and shouted. "Not now, you fiend!" Then he smiled and laughed.

"I've been called the most eccentric of my peers. I think the word they wanted was deranged. Never care too much what the rich think about you, David. Though, I guess that is unlikely to be a problem for you. I'm going to shoot straight with you. Your dissertation appears to be an in-depth critique of the RHC, which paid for this jet and everything on it, including Cassie here. I make it a point not to bite the hand that feeds me—at least not hard."

Rey tried to defend me, but I cut him off. I had to convince the Cannonball or this meeting would be finished soon. "But it's not a critique of the RHC," I started. "Well, I mean, that isn't the purpose. It is a theological study of the implications. The real question that I explored is what happens if death is eradicated. If people cannot die, what is the hope of heaven?"

"There is the kill switch in your model, David," Cutler rebutted.

"I'm no theologian, Sid," Rey said, "but suicide's a pretty big sin."

"Suicide? The kill switch isn't suicide. It is the termination of a program, like hitting the X at the top of a window," Cutler scoffed.

"A program that sustains human life. I understand there is a gray area here but to compare it to closing a program on a computer seems more than insensitive, Mr. Cutler," I said.

"David, do you know that the newest hearts do not contain a kill switch? They cannot turn off, and like your heart they filter cancerous cells. They know when to request antibiotics. They have, more or less, extended life indefinitely. In fact, we are working on an upgrade, where even if most of the body is killed, the robotic heart would send blood only to the brain, so we could transfer it into another host. The technology is a few years away, but you get the point. Death has lost its proverbial sting."

I was impassioned. "Then this research is even more

important, especially as we develop more technologies that extend human life even more."

"So you want me to publish a book saying that Catholics love human life so much that you see me as the devil for helping people live longer? Am I getting that right? You really think people will buy that?"

"I guess I do. They certainly will buy it. We all know philosophical works are big business," I said.

"We sure do, but that's no reason to publish you. However, David, I am going to publish you..." Rey started jumping up and down. He grabbed a bottle of Lilac Whiskey, chugged it, and yelled, "My big cousin is getting published by my boy Sid Cutler. Move over L.J., there's a new scholar in town. Rosario, baby! GB forever! GB Forever!"

Once Rey was subdued by Lilac Whiskey, Cutler smiled, stood, and for a moment, I thought he would shake my hand. Instead he whistled. Cassandra came back into the room, Cutler demanded more Lilac Whiskey. "Welcome to the Genius Brigade, David. And if you were wondering what I was about to say before being interrupted. That man there"—he gestured to Rey—"is why you are here. Publishing you will make me cash and shut him up. Get your research team together and write a final draft. Include some of the documents from the RHC archive that Cassandra's office will send you, and check in with me when you are ready for publication."

"Yes sir, thank you."

Cassandra poured Sid and me another round. Rey just drank from the bottle. Sid continued, "We have more business to discuss. Cassandra, print out a standard contract for David. David, you are welcome to stay to sign it once I'm finished meeting with Rey. That is if it's fine with you, Rey."

"Sure, this is my boy," Rey said.

After finishing the bottle of Lilac Whiskey, Rey was ready to eat. "So you going to keep your best talent hungry? Or are you going to offer me some of those legs?"

Cutler called Cassie on the intercom to bring crab legs and three bottles of wine.

"You know how to eat, Sid. If I never met you, I'd probably

have bought a Taco Bell franchise and stuffed myself with that every night. You'd have a fat poet on your hands," Rey added.

"I can attest to that," I said, uncertain how to approach the conversation which was shifting to Rey.

"Well, Rey, you can probably see that my diet has led to some added girth." He breathed deeply and shook off another evil spirit before addressing his significantly thinner and better looking counterpart. "David, you seem like a true believer," he said, "I am afraid that your ideas are, to quote someone from Rey's profession, 'suckled in a creed outworn.' But look at your cousin here. Rey can help you. He is like me, a man of appetites. Rey Pescador, the man of the world."

"Well, I can't disagree with you there, Sid. I believe in the sensuous particulars. That girl Cassie, damn me, if I could spend just ten minutes with her, you'd have another best-selling book to publish. Seriously Sid, if she wasn't yours, I think I'd be in love."

They laughed. Rey continued, "I'm a true believer too, you know. I believe in love and beauty and poetry and taste. And listen Sid, I don't really like you insulting my cousin and his faith."

"Rey, I understand the effects of Lilac Whiskey more than anyone else, but I will only ask you to maintain decorum once."

Cassie cleaned up Rey's mess at the side table between our chairs. Rey breathed in deep.

"Where were we?" Sid asked.

"Shit man, I can't remember. Cassie's legs just took over my mind. Actually, that's it. I was saying how I believe in beauty and love."

"That's it. I respect that. The problem is that your views, though marketable—hell, they are profitable— are still not scientific. Look at me for example: I am a man who enjoys eating. That's clear to anyone and the beauty of women, their touch, well, the animal instincts within me cannot resist to watch and be pleased by such creatures. But, I have never truly loved women. The reciprocity of a relationship moves beyond biological, to mystical. I have given contracts, in business, but only insofar as I can receive something more valuable to me. And that spirit, Rey, is what keeps our society advancing. So you see, love ... love is beyond my sphere of understanding. I am more binary than that,

Rey. The joy of food and drink is one-sided. I devour; I am pleased; I receive without giving, without my spirit, my body giving back in any way that could constitute a loss."

With Cassie gone, the billionaire devoured his crab legs like a starved dog while philosophizing about taste.

Sid continued his speech that was clearly planned, "Remember this, Rey and David: a powerful man can do nothing greater for himself, and for society than to receive in that way. You will have power, Rey. And David, I have plans for you that you wouldn't believe. I will give you power. But I will receive more in return, and you will start to understand the joy of receiving praise, worship, stimulation, and taste. I fear though that you will never understand it in quite the same way as me."

I tried to mutter something, but the Lilac Whiskey was clearly affecting me more than the other men. It was a bizarre intoxicant.

"I doubt I will," Rey said. "The whole world is a damn mystery to me, Sid. I'm not a philosopher like you or David or L.J... Hell, I don't have an education; I can barely put a coherent sentence together, unless it's in poetry because poetry has no rules, and because the muse is kind to me. But fame, who wouldn't want that? I used to walk down the streets of Chicago, like every other kid, just hoping not to get killed. I guess I figured, living with monks, I would be safe. Or maybe I wanted an excuse out. I wanted something to do after compline. It gets so damn quiet. My goal was to survive and meet some girls along the way and to win state in track. Now, I step into the street and women flock to me, Sid. Gang-bangers tell me that I speak for them. Scholars ask for my autograph. If it's quiet, I can walk out to the street, any street, pick the most beautiful girl and have her over."

All the while Sid ate his crab legs. Rey sipped on wine mesmerized at the unashamed consumption of the human planet across the table.

"That can't be all you want, Rey," Sid said, "someone to talk to at night, sex. That's how you're painted in the media, but there must be more. I can give you a billion dollars right now. That would keep you happy with hookers for a lifetime. Why do you really want fame?"

"I don't think that's what he wants at all," I managed to say to everyone's surprise.

Rey paused for a few moments. He didn't take another drink or look at his food. Rather, he did what he did in these rare moments that he tried to voice something for which he had inadequate words. He looked down, pulled his lower lip in slightly, then looked up and to the right without raising his chin. Then he found the idea somewhere in his parietal lobe and started speaking, "I guess I want fame because, I mean, it's hard to describe in words. I mean, in conversation. I could write a poem about it easy. I guess there is something that comes from the words. It's like poetry is sex: to create a poem that enters the mind and gives birth to a thought, requires poet and audience. And that idea may change everything, or nothing. But without an audience, without fame, what the hell is the purpose of it all? Never mind, that doesn't make any sense, but that's what I think."

Sid had finally finished his crab legs. He pushed himself away from the desk.

"And that is why, of all the people on the earth, I might just need you, Rey. You have the one thing I don't—the ability to give yourself to another to create something powerful. I am not cynical, Rey. I believe that you desire fame more than anything, and I believe your motives. Your soul is the key, Rey. It is the seed of your poetry. In it, with the proper marketing, is the ability to influence the world, to give birth to your passions: the passions of taste and beauty, of hedonism."

"No, that's not it. It's more than that. Sid, I want more than that, man. I want to be great. I am going to be the greatest poet, writer, prophet ever born."

"I didn't say you wouldn't become that. Your fame will bring it."

"That's not it. You aren't getting it, man. It's not about the crowds and the women. It's the word. You aren't getting my point."

"I think I am. You are saying that fame…"

"Listen to me, dammit! I'm saying that I'm done. I don't need crowds and tours. I will do one final goodbye show, then I'm done with public fame. I'm quitting it. I'm going to move back to a monastery or a freaking island somewhere to hear the voice of God. Then, and only then, I'm going to sing it to the world."

"You are done?"

"I'm done with the tours and the shows. I'll still write."

"You think that you are done?"

"I am telling you that I'm done. Did I stutter, Sid?"

"Rey, your whole half-ass existence is a stutter, you miserable, arrogant sonuvabitch."

Rey looked for a glass of pink liquid. He had finished everything that had been poured. There was, however, a final bottle of Lilac Whiskey on a bookshelf under one of Cutler's swords behind his desk. Rey went for the bottle, but Cutler blocked his way.

"You think you can drink my Lilac Whiskey." Cutler laughed. I've never heard a laugh like that, equally arrogant, ecstatic, and deranged. Sid continued, "Or is it my sword. You're going to kill the dragon on this mythic quest. Sit down and shut the hell up, Rey. You are not done. You are my kind of man, Rey. I understand you perfectly, and you understand that you will now sit and listen."

Rey sat.

Cutler breathed as well as he could with the constant pressure on his diaphragm. He laughed again and chewed on the last pieces of crab in a shell, "David, I hope that you will still work with me. Rey, I know that you will. We have history, Rey. I thought you looked up to me. You can understand my anger of you quitting like this, can't you?"

"I can," Rey said.

"You're right that you're done, though. Done with the crowds, whether you want them or not. Until you prove yourself again to me, you won't be able to fill a stadium again."

Rey laughed arrogantly. "You know that I can fill a stadium without your help."

Sid continued, "You will not have your final show in Chicago. I've filled that spot. Consider your contractual obligations toward me complete. In fact, you can publish with whomever you'd like. But know this, when you want to come back, and I suspect you will, I will not be as welcoming as the first time. I will demand more of you."

Rey looked at the ground, then in the eyes of Sid Cutler. "I'm sorry it came to this Sid. We had a good run."

"This isn't the end of anything except this meeting." Rey and I stood.

"David," Cutler shouted, "you are not excused. I have a contract for you to sign."

Rey and I looked at each other. How could I sign with him now? How could I not? Rey said, "Go for it, Cuz, you need this."

I signed a contract for the publication of my dissertation to be published by Cutler Corporations best academic imprint. By the time I walked out of the office, Rey had escaped to a bar. I called Brenda. We had work to do.

AGAMMEMNON

APRIL 2008

Two months after meeting with Sid, Rey and I were still in Chicago. I was working on the dissertation and planning lectures for a series of conferences. Rey was trying to clear his head to prepare himself for something beautiful.

Rey lay in bed and imagined himself on stage: the rush of eyes etching his face, his hair, his frame, and his smile into their eternal memories. He imagined his voice through the artificial power of a microphone. All of human technology and knowledge had worked together to create a society where he could exist and speak to these people in this way with the pyrotechnics and music and film and every other medium complimenting his perfection of verse.

He imagined himself throwing the microphone to the ground. His voice, a baritone, the color of Lake Superior with its ebb and flow and power, penetrated the twenty thousand humans.

Rey owned the 80th floor of the John Hancock building, the ultimate party penthouse in the Midwest, but he almost never left the guest room where he slept when he was alone.

The sun was rising over Lake Michigan. So Rey just sat up in the guest room bed and watched it peer over the water at him. The vaulted ceiling and walls were the same pure white. Rey spoke to the source of light, "Good morning, you old bastard." There was no response from the sun, but hearing his master speak from the room next door, Carl bounced into Rey's room and onto the pillow next to Rey.

"Morning Carl I love you, buddy."

The monkey had become Rey's most consistent companion. Rey had other friends. L.J. and Rey were close, but conversing with the child genius was often frustrating. Whenever we were in Chicago, I had work to do for the university. That left Rey with the carousel of fans that flooded his world of restaurants and bars, or talent agents, editors, and accountants who followed Cutler's prodigies with calculators and wristwatches. So Rey's brief conversations with Carl, that began almost as a joke, continued. Carl was his confidant. Rey loved the little monkey so much that he created the concept album *Carl<3!* Every song was dedicated to the primate. Most thought it was a joke, and well, what do I know but the fact that Rey loved that little guy as much as any man loved a pet?

Even after the meeting with Cutler, the carousel of fans spun steadily, but Rey became increasingly hollow without the stimulus of crowds chanting his name. Individual fans helped a little, but mostly he missed rapping or singing or simply reading his words from a black and white page then reveling in the euphoric praise.

That morning as he lay there chatting with Carl, under the absurd black and white poster of the cover art of *Carl<3*, Rey longed to pray. He had a crucifix on his bedside table. He thought it would be enough to focus his attention on the almighty creator of the universe for a while, but he just lay in bed and thought about praying for a long time, watching the sun move higher into the sky and turn yellow and then almost white. He decided he would pray soon. He would go back to the monastery and pray and hear something beautiful.

Being both bored and a monkey, Carl didn't rest in existential angst with Rey for long. He escaped the guest room and rummaged through gourmet food in the garbage throughout the apartment. Carl had developed a phenomenal palate, a love of psychoactive herbs, as well as a rare ability to hold incredibly long "conversations" with Rey. But most of the time he just humped chairs and other stuff.

Carl eyed a chair, and Rey still lay there thinking about maybe praying and knowing that somewhere someone might be praying for him: a monk, a mother whose daughter had his poster in her room and feared his influence, or maybe some evangelical who promised to pray for celebrities for a year so that God would change their blackened souls and bring them back to him. So Rey cleared his mind and watched the sun and rested in the fact that his prayers were prayed by someone and that God cared enough to send the sunlight into his room to ease his loneliness.

He didn't have to have the microphone in hand.

He didn't need to perform to feel happy.

He could certainly quit at any time. And I guess he did already. After his final meeting with Cutler, he was not welcome to the first show of Sid Cutler's newest tour of the arts and athletics (there was boxing and dance in this one). Sid decided to truly piss Rey off by picking a venue three miles west of Rey's apartment.

Around 11:00 am Rey finally climbed out of bed, dressed himself with brown corduroy pants, a navy blue A-shirt, and a matching corduroy jacket, unbuttoned to emphasize the magnificent steel medallion featuring an artist's depiction of the singer on the boat who gave Rey Lilac Whiskey for the first time.

Descending from the penthouse he walked the streets of Chicago: a poet king in a second-class city filled with metal hearts and handguns. He had just fired his driver and most of his staff. He would soon live Spartan-like on an island or something. That was the goal. He hailed a cab on Huron Street.

The cabbie was a thirty-year-old white man with a socialist beard. Seeing Carl, he said, "You can't bring a freakin' monkey in my cab."

"Seriously? No one has ever complained. Sorry, man."

Seeing whom he had denied service the cabbie apologized. "It's no problem," Rey said. "I have a car. I just feel like riding along today."

"Really, it's my bad, Rey. Get in the cab. I'm sure Carl won't make a mess."

"He might."

"Where are you going?"

"Mount Greenwood."

"Really? South Side. Big party there tonight?"

"I don't think that's how I would describe it."

They were quiet for a while. Rey closed his eyes, with the

window unrolled and let the sun and wind remind him of his childhood. Then he said to the cabbie, "How about you, what's your story?"

"From Oak Park. I'm working on my dissertation at UIC in Philosophy."

"What's your plan after that?"

"For a while I wanted to be an academic, but everyone wants to with the cash it's bringing in these days. I probably can't hack it, so now I mainly deal in transportation."

"Nice."

The cabbie parked in front of St. Mary's. Carl grabbed a 100 dollar bill from Rey's inside pocket and handed it to the cabbie. It was Rey's favorite of Carl's tricks. Whatever the bill was, Rey would double it, and put that much cash in his pocket. Then when it was time to pay at a bar or restaurant or cab, he would click his tongue, and Carl would deliver the cash. Waiters found it hilarious. I found it tacky.

Rey and Carl walked nearly every street of our neighborhood, and nearly every street seemed the same as it had always seemed. Bungalow after bungalow, brick after brick, Rey peered into every window for someone he knew or someone who knew him, but a Tuesday morning meant the community of police and firefighters and small-business owners were either asleep after a night shift or at work making sure they had the funds to keep the lawns perfectly combed and the brick facades without a crack. Every third house or so had a flag: American, White Sox, Blackhawks, or clover, mostly. Every block or two he'd see a Cubs flag proclaiming in the wind that a social deviant lived there.

What a beautifully ordered world.

After an enormous detour, and a long lunch at Brazel's, with beer on the house, the tipsy man and ape finally reached the monastery.

It was about 4:30 in the afternoon when they climbed Rey's favorite tree and slid open the window to the chapel and climbed home, the first time in almost a decade. He proudly showed Carl the chapel. Carl nodded in joy. Nothing had changed. They lay on the ground under the small altar and fell asleep under the simple icon.

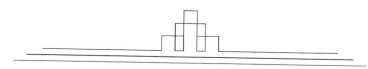

AGAMMEMNON PART 2

CH 19

APRIL 2008

Carl woke Rey at 7:20 PM in the monastery. Rey had napped through dinner and the first few minutes of the concert. He heard nothing beautiful. He received no praise. Carl had explored the monastery befriending a handful of monks who let the poet rest upstairs.

Rey didn't pray.

I'm not sure why he went to the United Center. Though I have two suspicions. Maybe it was neither of these, maybe it was both. The first is that I think Rey believed that in order to fulfill his mission, he must confront Sid Cutler. He must revenge the man who ruined his life: who got him kicked out of school, who gave him Lilac Whiskey, who made him want fame, who did all these things—this man must be made a fool in front of 23,000 people. He must steal the microphone again and let the world know that Rey's holy mission was greater than Sid's goal for him.

The other option is less fantastic, so probably less true. Rey simply decided that he needed the crowd to cheer for him one last time. *Just one last time, so I can get it out of my system.*

Either way, Rey sucked in the April sunset, kissed his medallion, and opened the window wide enough to birth a beautiful Latino hero and his valiant, monkey sidekick.

Above the concrete floor, he held onto the tree trunk. He pushed his chest to the city.

Then Rey shouted, "Chicago Transit Authority, deliver me to

my foe whom I will thwart in battle."

It was neither the first nor most dramatic time he invoked the Chicago Transit Authority. It would have been another day in the life of Rey, except that his foe was not some Chitown poet or rapper. His foe was Sid "The Cannonball" Cutler.

Fear Sid.

If you were riding on Bus #112, the Red, or Green Line that evening and happened to spot the poet king, you would not have seen his eyes. They were closed. But if you were close enough you would have heard him mumbling again and again.

Where is she?

Where is my muse?

Where is she?

Where is my singer?

Her legs, the Lilac Whiskey, the rolling ocean: he ached for it all. Once the elevated train delivered him to the stadium, the electricity in the microphone and the tangible energy from the crowd would numb his desire. It would comfort him one last time.

He chanted during the long ride. He invoked, he summoned, he fumed.

It was over an hour, though Rey was out of body most of the time.

When Rey reached the Madhouse on Madison, he chose to enter through Gate 4, nodding to the bronze statue of that other flying Chicagoan as he ran into the building.

He jumped the turnstile. And ran into the blackened arena.

Where is she?

Where is my muse?

Where is my singer?

He heard one voice. It was a singer. It was not his muse. It was now clear Rey had a foe to battle before Sid Cutler, Sid's current champion, Charles H. Spurwell.

He was currently casting a spell on the crowd.

Spurwell's stage name was Agammemn0n. He was a rapper, a gangster, whose mother and father were a Fortune 500 human resource executive and an important Chicago litigator, respectively. Charles determined that he would make his fame and fortune without the crutches of his parents' education, hard work, or political correctness: he would become a rap star, an artist.

Rey hated no one in Chicago entertainment more than Spurwell.

Standing in the blackness watching the illuminated rapper, Rey lifted both arms to the sky, ready to invoke the muse one final time when a blinding light struck him. The spotlights had found him there in the aisle muttering to himself. He was fifty feet from Agammen0n.

They were ready to rumble. Rey walked to the front of the stage, Carl still on his shoulders. What started as a slow chant *REY, REY, REY,* had grown into pandemonium.

"What are you doing here?" Rey asked the rapper. A stagehand threw Rey a microphone, curious to hear the interaction between the two superstars. Rey caught it, of course.

"What the hell are you doing here?" Agammemn0n replied.

"I'm here to speak, to create, to deliver. You can go home now, kid," Rey said.

"I am the main event. You missed your chance birdman. I read those articles where you said you were done with us. You said, 'I don't need fame. I don't need your applause. You need me.'"

"Birdman?" Rey asked laughing. "You are seriously going to call me Birdman?"

"Calm down. You poet queers are always getting all pissy." At that point the crowd booed at the rising rap star. Spurewell confronted them. "Y'all gonna boo me? I love you. You know that I love you. But if y'all wanna queer-ass poetry from a man who says he doesn't need y'all, then go ahead."

Half the crowd cheered. The other half booed as Rey took off his corduroy jacket and Carl jumped backstage to find treats.

"All right, all right," Agammemn0n said. "This poet thinks he's got some rhymes, so let's battle, freestyle."

"I'm not just here to rhyme. I'm here..."

"You here that, Chicago? This guy can't even rhyme. This 'poet' is scared of me. I'd say, 'the main event' is a lame event. You know what, Rey. I'll explain it to you real slow so you can understand."

You chokin' all the time like a poem that don't rhyme,
Chokin' all the time cause old boy can't climb
The steps to the throne on this tour of mine
Old boy runs like a Cheetah, and he'll say 'pleasetameetya.'
Callin' to the bitches all soft, cause he's full of Velveeta.
I'm the silver tongued O.G., up on the stage
You better sit back down and take notes on a page.
You be chokin' like all the time like a poem that don't rhyme.

The crowd erupted. Rey was king no longer. Rey had never been happier. Looking over at the drummer behind him, he nodded his head at a slow steady pace. The crowd continued to chant Agamemn0n, Rey called above their steady voices, but they ignored him, "Listen! Listen! Listen, I am Rey Pescador!"

At his voice, silence.

Now listen Agamemn0n, it should be I'm-a-dead-man
You're right 'Memnon was the OG 'til he came back
*   from Troy,*
Aegisthus stuck him with a sword, he got avenged by his
*   boy.*
If you're Agamemn0n, then I am Menelaus.
Hangin' with the finest girls, while you rest in Hades.

That's RIGHT, OH YEAH!

I've seen light scatter through a corpse in chlorine.
I've played poker with the drug lords of Mexico City.
I've washed my face with the water from the fountain of
*   youth.*
I've told a thousand crazy stories, but you know they're
*   all true.*
I'm like Odysseus, but without a home, the muse is kind
*   to me.*
She bathes me with her oils, then she puts me to sleep.
You know they'll put me to sleep, if they hear my heart
*   beat.*

The beat continued. Rey continued. A female background singer joined in singing, "I'm going to put you to sleep." Rey's familiar voice won the love of the crowd.

I wish I could have seen the look on Sid Cutler's fat face, which he was surely stuffing in some press box.

Even Agamemn0n had the sense to know that he had been defeated. He looked at the crowd, slapped Rey's hand in congratulations then shouted, "To Mr. Rey Pescador, my boy. Give it up ladies and gentlemen. I taught him that shit. I'd stay, but I got some honeys waitin' for me in back."

The rest of the show was no more noteworthy than any Rey Pescador performances until the final poem. In the first stanza, a girl ten rows from the front yelled something about Lilac Whiskey. Maybe fifty people in the United Center heard it, but one was Rey Pescador. He continued to entertain, but walked to the very front of the stage where he could almost see the singer, his muse from the yacht. She was there, he knew it. She was right there in the center of the arena beyond the spotlight's haze. He wanted nothing in the world but to be with her on the beach or in his penthouse or anywhere at any time. Then he shouted mid-poem, "Cure me, you know you can. Cure me, cure me, cure me. Give me that drink you gave me on the lake. I can see you. I can smell you." He shouted, "You are my muse. Put me to sleep."

He sensed her smiling at him, though he couldn't see her face in the darkness. She turned her back, and Rey knew he had only one option. He had to make the crowd erupt. He did a series of three back flips to give him room for take-off then shouted his favorite line from Keats, "Beauty is truth, truth is beauty, and I'm Rey Pescador. Good night."

He sprinted and dove into the crowd. Pandemonium broke out. The musicians came back on stage and they played. The lights turned on.

He could see the back of her hair across the floor. Mobbed by hundreds of men and women, the hero pushed through the bodies toward her eternal voice. She was the only thing to keep him tonight from feasting on the praise of his fans. They vanished from his mind, though pressed upon his body.

He could no longer see her. He saw nothing.

He was deaf and mute and blind. All he could register was the faint taste of Lilac Whiskey. He said it tasted like a memory, like the memory of waking up on Christmas morning and seeing the white sunlight bounce off the snow, but that seems cliché.

He may have lost consciousness until the terror began.

A dozen Chicago police flooded the stage. A lieutenant grabbed the microphone and issued a state of emergency. You remember the warning, "Terrorists…anti-RHC… and protection mode."

All ran home or to hotels to protect their undying hearts from an electro-magnetic pulse, or whatever the hell it was. You probably are too young to remember that with each original RHC heart came an anti-terrorist generator that powered a suit that protected it from electromagnetic-pulses. People now grow up taking the generators for granted, but when I was a kid, this type of attack would have cost far more lives.

Rey looked at his city that was searching for its generators. Then he thought, *Fear Sid*, as tens of thousands scattered before him trampling each other, some dying in the frenzy and stampede of the crowd.

He had angered the man who could end every human life.

Rebecca, where were you that night that the Department of Homeland Security shut down the three biggest cities in the country under clear evidence that a magnetic pulse would destroy every heart not plugged into the antimagnetic suits?

I was at dinner with my parents when the televisions turned on and announced that yes, this was real, and yes, we all needed to plug in. I was so young still—thirty-five years old—that I never considered leaving the suit off and taking this as my opportunity to die a natural death. Plenty did, thousands died that night in each city. Everyone had a chance to protect himself, but thousands chose to escape the world of Sid Cutler.

The night passed slowly. Rey could not sleep. He was alone with nothing but the foretaste of that elixir in his throat.

He walked the streets of the West Side searching for that singular experience of a short dress and a pink bottle. Even the homeless were hidden in the safe stations throughout the city. Rey nearly stepped on the first corpse at Madison and Western. Its eyes had bled creating a puddle on the ground. Rey was almost sick. The grotesque image of a grin remained on its face. Rey wondered if it was suicide. He abandoned the sidewalk with its corpses for double yellow lines of the street's center as he walked toward the Loop.

It took an hour for the polished glass and iron of the business district to rise around him into the night sky that usually collected all of the lights of the city and slung them back down on him. But tonight there were no lights to collect, so the bright reality of moon and stars shone on the poet king.

Rey wondered how many people waited in each building wearing clothing that plugged into the wall. Could Cutler be capable of that sort of violence, and if not, was Rey just so vain he thought his manager would kill to punish him?

The bright galaxy above comforted Rey as he prayed for each soul that chose to wait on the sidewalk, and hear its heart stop ticking. God have mercy.

Blocks from home he saw beautiful life, a slender woman standing in the street.

She was singing.

He called out to her, "Muse! Muse!"

She ran. He chased her.

Chicago's first RHC lockdown was certainly the bloodiest. The martyrs all died that night. The city slept for the first time as every counterproductive cell oozed from her body into the sewers below.

Cabs were at bay. Boats docked. The 'L' shook no apartments. The only movement was blood draining from eyes, Rey, and the woman he had sought for seven years.

He caught her, just outside the John Hancock Building.

"Who are you?" he asked as he slowed to an arrogant jog. He tried to hide his panting, but he was out of breath. "Are you in my mind? I know you are real; I can sense your reality, but are you only real in my mind? Would someone walking by, if anyone could walk by, stop and see you and smell and taste you? Could I?"

"You tell me."

"I will. I love you."

"Really? Then it's time for you to show it."

"Well, I think I showed I would drown for you."

"What good is that?"

"You tell me," Rey said again this time. He was growing frustrated. By now he was standing next to her. She pivoted toward the lake as fog rolled onto the street. Rey doggedly followed her.

Looking upward, Rey realized that the stars were now hidden by the fog. "Shit," Rey started, "I've always wanted to spend a night with a beautiful woman staring at the stars above the city, but the electric light shrouds them. For the first time the lights are off, and I have you here. But this damned fog."

"Well, there is one solution."

"What's that?"

"We go above the fog."

"But we'd have to be pretty high up there. How high do you think the fog is?"

"I really have no idea."

"What if we went to the top of the John Hancock? To that building there. To the roof."

"That should be high enough."

"Good, I can get us up there."

"I'm sure you can."

"I want you to go with me, to see the constellations."

"I'm sure you do."

They cut through the fog until they reached Rey's building. It was pitch black inside as well. Rey kissed the singer before reaching the elevator. He tasted the Whiskey. She stopped him after a moment and said, "Let's wait until we are on the roof, Rey."

"All right. We may have to take the stairs. It will take a while."

"The elevator is powered by a generator."

"What makes you think so?"

"I just know. So tell me, how will you write about this meeting? With all of the mythopoetical crap that you said about our last meeting?"

"I always write the truth."

"So you will write that you have a human heart."

"I don't."

"Then why were you out here. You will write that you are suicidal."

"I will tell the truth."

"How?"

"I will strip it to its bare elements. I will write about the reality of the situation."

"Which is?"

"Could be numerous things: I might highlight the fog and the fact that you are the only woman I see. I might highlight the idea of technology breaking down around a man chasing after his desires, that in the moment of the chase, not even light pollution can mask the stars."

"So this is a chase to you?"

"Everything is. I am a hunter, a fisher, an original man."

"And how does the story end?"

"I don't know. You tell me."

"I want you to predict. Do you catch what you chase?"

"I already have."

"Have you?"

"Of course. We're here, aren't we?"

"We sure are, but is here where you want me, right here in the lobby waiting for the elevator to bring us to the roof?"

"I want you here and on the roof and in every bedroom of my penthouse suite, but even I have my limitations, so I'd rather wait for the elevator to the roof and look out on the city and kiss your long neck and have you sing to me."

The elevator door opened. They stepped in. She hit the stop button immediately.

"I'll tell you how the story ends. It ends with the King Fisher taking flight."

"Diving after his prey?"

"Of course. Close your eyes."

"Why?"

"I want to teach you to fly."

"It's about time."

He closed his eyes. She opened the door and hit the button for the top floor. She told him to keep his eyes closed. She whispered it into his ears. Just before the door closed she exited.

He was alone in the elevator.

At the top of building, when the elevator opened, Rey saw that the stars were still hidden behind the layers and layers of clouds weighing on him. The wind blew. The poet walked toward the north end of the building stopping at a fence that kept people from the edge and surveyed the fog over the black city alone.

There on the roof the wind was a tenor chanting over his head. In it he thought he heard the voice of God. He wanted the voice of God, but also wanted the singer with him. He wanted flesh and blood and chemicals and sinews. He shouted into the sky, "Make me whole!" but heard no answer. Then from the West side of the building, the faintest sound of a human voice flew to the roof. She was still there, at the bottom of the building singing to him.

Rey climbed the fence wondering if he could jump, if the clouds would catch him like the hands of the United Center crowd and drop him off at the singer's feet, or if God would simply send his soul to heaven or if he would go straight to hell.

She sang and sang and sang and sang; then she shouted, "Fly, Rey Pescador. I will catch you."

Rey sat and cried with his feet dangling over the edge. Then he stood in the fog and held his arms out knowing either she or God would retrieve his soul forever. He shouted as he leaned forward pushing his chest off of the building, taking flight. But his words were held back by the wind, the wind pushing the words of God into his chest, holding him from sure death.

He hung above the building and breathed.

"I don't need her," he thought. "I don't need her."

She sang and sang and sang and sang again. He needed her. He wanted to taste the Lilac Whiskey and hear her sing him to sleep. She would catch him. He must dive after her. He walked backward about twenty five feet to the edge of the fence. He needed to reach a maximum velocity to jump far enough to overcome the wind and land on the sidewalk, rather than the side of the building. Luckily, Rey knew that he was rather swift.

He sprinted to the edge and leapt off the 1,000 foot building. The singer would never catch him. He would never reach the ground.

God swirled him in the wind then slammed him through the glass of the 80th floor. His flight was parabolic and hyperbolic. He was bloody and bruised. When the lockdown lifted, the paramedics attached him to a gurney and brought him to the hospital. He survived the flight but cursed God for keeping the singer from him.

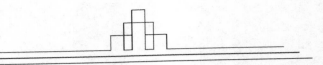

SIX DEADLY SINS

CH 20

SEPTEMBER 2008

"Where were you last week?" Cutler asked me in his office.

"In the desert, with Rey."

"Has he learned the lesson?"

"I'm not sure what the lesson is."

"It's simple. This is it. When you piss off a whole country and then run and hide in the desert riding horses and proclaiming your greatness, America will not forgive you."

"America is pretty forgiving, especially toward celebrities, Mr. Cutler."

"Rey Pescador's career, as we know it, is over. That is the lesson. The lesson is over."

"Well, if that's the lesson, then I don't think Rey has learned. I'm sure he still believes he will save the world somehow."

"Rey will save nothing. But I have finally found a celebrity who can save us. Rey was all right as a distraction, but this man here will take the place of Rey and God himself," Cutler added. I'm not sure which idea pissed me off more—that Elijah would replace God or Rey— but I must have physically responded.

"Ah, I have elicited some emotions from the scholar. Let's dive into those. A good leader is able to dive deeply into his followers emotions and understand their roots. And I am the best damned leader ever."

"I'm not angry, Mr. Cutler, just surprised."

"Sometimes I forget you are a true believer, David." He

certainly did not forget, but he did shout in horror at his neck spasm.

"Sometimes I do too, Mr. Cutler." That part was true.

"So you are witty like your cousin, Mr. Rosario...oh wait, I can see that you want me to call you Dr. Rosario. Well, David, I don't call those who can't heal, those who were simply so pedantic they had to prove they were better than everyone else doctor."

"I'm sorry if I offended you, Sidney."

"I will not hear your confession"

"Sidney, I really didn't mean to insult you."

"David, what do you think about me?"

"Well, I mean, that's not an easy question to answer. You are incredibly talented, influential, and rich. I'm honored to work with you."

"Good, because I have a plan for you, a long-term plan. You will help me immensely, and I have something for you that you have always wanted. But we will get to that. Let's have a drink."

Everything in the room weighed on me. Cutler had always terrified me, but Rey's warning in the desert was finally starting to sink in. Sidney stood and poured wine.

"David, you probably don't realize it, but I like you," Cutler said. He smiled at me during a terrifying pause. "I'll go one step further: you are more like your cousin than I realized—a man after my heart."

The sun was bright, and despite the absence of windows, it crept under the door from the lobby and lit a small area of an ottoman era rug. I drank more wine as I walked the room examining light and the decorative antiques on the wall, mostly knives and swords and ancient maps.

"When is this from?" I asked Sid about one sword, taking it off its shelf.

"Imperial Japan. A famous man was killed with that sword. Famous during his time like Rey, though like Rey's future, he was forgotten by history."

"Rey'll be all right."

That laugh again. I hated Sid Cutler's laugh. Maybe I've just read too many books on antique, flesh-and-blood hearts, but I swear my chest constricted, and my metal heart ticked more rapidly in horror at that laugh that lingered over my soul like cigarette smoke in a closet.

Cutler continued to insult my cousin, "Rey will not be all right. He would have been better off if he died jumping off the Hancock with all those other miserable idealists in April."

That was it. I believed Rey Pescador. I believed that all those people suffered from Sid Cutler's colossal hand. I wanted him dead. More than anything I wanted him dead. More than anything I wanted to be the one to kill Sid Cutler. I wanted to stick that sword through his enormous belly and watch the layers of fat cover it like a fountain's ripples after dropping a penny.

"See what I mean? David Rosario, you are a man after my own heart," he added. "You could even be my son if you were whiter and well, larger. You are filled with my passions. I see that lust of murder. You know it's not good for your soul, murder. Of course you know that. You know everything. It is your great source of pride."

I said nothing. I only sipped more wine and weighed the sword in my hand.

"I know you, David. I know your thoughts, David. Your vices. You drink too much. You eat too much. You wear your intelligence on your sleeve with pride greater than Rey's, and you envy what he has. You are the great sloth of my employees, spending your mornings with red wine while we work. Yes, David, I know you well. You are my son. Once you age, and your metabolism changes, you will be like me. A round man behind a desk controlling everything in his world to make sure it profits him. I've been keeping track, David, and that makes six deadly sins I count in you. But don't worry; I'm not that man around your neck. I support each of these traits."

It all seemed true. Everything he said was true. I sat again in my chair and drank another glass of wine. I hoped the room would start to spin and disappear, but I was bottles away from that.

Cutler added, "One thing I don't understand, David, is why you are always alone. Why don't you enjoy the pleasure of a woman or two? Is that laziness, or virtue?"

I was still unable to speak.

"Well, as heartfelt as this is, our meeting is done. David, since you are my type of man, I will give you our type of gift: a bottle of Lilac Whiskey. You will never drink anything like it again. Take it, and close the door as you leave."

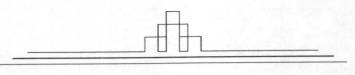

MY SEVENTH SIN

CH 21

OCTOBER - DECEMBER 2008

Perhaps Rey's sin—his death rather—was that of a sheep whose shepherd had fallen asleep. Perhaps it really was my fault. Perhaps I merely overestimated my influence on my little cousin. Either way, a year after visiting Rey in the desert, I sat behind a locked door hoping he would die. It is my second greatest regret.

Actually, I shouldn't be telling you about that yet. I am skipping too much this time. I need to start earlier. It's amazing that it was just over a year after Africa that the Genius Brigade dream broke into pieces. He enjoyed himself as much as ever, but his parties were no longer old-fashioned, A-list affairs with high-end scotch and cigars.

Rey befriended Agaemmen0ns and sought counsel with his gangsta rap colleagues. Fights broke out. Shots rang in the 80th floor on at least one occasion. The newspapers were not kind. Rey's fans were still uninterested, but he had money. He still had quite a lot of money.

On October 23rd, Rey called me in tears. He spoke only gibberish, so I tried to console him. "Calm down, Rey, what happened?" He didn't say anything. I was afraid that my father or mother had died. The poet was hysterical and hung up. Five minutes later he texted me: "get to the 80th floor STOP too upset to talk STOP."

Rey never understood texting.

When the elevator opened at the 80th floor, a cleaning crew was sitting outside Rey's front door. I didn't even knock; Rey opened the door immediately and hugged me for a long time.

120

We walked past the living room and library into the kitchen. Amidst the empty bottles, clothes, and broken dishes, I saw the most grotesque site I've seen: Carl lay dead, his little arms stiff in rigor mortis around a baking pan.

"Shit Rey, what happened?"

"He overdosed. Some piece-of-shit filled brownies with weed and thought it would be fun to lace the powdered sugar with cocaine."

"I'm sorry, man." I hugged him again. He teared up a little, but was no longer hysterical.

"That little guy loved brownies and weed, but he couldn't handle cocaine, David. They should have known that."

"I know, man."

"We need to have a funeral."

Carl's overdose affected Rey more than anyone realized. The first book, album, and film, of his new publishing house were all named *Disappear*. They proved prophetic in a way Rey would never have considered.

L.J. was traveling through time and space (well, probably just space, but even after years of friendship he wouldn't admit it), and I was researching for my second book in Chicago while Rey drifted from town to town, girl to girl, trying to rediscover his purpose, as everyone but Rey discovered that he no longer mattered to America.

On the other hand, I had never been happier than I was then, spending every day researching and planning to change the world with Brenda.

Brenda with terrifying legs and arms possessed such reach that while standing in the fires of hell she could hold me in the Crystal Sea for a moment. I imagined her often. I wanted the life of a scholar, not a priest. I desired the life of a good man, not a saint. Forgive me, Rebecca; I wanted Brenda. Her engagement with Brian/Todd/Paul broke up before coming back to Chicago, and I decided that I would marry her. Maybe it was too much time with Rey, or maybe I'm just more delusional than I realize, but I believed it was that easy: you just decide, hey I'm going to marry this woman, and it happens.

We mostly just worked together. But some nights we ate

dinner. Usually, we ate out, but every few weeks, I would cook for her. Somehow, I could not even begin to woo her. I had had plenty of romantic relationships before (not to say I was Rey Pescador or anything), but with Brenda, I couldn't make a move. A few times I complimented her shoes, but seriously, her brother might have done that.

After Carl's death, Rey ate dinner with Brenda and me for the first time. While she was in the bathroom he said, "David, I'm surprised you don't like this one: smart, hot, even believes that crap you write about the RHC. "

I was going to marry her. I did not tell this to Rey Pescador. He would have made it his mission to get us hitched then and there. He probably had a license to do it. Dinner was bizarre. That's all I'll say about it.

We ate. We talked. She left.

I fell asleep early, around ten. I must have slept through Rey's invocation of the muse because he wrote a few poems while I was out. I guess after two decades I was used to that crap. He left the apartment, the poem still sitting on the table.

A knock on my door and Brenda was there again at 1:00 am.

She had left her purse or something, maybe it was her phone. I can't even remember. I was so groggy. Someone must have bought her more drinks because she was tipsy. I was tipsy and half asleep. She walked into my book-filled apartment: no cases, just piles and piles of theology texts. I saw her legs in a beautifully short skirt. She must have changed after dinner with us to go to a bar.

Rey's poem was on the table. He had to leave it there next to whatever it was she had forgotten. He had to write her name in calligraphy. There was no way she could ignore the thirteen-line almost-sonnet titled "Brenda."

As far as the poem's content, let's just say Rey did a lot more than compliment her shoes. I would include it here, but I think I destroyed it a few months later.

After reading it, she pressed her body closer to mine. "Did you write this?" she asked.

I said nothing. Have mercy.

"Do you mean this?"

I saw her legs. Forgive me.

"Do you want to know my thoughts?"

She moved toward me.

I waited. It was his sin I took. She showed me exactly what she thought about Rey's poetry. Have mercy.

For the next two weeks, we researched together and made love. I wanted to propose. I know it was too soon, but even after years with Rey I was a pretty traditional man.

I loved her. I couldn't imagine living without her.

One day, Brenda did not come to the library when we planned to meet. She texted me. She was going to California for a family emergency. She returned no calls after that. A month passed. She wrote a letter. She was pregnant.

Oh God.

I don't know what the normal response to that would be, but like I said, I wanted to marry her. I wanted a family. It was the happiest I had been in my life. I love you Rebecca, more than I ever loved Brenda, but that was my happiest moment, just knowing that I was going to be a father.

I toured the gold coast. I bought a ring, a big ring. I bought the house in Hyde Park. Brenda bought plane tickets. She would be back on the second Friday in December. I imagined all of the things expectant fathers imagine. One minute I was father of the year taking happy bike rides to Grant Park. The next minute I was totally incapable of raising another human being, having a mental breakdown and leaving my family because they were better off without me. Then my mind flipped back to coaching a championship little league team.

Brenda didn't fly back to Chicago that Friday.

She did write another letter. Her parents were old-fashioned. She didn't want them to know anything. They would never forgive her. She just couldn't do this right now. I wrote a letter. I had a ring. I would fix it all. We could live in Hyde Park or anywhere else. Her parents would understand. Or if she didn't want the child and didn't want me, I could raise the child. I wanted her to know she wasn't alone.

She wrote a letter. She explained that I wasn't listening. It wasn't a conversation. She had terminated the pregnancy. It was done.

I wrote a letter. I put on a black suit. I bought a bottle of Whiskey. I took the Red Line downtown. I climbed a bridge to be no more.

Lord have mercy.

There in the frigid air, I waited for the whiskey to take full effect. The city was sublime and beautiful. All the steel and concrete highlighted the black water that would be my grave. Just as I would have passed out from the whiskey, I hobbled over the retaining wall and off the bridge.

It was the second time that Sid Cutler had stopped my heart.

When I awoke, Elijah Grey stood there with demonic eyes. All right, I can't really remember his eyes, but the image I have created from that moment is still lucid: the irises are gray against the sclera juxtaposed against his black face. Those eyes watched me for a long time. Never before, or since, have I wished for death more strongly.

Elijah watched me for a while. I slept. He was gone when I awoke.

Alone in a hospital room filled by machines and a large African painting of the passion of Christ on the wall past the foot of the bed, I laughed at my fortune. Of course, it had to be a Catholic hospital. I cursed my luck. Of course, the chaplain had to walk in and start talking without considering that I might have an extraordinary headache, "David, do you remember me?" the grandfatherly priest asked.

"No, father. I'm sorry. Have we met?"

"I have known your father for a long time and am a fan of your writing."

"Thank you."

"Is there anything that you would like to talk about?"

"Not really."

"Are you sure?"

"It's been a long month. I kind of want to sleep."

"There is time to sleep. I want to talk with you first."

"What do you want from me? Do you expect me to confess? Then here you go. Forgive me father for trying to kill myself. Can I sleep now?"

"I expect more than that."

"All right, what is my penance?"

"David, you are alive for a reason."

"To do the will of Sid Cutler, I suppose."

"I don't know what that means, but it surely is not what I was talking about."

"Give your life to the service of God, David. The church needs you. There are so few with your faith."

"I just tried to kill myself after my girlfriend aborted our child. If that doesn't disqualify me to priesthood, I don't know what does."

"And now you sit here forgiven. If that doesn't qualify you for priesthood of God, I don't know what does."

Maybe it was the pain medications, but I could hardly respond to the priest. I lost my energy to fight and just stared at the painting in front of me and wanted to give up everything I had ever fought for and rest in that moment. The only action I could imagine doing was opening my mouth and saying, "OK."

So that's what I did.

Since that moment I have been asked a thousand times why I became a priest, why someone who had so much would take a vow that would disrupt everything. I still don't know how to answer it, but if you were there in that room in that moment with Christ staring at you from that crucifix, you'd probably give your life up too. I swore to the father that I would be ordained. He called the Bishop. I slept.

Elijah Grey was in my room again. It was the only time I would ever hear him speak. "I healed you, brother," he said.

"I am not healed."

"But you are. You must do me a favor."

"Must I?"

"I have saved your life. I need you to work for me."

"I would, but I just got an offer from the biggest organization in the world."

"What are you talking about?"

"I am going to be a priest."

"Listen David, I saved you on behalf of Sid Cutler. Without him you would have died. You would have been damned, David."

"I am damned. Cutler did nothing for my soul."

He paused. He waited.

"I would have it no other way, Dr. Rosario. Only, in exchange for the second chance that I have given you, that we have given you, I will ask for a favor. You must agree to never speak with Rey Pescador again."

Rey Pescador.

All the name evoked was images from that month, the poem, the bridge, the whiskey, and Brenda's long legs. I thought about the image of a son or daughter on an ultrasound. I thought about youth baseball and the Hyde Park house filled with food and laughter. I took all of my anger and placed it on Rey. Surely, he wrote the poem. Since I was seven he was ruining my life. It was his sin that I had taken when I slept with Brenda. It was his influence, at the very least. So I looked at the demon in front of me and bowed to his request.

"Kill that bastard for all I care. I will never speak to Rey Pescador again."

THE BOTTLE

2037

Some mornings when my memory is especially flooded with the images of these years, I almost expect Sid Cutler to stumble into my room. No doubt he is out there somewhere, in one form or another. I'm sure he's busy, but he still makes time to visit me in my dreams sometimes. I awake, make coffee, and try to ignore the images. In many ways, my life is one long attempt to spite him. Maybe that's why I kept the only gift he ever gave me: the Lilac Whiskey.

Last night after writing you these stories all day and thinking about Brenda, I opened my foot locker and touched the bottle, but I knew that it would make me forget that I need to finish this story to you. Maybe that is why I reached for it to start.

If I know Sid Cutler, it's the very best Lilac Whiskey money can buy sitting right here in my tiny motel room, like a pagan idol.

That pink bottle was made to forget, but to me it is a remembrance that Sid Cutler would kill thousands to get to Rey. He would do the unspeakable. Then he would have you drink enough Lilac Whiskey not to forget what happened, like the legends suggest, but to forget to care.

Once I figured that out, I learned that memory, even the memory of pain, is a gift.

Sorry to preach. As they say, old habits die hard.

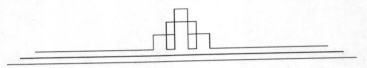

WE ALSO SELL MATTRESSES

23

OCTOBER - DECEMBER 2009

Most of 2009 was not worth writing about. I was with men in collars being hastily ordained and touted as an amazing miracle for the church. Rey was trying to fan the final embers of fame.

By the beginning of fall, as far as America was concerned, Rey Pescador, the King of Consonants, was just another Latino with perfect skin. Of course, it took Rey longer to realize it.

In late September he even called Sid Cutler. He was ready to go back to the Cannonball.

Cutler did not return his call.

I was still not speaking to Rey, and Brovault was just being Brovault.

Just as Rey's career had deflated, so had the mind of his desperate, new publicist, Emory McGill. He booked Rey in a series of small time gimmicks. He even got Rey a gig advertising while playing minor league baseball. The idea was to make a few dollars off of tattoos on Rey's calves. While he stole bases, the camera would show the advertisements. Rey believed completely in his own athletic ability and never doubted that he would make the pros within a year or two. He never did, and no one saw the tattoos on his calves, because no one recorded Single A ball in Toledo.

My favorite image of Rey's fall was when I was driving on Interstate 70 through Indiana on my way to a lecture at Miami University of Ohio about the imperative of the human heart. I saw an abnormally large billboard rise from the cornfields. Rey Pescador was, of course, resting there in the Indiana sky.

If the *Tribune* image of "Cutler's Brigade of Geniuses" concretized Rey's ascent, this billboard did the same for his descent: a normal featured housewife sat in the bed with the blankets pulled up to her chest, and Rey looked at the camera, book in hand, pipe in mouth, wearing a black, silk robe pulled up to his neck. Underneath was the tactless caption: *With GB Mattresses, I might even get into the bed with you.*

Rey's once prized signature anchored the billboard. I almost crashed my Honda. I've never laughed that hard on an interstate before. I found the closest McDonalds, got some burgers, and drove back to look at the billboard and relish the moment. Amidst a million rows of corn the former King of American Art became a five-dollar-a-night corporate whore. It was tasteless, low quality, and disturbing. It sold mattresses, though. At the beginning, it sold quite a few mattresses.

If glory fades, so do mattress advertising contracts. After a few months and a few more bad investments, the mattress money dried up, and Rey's publicist decided that he needed to reintroduce Rey to the fickle, powerful, and wealthy world of literary criticism. Emory decided that the shock-and-awe approach was the simplest way to bring the literary world back the beating heart of Rey Pescador. Rey Pescador would become a farcical martyr in the greatest book burning in the history of the local access TV.

Rey wasn't convinced when Emory first suggested burning Rey's books. "Well. Hmm. I guess we could burn the tower of books," Rey said. "How high did you say it was? Ten feet? That's got to be ten thousand books. Thirty bucks a pop. It doesn't seem worth it. Sure, I'll get the royalties, but that's only five percent."

"You only get five percent?"

"Cutler isn't into handing out money, and I don't really care about it. Also, when you sell 20 million books a year, it's still quite the sum of money. Plus the ads. You forgot the ads."

"I forgot nothing, Rey. Second hand book-sellers are basically giving your books away. And we only need enough to create the illusion."

"And that's supposed to make this better? I don't do illusions. I deal in the truth. You know that. This whole thing is making me angry."

"I'm trying to make you famous again; I don't care if I make you angry."

"I guess the other options would take longer. This burning thing will get a lot of press, a more efficient rise to the top than getting the critics back on board."

"I will not argue that, Rey, but did the poet just say 'efficient?'"

"You're right. Maybe we should just call the whole thing off. Doesn't it seem a little—what's the word— heavy-handed? Why don't I just do the Super Bowl halftime show or something?"

"I know you're used to people telling you whatever you want, but I'm here to tell you that the Super Bowl is out of the question. I can't even get the mattress store back in touch unless you agree to take your shirt off."

"Well, I'm not taking my shirt off on a mattress or on a funeral pyre or anywhere. This fire thing is beyond metaphor; get another idea."

"Rey, you want to reinvent yourself. You are a poet; this is how you do it. Climb on top of a pile of your old works, rip off your shirt, light a match and watch them burn. The public will know that you have changed and will want to see the new Rey Pescador. If Cutler has shown us anything it's that new matters more than anything else."

"The proverbial phoenix rising from the ashes." Rey looked away and finished the final drag of the cigarette.

"You get the metaphor." Emory grinned with satisfaction.

"Of course I get it; I just said it was heavy-handed."

"Rey, let's get a drink of whisky; we'll talk about it tomorrow."

The next week Rey visited me for the first time since my ordination. He strolled into the confessional, tapped three times, coughed and asked, "Cousin, is book-burning a sin?"

My answer was simple. "Go to hell, Rey."

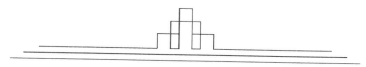

THE VOICE OF GOD

CH 24 •

DECEMBER 15, 2009

Rey looked at every mirror that he passed, whether it was at his home, or in public. I define mirror loosely. New car windshields, storefront windows, and the chrome mannequins found in storefronts all demanded his gaze. He never peered for too long, just enough to ensure that his hair remained carefully positioned on his scalp, and that his skin was a rich caramel hue. It was. On December 15th, he was enjoying mirrors on the street when he heard a voice from the sky that may have been an airplane engine, or a stereo blaring from a high-rise on Michigan Avenue.

Either way, Rey knew it as God speaking audibly to him.

This voice, this sound, had affected him profoundly. He stopped briefly and considered confessing his sins. Rey often considered such things. But the light splintered his eyes as it bounced off the windows, and he became distracted in the one-two of his step and the fragrance of his cologne. His leather bottom shoes sounded soft on the concrete. Moving in such simple rhythm one - two, he glanced at the women on the street, carefully categorizing their bodies. Each was as beautiful as the sunlight peeking through the buildings. Though Rey seldom noticed the nuance of sunlight anymore.

The women peered back. In Rey's mind they fell in love; they struggled to breathe. Most didn't. However, one dropped her groceries. This hardly startled Rey Pescador. If he stopped for every soccer mom who nearly fell over when she saw him cross the street, he would never make it home.

Despite not being able to sell an album or book to save his

life, the general public, especially in Chicago, still remembered the soon-to-be spectral image of Rey Pescador.

The groceries scattered. A bottle of wine burst with its beloved contents seeping into broccoli, cauliflower, and two boxes of cereal.

Out bounced an orange. A rather determined fruit, it rolled in between the V made by Rey's shoes. It woke him from his stupor. He picked it up. There on one knee reaching for the orange, he noticed the woman's black heels, her long arching calves, leading to a frustratingly long skirt. Altogether forgetting the voice of God in the sky, he muted all his senses but sight. He handed her the orange and looked at her face. He did not first notice her high cheek bones, red hair, or complexion. He only noticed her sunglasses, or rather his own reflection in her glasses.

He paused long enough to enjoy the image, like a sip of wine, but he found himself less alluring than ever, changed in some vital way. Of course, his skin had not aged. It was something that he could not place. Perhaps it was the loss of the illusion that he was essential to the world.

The woman's hand finally grasped the orange, and he finally noticed her face. It was the first time in years that Rey Pescador, the Bard from the Barrio, felt unsure of what to say to a woman.

Rey and the woman stood admiring one another for a moment. He looked beyond the dark tint of the sunglasses trying to determine the color of her eyes. Wishing to speak, to grab her hand and kiss it with a ceremonial bow as he had done so many times; wishing to say his most basic, and successful, pickup line: "Hola, I'm Rey Pescador; beinvenidos to my swaggy world;" wishing to recite a poem or serenade her; wishing to act, but unable to for the first time in years, Rey simply muttered: "Here is your orange. I ... um ... think it fell."

Then without asking her to go for coffee, a drink, a quick wedding ceremony, or to take off the damn glasses so he could determine the very color of her soul's door, Rey backed up slowly, turned, and sat on a nearby bench. The sunlight scattered through the buildings both casting shadows and illuminating streets.

The bewildered woman looked at the orange and then at

Rey. She placed the orange in her bag and collected the rest of her belongings. Before she left, she looked at him one last time. He seemed tired, though his hair was slicked back perfectly, and his designer clothing seemed to shine in the shadows near the bench. The famous, apparently manic, man whom she had seen on countless talk shows, HBO specials, and poetry videos just sat and glanced at her nervously again, only to stare at the sporting goods store in front of him.

"Thanks, Mr. Pescador," she said as she walked toward the door to the stairs of her apartment and left the scene.

He slouched, looking at himself in the window in front of him. His tan was fading and with it his hair. He smelled of cigarettes and two bottles of cologne. Then he noticed for the first time: the magazines on the shelf featured a six foot four, 170 pound healer named Elijah Grey. The western hemisphere now crooned for him even greater than they had for Rey "Windy City Wordsmith" Pescador.

One headline read, "Finally a Star that Can Heal Us." Grey's smug, square smile and sparse mustache slightly spun toward the sky. It was as if Rey had never existed, as if he never won their hearts and changed their world. He feared there would be no more cable specials, magazine covers, book talks on CNN, or trips to the White House. Perhaps the lazy subconscious of popular culture realized that a possibly deaf/mute 25-year-old healer could give them more than a twenty-nine year old Latino poet who offered little more than words and an undeniably perfect complexion.

Rey forced himself off the bench and walked to his apartment.

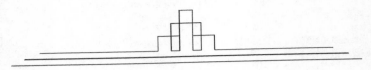

A BATED HOOK

CH 25

DECEMBER 23, 2009

Rey smelled her before he saw her. She was there behind him. He did not turn; he did not look away from the bottles in front of him. The effervescent desire that he tasted, that he breathed, ten years earlier in the fresh water of Lake Michigan, in her lips, her tongue, had never plagued him more than that evening. He remembered the light that crossed the water, the island, the moon.

Earlier that day Emory McGill quit. The book burning was a colossal failure. Critics throughout the country determined that Rey had lost his mind. Some blamed the fame; others the alcohol; others suggested the fountain of youth had demanded his sanity; still others determined it was the results of STDs.

My favorite critiques were the arguments that Rey Pescador never wrote any of his poetry. It was the closest to the truth. They argued that his poetry was the invention of L.J. Brovault. One astute reporter presented an expose that newly minted priest, the Rev. Dr. David E. Rosario, was the true author of *Nepenthe Incantations at the Fountain of Youth*. He carefully analyzed the voice of Pescador and, with the help of a robotic critic, cross-analyzed it with the writing of everything published in the last one hundred years. My voice was the closest to his. What he failed to notice is that only the introductory prose sections were similar in voice. I did edit and rewrite much of the introduction: Rey's prose was always flawed, but the poetry itself was not in any way influenced by me. To tell you the truth, his poetry—not the rap, but the fine art stuff—is still beautifully incoherent to me.

After Emory McGill, his sole support, left Rey's Chicago

134

office screaming, Rey stumbled down the stairs and into the bar section of Rush Street. Sick on his own lack of purpose he fell on the sidewalk and vomited. Women in pumps and men in leather bottom shoes avoided the fallen star: the Wednesday night before a long Christmas weekend created such casualties. The air, a cosmic icebox, pierced through his shirt sleeves, past the wool tie and hit him in the chest.

If Rey had fallen just three years before on any busy street corner in the world, he would have been caught.

He was now without pity. He received what he deserved, nothing.

Remembering the woman with the orange, the woman of the fall, the woman who taught him what he was and the afternoon where he heard the voice of God, he looked to the sky and prayed, "Is that where I look? Up there? Do I just speak to you like this? I heard you before. Twice by my count. Speak to me now. Speak to me. I'm listening," but God was silent to Rey Pescador.

The crowd surrounded the madman. A thin, bearded man, surely some sort of account executive, in a Green Bay Packers sweatshirt and a Santa Claus hat approached the poet, "I know you." Rey smiled, he thought quickly; he ran through his poems, his acts. What could he say to make this occasion serendipitous? He was The Poet. They crowded him like this so many times. The gaunt man said again, "I know you, asshole. You're the guy from the mattress ad. You hit on my wife at a bar last week you sonuvabitch." He kicked Rey in the stomach and continued.

"What's your name again? You had that fruity signature: some sort of fairy poet."

Rey, out of breath, looked at him. "I am, uh, Rey Pescador. I am," he breathed deeply and sighed, "Rey."

"Ah, yes. You are El Rey. The king, everybody; he thinks he's the king of poetry. Well the king of poetry is a little princess in my book." He kicked Rey in the face and looked with satisfaction at the drunken businesspeople around him.

Rey, a half-dead bull taking aim at a fighter, played dumb for a moment and then erupted at the account exec. He threw him against a boutique window and punched him as hard as he could.

The kick had certainly affected the poet. Rey's teeth were bleeding; the Packers fan's nose bled. He turned to the crowd. "Now leave! Leave now, unless any of you can send a message to God, leave!" This did not diminish the crazy factor.

He fell into the closest bar to unmute the voice of the Almighty. The bartender recognized Rey's red and olive face. He recognized his pain and poured him a beer. "This one is on me, Mr. Pescador." Rey had been poured free drinks for ten years now. Usually people gave him drinks out of awe, but Rey recognized pity from the bar tender. He waited and watched a soccer match on the television. He felt his heart slow as he drank. He wondered where and when he made a wrong decision.

"You want another one?"

"Yeah, let's make it stronger."

"What's your drink, whisky, vodka, gin?"

"That's a loaded question." He looked at a bottle of red wine. The room was dark: it was smoky. "I want something that will let me hear the words of God."

"I'm no priest, but I do have some strong stuff. You just let me know what you want. We have quite the variety."

For all Rey knew, the bar could have been filled with a thousand people. He had seen and heard only one, the potbellied barkeep with a short sleeve dress shirt and polyester black tie. Then he smelled the Lilac Whiskey. He could taste her. He could feel her breath warm his neck.

"Give me a Lilac Whiskey," he said, thumbing the pint that he had just finished.

"I don't think I have that. Hell, I don't think I've ever heard of that."

"I've had it here before. It's in the wine cabinet at the top left. I see it. I can see it from here. I can smell it."

"I'm telling you, there is just wine there. Calm down."

"Give me the damn drink."

"Listen, Mr. Pescador. I know who you are. Hell, everyone does. Calm down. I'll get you that bottle, but it's not called that."

He lifted the pint, stared at it, and saw her reflection. The light-footed singer hummed a tune. He pulled out his wallet, gave it to the barkeep, then in one fluid motion and with the force of a one-time Single-A Toledo base stealer, threw his pint against the crystal shelves, turned around, grabbed the right wrist of the singer with his left hand and, reaching around to the small of her back, grabbed her right hip with his right hand.

"I love you. You do know that?"

"I do."

If there were other patrons in the bar, they had now left. The barkeeper escaped the shrapnel. Rey turned her around and sat her up on the bar. He placed his palms just below her hips, to hold her on earth for a moment.

"Why do you torment me?" he asked.

"It is my job."

"I will give you a new job. You will give me Lilac Whiskey. You will be loved by me." She smiled at his tacky response. He looked at her teeth and lips and down to her neck and chest. She was still thinner than anyone he had ever fallen for, but there was something about her that drew him to her.

"I am loved by you, and I will give you Lilac Whiskey, but that is not what you want." She dangled her hair in front of his eyes. Her voice was soft, hypnotic. She laughed like the right side of a keyboard.

"Do you even know what you want, Rey?"

"Of course, I know. It's what I've always wanted. I told you on the beach. On the island."

"You do not truly want me, Rey. You want your fame back."

"My fame is merely a vehicle to your love."

"Rey, you are so full of poetic bullshit that you can't see straight. I've read your books, the books of the Genius Brigade. You guys scream mythopoetic at every juncture. Imagine the absurdity of the fountain of youth in the year 2000. I can't believe you Rey." She paused for a moment. "But I can give you what you want."

Her hands moved through his hair. She looked at him, truly looked at him for the first time. She touched his face and smiled. For a moment she was frightened. "Your face hasn't aged a day. Oh my God. He never told me it was true. How could it be?"

"It was all true," Rey said.

"Maybe I could give you all that you want."

"I know you could."

"I can give you love."

"I know you can."

"I can give you fame."

"I know you can."

"I can give you happiness."

"I know you can."

She kissed him. He tasted what he had searched for his whole life. He felt the back of her hair. He saw down her shirt to her belly ring. She had no scar. He climbed the bar to her. "Wait," she said. He held himself over her as she said, "I can give you Lilac Whiskey as well, but it will cost."

"I will give anything."

"You must give everything."

"I will marry you."

"Not to me. You know who I work for. You must give him everything."

"Doesn't he already have my life?" Rey asked.

"He wants to make things official."

"Will you be there with me?"

"I will."

"When?"

"Next Saturday at noon." The light of police cars now filled the room. Rey whispered to meet him at the 80th floor. She smiled; she laughed and disappeared out the back door.

Rey scanned the bottles of wine. One was missing. He punched his hand against the wall, and then laughed. "It was all true," he said, grabbed a bottle of Cabernet, and fled the scene.

PART 2

THE YEARS OF LILAC WHISKEY

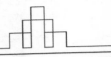

SIN OF OMISSION 1

⌐CH 26 •⌐

DECEMBER 25, 2009

On Christmas morning after Rey's elaborate seduction in the bar and a night of Lilac Whiskey inspired euphoria, the singer flew from the 80th floor of the John Hancock building. Rey claimed that she literally flew; though I suspect she only did so literarily. Rey's version included her growing grotesque wings and floating from high rise to high-rise until she gently touched the city floor.

When Rey first told me that tale, I said it was too much—that you can only have one story of someone flying off the second tallest building in Chicago. "That's the point, David. It's all connected," he said, as if that was enough to suspend my disbelief.

"You need to realize the point, David," he continued. "She wasn't just a singer."

"I got that, Rey. It's very clear."

"All right, so you understand that her mission was to deliver me to Sid Cutler."

"Yes, Rey."

"Then let me tell you what happened next."

"Tell me."

"Well, I had a clear mission at this point, David."

"Of course, you did."

"I had to rescue the beautiful singer, my beautiful poetry, and this beautiful world from the grip of Sid Cutler."

"Of course, you had to. Who else could?"

"Are you mocking me?" Rey asked

"Just keep telling the story."

"All right. Let's get back to it. I had one week before the meeting with Cutler. He wanted my eternal soul. I feared him. I feared that he would trick me, so I needed consultation from the wisest men I knew."

"From me and L.J.?"

"Exactly, if L.J. could locate my soul with his triangulator, I figured he could find a way to protect it in like a safe or something while I battled the devil."

"That makes perfect sense."

"It does, right?"

SIN OF OMISSION 2

CH 27

DECEMBER 25-31, 2009

In his 1977 mother-of-pearl Cutlass Rey cruised from Chicago to the desert north of Ciudad Juarez, stopping at only a handful of truck stops and Taco Bells until he reached the dilapidated farmhouse that had become L.J.'s hermitage.

The little white house welcomed Rey with memories of an America that he had never known. It was hot. Rey hadn't considered that. No cars were in the driveway, the garage swayed in the breeze, and Mrs. Lindberg—L.J.'s assistant/surrogate mother—sat in a chair on the porch smoking a cigarette. Rey removed his hat and greeted her. She simply said, "Hey, he's upstairs."

The front room was nothing but four plaster walls, three windows, and hardwood floors. Several bottles broken smoothly in two rested in the corner a few feet from a litter box that needed cleaning. Rey searched the dining room and kitchen then bounced up the old, wooden stairs. The second floor was one room with angular ceilings. In the middle of the water-damaged hardwood, in between three piles of books, lay L.J. Brovault. The slatternly scholar was wearing only mesh pants and glasses. His hair and beard were long. He was thinner than ever. He held a pistol in his right hand and a book in his left.

"Don't shoot, it's me," Rey said, jokingly.

"Hey Rey, why are you here?"

"What's up, bro? Long time no see. You've got quite the place here."

"What do you need, Rey?"

"Shoot, man. Now I feel bad."

"Why?"

"That I came here because I need something."

"It doesn't bother me. Why else would you?"

"A friendly visit. I should have come before on a friendly visit."

"I'm telling you that I don't mind."

"All right, you sure?

"Yeah Rey, I'm sure. It's good to see you."

"You're telling me. I've had a rough year."

"Me too."

"Listen, I need you to triangulate something for me."

"What is it?"

"The human soul. My soul. Either one, preferably the second one, my soul, I mean."

"That could be tricky, Rey."

"I thought you could triangulate anything?"

"I can, as long as it exists, but I've never seen evidence of the soul's existence in my research."

"Well, if the soul doesn't exist, that would be ideal. I mean, that would be amazing."

Rey sat a few feet from L.J., stretched his back, lay down, and looked up. The open-truss ceiling had visible holes in it.

"Do you sleep in this room, L.J.?"

"Yes, when I need to rest; though the human body needs much less sleep than most believe, Rey."

"What do you do when it rains?"

"It doesn't."

"Never?"

"Well, it doesn't rain while I'm in the room. I usually go outside to bathe in it."

"What the hell happened to you? I'm the one who lost my fame. You still have millions and you are sitting here in filth."

"I don't want to talk about my house. There is a reason I don't invite people over. How did you find me, anyway?"

"I received a letter last year from Mrs. Lindberg. She was worried about you killing yourself or something. I would have come then, but I was in the desert with my own issues."

"Let's not talk about that stuff, Rey."

"You wouldn't do that, would you?"

"What?"

"Kill yourself."

"I don't think so."

"Good. I like having you around. And they say things are harder in the next life if you squander this one."

The two lay there as the sun set.

"Let's go to my triangulator," L.J. suggested. "I think it's time."

"It's about damn time!" Rey shouted.

The triangulator's housing was a surreal equilateral triangle. The three cinder block walls were painted red, blue, and green. L.J. Brovault scampered up the rope over the eight foot tall green wall and waited for Rey to enter.

"Where's the door?"

"There is no door, you just climb in."

Rey climbed in and lit a cigarette. The only thing in the tiny roofless room was the hammock and the triangulator. It was a weird machine. It was all metal, as far as I can tell, and it stood about four feet from the ground. It had three arms and a small digital interface. L.J. plugged some numbers into the interface and then lay on the hammock. The two geniuses watched the arms of the triangulator spin ceaselessly. Above, a cloud covered the luminous crescent upon which Brovault himself claimed to have walked only a few years earlier.

After a few hours, the triangulator stopped. By this point, Rey was sleeping in the dirt, exhausted from his trip. The world was silent. Brovault excavated from the hands of the mechanical creature a piece of paper upon which the location of the human soul was written.

Rey woke up to L.J. shouting, "I am but a beast." Then L.J. removed his mesh pants and climbed out of the door-less room into the darkness.

Rey climbed into the hammock and slept in the cool desert night. When he awoke, L.J. was climbing back into the triangulator's housing. "What did you find last night?" Rey asked.

"Nothing. It's nowhere."

"You mean, my soul is lost."

"No, I mean there is not any human soul. There is none. There is no such thing."

"And there was no error?"

"There never has been."

"So what now?" Rey asked.

"We're all damned?"

"Or none of us are."

"I guess. So what is the poet's plan?"

"Well, first we should get out of this creepy room. Though, I must say, I slept great last night."

"It's not creepy."

"It really is, kid."

They climbed out. Then the pair walked toward the house stopping at Rey's Cutlass in the driveway.

"Well, L.J., the way I see it is this," Rey started. "I have two options. The first is that I use myself as bait, put my soul on a hook, meet with Sid Cutler, sign his deal, and then kill him."

"What is the second?"

"The second option is simpler. I stay the hell away from that fat piece of shit. What do you think?"

"I don't know, man. This is the type of equation that I can't solve."

"I guess not. But I think I know who can."

Rey jumped into the Cutlass. L.J. turned his back and started to walk away. "Hey L.J., listen to me, the desert is fine for a season, but when all this is over, I'm coming back here, I'm going to bring you back. I'm not going to let my best friend live in the desert like this."

"Why not?"

"Because, my emaciated amigo, that is what friends do."

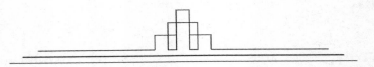

THE SIN OF A SHEPHERD

CH 28

DECEMBER 31, 2009

Breathing steadily in the cold, I looked through the window as God lit the restaurant where your carefully manicured hands carried trays of pancakes to people like me. The noise of the city bounced on every surface to remind us that the city was moving and alive. Delivery trucks moved bagels and bread north to south. Cab drivers opened doors and started engines. Though it was morning, everyone braced himself for the long night.

Two men on bicycles passed me before I got to the door. They locked their bikes to a "no parking" sign and proceeded. The stench of sweat and December flooded the entryway. Before entering I looked at the sky, it was bright blue, scattered with cirrus clouds, one of those skies that tells you how bright the cold can be and makes you feel like you are at the northern tip of a long flat world.

The bikers invaded the corner booth until you motioned toward me and explained that the particular booth they wanted was reserved for the priest. You floated toward me, grabbed a menu, and your crimson fingernails triggered rods and cones that reminded me to breath.

I miss sitting there almost every day, a reluctant priest, a renowned sinner; a lonely miserable 35-year-old man infatuated with you, the angelic waitress.

Writing about it now, the whole situation was pretty miserable, I guess.

A window met the small, red-upholstered booth where I unpacked my books and journals while you served others. I wrote

146

about the sky and the window and the tip of the northern world. I drank ice water until you walked toward me in canvas shoes and jeans—a tidal wave of meaning to an overly cerebral man. Your hair back, except for a single strand, your white apron, your restaurant pad, the pencil in your hair, and your smile all left the synapses of my mind understanding how silly my infatuation was, how simple and cliché it was for me to find solace in the idea of this beautiful woman, whose job it was to please me in the most tangible way she could.

We talked about the New Year, about our New Years. I'm sure that you had that same conversation with everyone else that day. I'm sure other men fell in love with you as you placed a cinnamon roll on the table or held you long arm in front of them to fill coffee cups.

But despite you being the loveliest woman in the world, no one has ever loved you like I do. That much I've proven.

I studied there for a few hours. I was trying to discover what the difference was between our organic ancestors with organic hearts and us. But I was distracted from any real epiphanies by thoughts of Rey, the final man with a human heart. Could he love you better than me? I doubted it. He was too distracted by the absurd. He was too much. I wrote down in my journal, "Rey has mastered the outlandish, the absurd." Underneath that I wrote, "I, David Rosario, will master the commonplace: the cup of morning coffee, the conversation with a pretty waitress at a normal diner." That was my goal as a new decade was ready to commence.

Around 4:00 PM I left cash on the table and exited to the gray city on the final night of the year. The frozen sidewalk unfolded before me and caught my shoes which clicked. The salt underfoot crumbled as I pivoted to look at you one last time that year.

Three blocks of salt and sidewalk later, my armchair greeted me. My wine consoled me during thoughts of you and Brenda and of the bottle of Lilac Whiskey that sat on my nightstand. That same bottle, still sealed, not yet hidden, tempted me as it still does. Perhaps if I could have forgotten Brenda, I could have lived a normal life.

As I lingered in thought between past and present and

watched the dark orange glow of mid-winter sunset, I heard Rey Pescador cough between the sound of horns of trucks and cabs that braced for the celebration. Though it was still early, I had begun the descent into a lonely celebratory evening like a plane slowly falling to ground. Rey had touched ground an hour earlier from a literal plane that had delivered him home from the desert.

Perhaps Rey's sin that night was my sin: the sin of a shepherd who watched his sheep get eaten for sport. Perhaps it was my sin in that very moment as I sat there unwilling to open the door that tore Rey's soul from his body.

He coughed again before knocking. I saw his breath, just outside the front door. He must have seen me sitting there at my armchair against the yellow wall. He knocked again and again and then shouted, "David let me in, man." He continued, "David, I need your advice. It's serious."

He knocked and knocked.

"David, I know you're in there. I really need your help."

I drank a glass of wine.

After Rey stopped knocking and sat down, I didn't think of him or my promise to Elijah Grey or of Brenda. I thought about you at the coffee shop. I grieved the fact that a year after my suicide attempt and six months after my hasty ordination, I would fall in love.

I decided I should break my vow of celibacy. I started to imagine how I would do it. I imagined your face, your lips kissing my neck and scarred chest. I imagined my hands on your shoulders and hair and then I thought of your smile. I tried to think of the colors and sounds to make my fantasy as real as possible.

Then right there in my armchair, I imagined your face and its surreal joy. I realized that was why you fascinated me so much. How many people exude joy like that? I couldn't keep fantasizing about your body. I couldn't think of you merely as an idea when I thought about that joy. Or was it joy at all? I wondered. What if it was merely the genetic composition of your physical features that corresponded with a pleasant demeanor to receive tips that mimicked joy despite a deep sadness? What if your lips curled naturally, and your eyes were a paradox, too bright to be dimmed, yet the palest blue I had seen? I wonder if people thought they were gray.

Either way I found it lovely and wanted to explore the root of your countenance because never had I seen anyone who could even mimic joy like you did while serving coffee to fools like me.

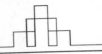

THE DEATH OF REY PESCADOR

Ch 29

DECEMBER 31, 2009

While I sat there, Rey smoked three cigarettes on the front porch of the Hyde Park house, watching the snow that mocked the smoke dance along the asphalt until it vanished into nothingness. He knocked and knocked again. Then he sat on the chipped green paint of the top step even longer. When I finally noticed the snow—if you can call it that—I thought it was smoke. I thought Rey was still there an hour after the first knock.

I opened the front door and said, "All right, you idiot, what advice do you need?"

But all three cigarettes had been extinguished though the last one still smoldered. He was gone. By that point he must have been looking at the city's lights like he never would again, through the window of a cab that transported him to Midway Airport. From there, jet engines hurled him to New Jersey where men in white suits escorted him into a helicopter that spun its wings and delivered him to Cutler Corporations new headquarters.

No more than four hours after knocking on my door, Rey surveyed Manhattan from that ungodly high-rise with the ache of body and soul desiring something unspecified that the city promised but could never fulfill. Normally insignificant dissonant stimuli shook the sinner: a squeaky door, a silver tie slanted left, a brown logo juxtaposed against the amber liquid in the Whiskey decanter that Sidney now poured into his own glass as Rey sat on the high-backed armchair and drank scotch.

Rey looked at the blood from the steak on the white plate. Of course, Cutler did not notice the blood. He ate. He spoke. He coughed and wheezed and chatted and consumed always at the same time. Then he took a long drink of water. Following that was a few minutes of silence other than the disturbing sound of Sid Cutler devouring his food.

While Rey observed Cutler, he knew that he could never sell his soul to this man. Surely this was the devil incarnate. Finally, Rey broke the silence and small talk, "Mr. Cutler, I just realized something."

"Yes?"

"You could call it an epiphany even."

"What is that?" Cutler continued to chew as he said this. That alone was enough for Rey.

"Let me finish this beautiful steak first," Rey said.

"Whatever you want, kid."

Say what you want about Sid Cutler, he made Rey probably the best steak anyone ever had. At least that is what Rey said. He talked about that steak more than just about anything he's ever experienced.

After the final bite, Rey thumbed his knife and decided that now was as good a time as ever to turn down an offer that he certainly could never accept.

"The thing is this, Sidney. You and I both know that I am an addict. Withdrawal isn't treating me so great. By taking my fame away, you've made things quite painful to me. We both know that what you have offered is the only logical option for me."

"I'm glad that you realize that."

"I thought you would be, Sidney. Do you mind if I tell you a story?"

"Sure. I've got some time."

"Don't worry, I've been told that I have a knack for the spoken word. It won't be a waste of your evening."

"I never thought it would."

"Could we get some more whiskey in here?"

"Absolutely." Cutler personally took another bottle off of the shelf on the wall among the ancient swords and weapons and maps that were consistent with Cutler's other offices.

"This is a good scotch, kid. You will like it."

"I'm sure I will."

"So tell me this story."

"Of course. Damn, this is good Scotch. All right, well, here is the thing, Sidney. When I was a kid my favorite thing to do late at night when I couldn't sleep was read these stories about Saints, *The Golden Legend*, stuff like that. You ever read any?"

"No. I thought this was a story not a book report."

"It is. It has a beginning, middle, and end, but if you want me to sign your parchment, you need to listen, to understand the soul you are getting."

"Keep talking."

"I don't often talk about the monks who raised me. I don't think I've told you anything about them. Have I?

"No."

"Okay. Well, one of them, the brother I was closest to until I was like eleven, and he moved to Europe or something, was named Brother George. He was probably the most cerebral man I've ever met. He hardly ever did any of his duties, but he gobbled up novels and even told me stories even after compline when everyone was supposed to be silent. The thing about George was that he almost never read anything but these cheesy science fiction and fantasy novels. So he would pass them on to me, but for some reason they didn't interest me much at that point. But he also told me stories. He told me this one story about a thousand times, maybe the best story I've ever heard. Man, I'm feeling tipsy. What'd you put in this whiskey?"

"Alcohol."

"Good. That type of thing, putting alcohol in the whiskey, that is what I like about you, Sid. I want you to know that."

"So what is the big deal with this monk?"

"Well, I have forgotten about most of the stories he told me. I mean, I didn't forget, but I hadn't thought about them for a while. I've read so much and seen so much that the stories of childhood kind of drift out of the consciousness. The thing is, Sid, I think that they must inspire future action, right? I mean I can't imagine that you fill your mind with these fantastic tales, and then just forget, and they have no effect. Anyway, that's not really the point of all this. The point comes a few years back when we went to Africa. Ethiopia has some interesting stuff. You know they have the Ark of the Covenant? You scoff, but seriously, I believe it because of what I saw when we were there, we went to this freakin' awesome church. It was carved into a hill."

"Rey, I have another meeting. I've read your books and paid for your trips. I don't need you to explain your journey to Africa."

"This was a church of Jesus Christ. I think you should listen, Sidney. It's a good story, after all. So we slept on top of this church. It was in the shape of the cross. It was called Saint George's, which was cool because it made me think of two things: this monk, George, and the story he always told me about his namesake Saint George, who of all the Saints was especially badass. You see—"

"I've heard that story."

"You haven't heard this part. You of course know that George is famous for killing a dragon back in the 4th century or something. It was in Northern Africa, I think. Actually, I'm sure of it. Sorry, I'm a little tipsy, as I mentioned. So first George tames the dragon and stuff. Then he kills it and converts the whole town. The thing is you know how I slept on top of this for a while. But I've never told anyone that after that I had trouble sleeping. So in the middle of the night, when L.J. and Carl, and the others slept, I repelled down and through the window and wandered for hours through the corridors. There were all these paintings of George killing a dragon, which is pretty sweet. But there was this one that never made sense. It was George standing over the body of a man. Or at least it looked like a man. It was old, super faded and all. But the man was quite rotund. He seemed like the kind of piece of shit that might eat a steak without ever looking down. He seemed like the kind of man that might keep women around and treat them like objects. He seemed like the type of man who you could think you killed or something, maybe kick out of your town, but centuries later might show up again and offer you something with strings attached. He seemed like he might give you your fame back at the price of your soul."

Cutler laughed. "What is your point, Rey? I think I get it, but I was promised a story, and this is more exposition than I'm used to."

"Well, when Brother George raised me he said something

like, 'One day you will kill a dragon, Rey. You'll understand me when it happens.' So here is your story. There was a fat cannonball of a man who kept the whole earth content with faux health and entertainment. Then a kid was born by a miracle of the Virgin Mary. He grew strong and famous and slew the dragon."

Rey grabbed a sword from the wall and ran toward Cutler. He imagined all of the stories of saints or knights with their lances destroying evil. Now he was one of them: a modern day saint killing the shell of the devil and overcoming his greatest temptation at once.

Rey locked onto Cutler's eyes as he ran.

Cutler grabbed his chair and held it as a shield. Cutler was surprisingly quick for a morbidly obese man, but he misjudged Rey's speed and strength. Rey was incredibly fast. The sword pierced through the chair and into Cutler's belly. Rey pushed as far as he could, but the Cannonball laughed, pushed back with his incredible weight, and hissed. Even while injured, Cutler leveraged his enormous strength to overwhelm his foe. As he threw the chair aside and pinned Rey, men in white fedoras flooded the room to assist their wounded boss.

"Stay back!" Cutler shouted. "He is mine." Cutler tore open Rey's shirt and with his steak knife carved a C into his chest. At the end of the C, at the bottom, he pressed until Rey's sternum started to splinter.

"To think I let you keep this antique heart as long as I have."

Cutler put knife to bone and then paused and ordered his assistants to tie Rey to the chair as if he'd be able to escape anyway.

"Rey, you have always been like a son to me. You told me your little story, so now let's get back to what you came here for. You owe me your soul. The George thing was cute, but you are no George. You are the greatest sinner I've ever known Rey, and I am going to make you a deal because I am a more forgiving man than you could ever imagine I'd be. I will give you your body and fame for your eternal allegiance. Simply answer three questions and sign this document.

"Do you reject all other claims upon your eternal soul?" Cutler asked.

"No."

"Will you serve Sidney Alphonse Cutler with your body and mind?"

"Never."

"Do you wish to live in pleasure without memory of pain?"

"Sidney, just let me go."

"Then give me what you promised."

Rey tried to spit on Cutler, but had not the energy.

"Then you will wager that George's God can give you the pleasure that I have for all of these years. Does he even promise that? I have read the Bible more deeply than you, and I'm pretty sure of two things. First of all, his heaven would be hell for someone like you. Secondly, you'd never make it anyway. Do you want his heaven? Or will he damn you? Have you confessed lately? How confident are you that hell isn't your last stop anyway? You can reign with me, Rey Pescador, the King of Art and Pleasure, or you can hope for a lawn chair by the Crystal Sea."

By now the whiskey and endorphins had taken full effect. Rey hardly understood the questions or their implications. As his wound bled without hope of stopping, he imagined the face of Christ. He imagined himself a martyr, but thought that Cutler might be right. He couldn't imagine that he could ever be saved from hell. How could God forgive all of those sins?

He drifted in and out of consciousness. The singer who was Rey's muse finally entered the black space. She cried and gave Rey Lilac Whiskey, playing the part of mourning wife, nurse, and angry employee simultaneously. But Rey ignored her for the moment. Rather, he stared at the grotesque countenance of Sidney Cutler: the paradox of pleasure and fear. More than anything he wanted to kill the spherical executive.

His heart pounded. He thought briefly of me and L.J.: my closed oak door, and L.J.'s insistence that he had no soul to sell anyway. He thought of our childhood, the brothers who forgave him and fed him the host even after he was expelled. He remembered the marble crucifix in the chapel, the countless mornings as a child whose eyes, before reaching the cherubim on the ceiling, were pulled into the immense gravity of the suffering

Christ.

That gravity now was canceled in the weight of the singer's touch. She kissed his face and neck. She whispered into his ear.

Rey's heart beat more gently as his blood drained from his chest. He considered praying one last time to the silent God who gave and who took away, but he felt a heart pounding against his wounded chest. It was the singer's human heart. She whispered, "I am like you, Rey. I need you here. We can find a way to save you."

No one moved. Rey slipped out of consciousness, and the singer, fearing her beloved had been dealt the final wound, kissed him. She stroked his hair and sang to him. She whispered that she could give him children, and love, and fame.

"It's an absurd contract with a madman," she said. "It's not a big deal. Don't waste your life."

Her human touch and the thick aroma of Lilac Whiskey on her breath revived him enough for him to look Sid Cutler in the eye and say, "Take my soul, you piece of shit, but stitch my body and leave me with her!"

Rey reached his forefinger through the full crescent shaped wound, and then on the document before him, signed in his blood.

Cutler delighted in the document as Elijah Grey chanted incantations of healing. Cutler kissed Rey's forehead and said, "Welcome home, my son."

Rey said, "Don't ever touch me again you fat fuck."

Cutler punched Rey. Rey blacked out.

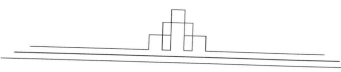

THE YEAR OF LILAC WHISKEY

CH 30 •

DECEMBER 31, 2009

On top of a giant unlit sphere of potential light, Rey awoke with 500,000 people waiting below eager to count backwards for ten seconds. Not sure how he got there and how his heart was still beating, he scanned the skies for an answer. Above him, was the helicopter that transported him here from Cutler's office and held him upright with strings and a harness. Lilac Whiskey numbed his pain. Elijah Grey had healed his wounds.

A bird ready to swoop from the branch into a stream, Rey watched the crowd patiently.   He had not been briefed on his first stunt as an excarnate celebrity, but his natural sense of the dramatic mixed with this most unnatural inebriation made briefing unnecessary: he knew that he was bringing in the New Year with a spectacle that would delight the anxious, bored, tired, and cold crowd. None of the half million people had ever seen such an absurd scene: a man with a human heart in a black tuxedo taking flight above them, and they would one day tell their grandchildren that they were there when Rey Pescador flew.

Cue lights popping. The massive cluster of bulbs ignited, and all eyes moved from the ground's cold cement to the lights. Rey's heartbeat nearly overcame his thoughts. The crowd began to ask who that man was up there on top of the famous icon of new beginnings. Rey Pescador, the patron saint of the spectacular, could be the only person up there at a time like this. Then Cutler, comfortable as always in his chopper, flipped a switch.

A single ray of light illuminated the hanging man who smiled at the crowd. Hidden in the shadows of the robotic bird, Cutler addressed the crowd, "World, welcome to the Year of Lilac Whiskey. I have given you your undying hearts; now drink my favorite vintage as a gift to celebrate the year that you forget all of your pain and guilt." The crowd erupted. Bottles were being passed. People drank the modified pink liquid that was now void of virtually all of its nepenthe. Cutler continued, "And now, to start the year off in style, the Captain of Consonants, the Sultan of Spoken Word, the Duke of Discourse: America, I present to you the Czar of Arts and Beauty, Rey Pescador."

At the birth of the New Year, the crowd erupted. Rey sang the national anthem. He read a poem. He dove into the ocean of hands. He emerged satisfied.

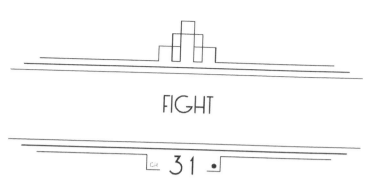

FIGHT

CH 31 •

JANUARY 1, 2010

Rey claimed to have no recollection of what happened after flying into the crowd. As far as I know, his next memory was exiting a limousine and walking through rows of fans into the locker rooms of Madison Square Garden where he offered unsolicited fight prep to Riley before walking into the ring as the MC of one of the last great boxing matches.

The first two fighters were both bald. I would say very bald, but I think it is a binary category, but if not, these creatures were very bald: one black, one white. They had no eyebrows, no hair at all. Their scars were larger than typical RHC scars. Tattoos covered their arms and backs. Their movement was angular and explosive. Only one walked out of the ring. Rey watched in near horror from the first row, and two seats down, Sid Cutler laughed hysterically at the synthetic blood that splattered his shoes. At first I thought it was impossible that robot fighting would be happening there, at Madison Square Garden on New Year's Day, but now it is a historic fact (though no one would cite Sidney Cutler in any research regarding it).

Robot fighting was as illegal as adding human organs to machines partly because robot fighting—the worst of it, at least—often included grotesque humanoid creatures. Creatures with human skin or human livers or pancreases, etc. (you get the picture). Politicians feared blending the lines of human and technology more than it already had been. They would add certain technologies to a human, but to add anything human to a machine—including a competitive desire—crossed some bizarre

159

ethical line for them. I don't think many people saw the difference between a humanoid creature and a regular person in those days. I don't think many people care about the difference these days. Both humanoids and humans have fleshy exteriors and metal insides. Also, robot fighting had historically always ended in death. Say what you want about America during the years of Cutler's influence, it was not a place that would publicly promote death.

I was relieved to see that the second fight was human vs. human. It would herald the new female heavyweight champion of the world. The third and final fight was dubbed as the fight of the millennium. While the women fought, Rey turned and stared at the crowd. He could not watch: the chivalrous machismo identity he had formed was never an act. To Rey, women were to be protected. Rather than watching the violent spectacle, he continued his obsession and searched the audience for the singer.

She told him that she would be there. He imagined her skin, her hand, her voice. He considered using his role as master of ceremonies to find her. He could simply say, "Beautiful singer fly back to me." But now that he was famous again that would never work. He would have a stampede of a thousand singers who were watching the fight hoping for Rey's attention. He couldn't remember where she went after Sid's office. In fact, at that time, just a day after the event, he could hardly remember selling his soul. It would take the next year of meditation to remember most of the details that he shared with me. I'm sure he made up the rest.

A woman was knocked out. The crowd erupted.

It was Rey's turn. His job was simple: smile, introduce the fighters, and leave the ring. He stood in the center of the ring and called to New York, to the world, "Welcome to the year of Lilac Whiskey, the greatest year the world will ever see. We have conquered death. We have perfected science. Now be entertained. I've got two fighters here ready to punch each other's brains in. We have one goal, to see the greatest fight in history. Now tell me, America, who do you love?"

The chant moved like lava from a volcano. It started in the cheap seats and echoed and reverberated until it consumed the stadium: *Rey, Rey, Rey, Rey, Rey.*

He looked out. He smiled and shouted back, "I can't hear you! What do you want?"

Poetry, poetry, poetry, poetry.

"That's what I thought," Rey said, as he took off his shirt, for the first time ever in public. His new, crescent scar ensured that no one would conclude that he was lacking metal. He grabbed the hanging mike above him and swung around the ring. The crowd overflowed. Then shirtless, inspired, and overflowing with vainglory, Rey climbed the rope still holding the microphone until he was about 20 feet high. He closed his eyes and shushed the crowd. He breathed deeply and shook the room as he cried, "Muse." Once again, it was two syllables "M(A)-USE." He cried again, "Muse, don't leave me." The crowd was enthralled by the soulless specter hanging from a rope once again.

Finally, he heard her. Just as beautifully as the night before. He could almost see her flying toward him. She had the purity that she had on the boat so long ago. She wore heels and a black dress. He laughed and said, "Muse, sing to me. Sing longer and sweeter and stronger than before. Surround us like a fountain. Breathe beauty into the cold, steel and ice of the modern world, the northern world." Then in a final bellowing yawp, he shouted one last time, "Muse!"

Then poetry engulfed the audience.

Electric pens swim to me.
Carve ink into my heart.
Etch MAN on the final man
for like my genesis a serpent came;
I drank its fantasy.

Inscribe on this heart a pale, dim
stain. Unintelligible, until
you drain the blood.
At last beat ends

the last man. Hanging
from a helicopter

*strings of wire intersect
the midnight sky of
commencement. Forgive
the modern world. Forget
the modern world. He dies tonight.*

*Then, capture my history in
cathartic electrons, in this moment
of brilliance. A flash of light:*

*a million humans illuminate
the ultimate soul in electric light.*

Rey shouted, "Are you ready for the fight? Hell yeah, you are. Are you ready for a fight? Hell yeah, you are! Hell yeah! Hell yeah!"

Rey finally noticed that Cutler was not happy with his improvisational poetry.

Rey yelled to him, "You getting antsy, Sid? I wouldn't want to make you wait to win a bet. But if you want money, then bet on me."

Then he lifted the mic again, "Who wants to fight me? I'll give 100,000 American dollars to anyone who can beat me in a one-round fight. Mr. Cutler, I'll let you choose among the eager men approaching the ring."

"Bad idea, Rey. You're going to get the shit beat of you," Cutler said.

"No I'm not, Sid."

"You want to bet?"

"Fine, how about 500,000? Paid to L.J. if I win, to cover an old debt."

"You're on."

Cutler selected the largest man from the crowd. He could have been a professional football player. Maybe he was. Rey stripped to his shorts, and danced around the ring. He was as fast as ever. He slapped away a few punches and jumped around the large man for the first two minutes. The football player was tiring. Then, Rey struck, first in the belly, then again, then he backed out.

Rey danced again and lifted his arms to the crowd. In the midst of Rey's hubris, the football player attacked. Rey swooped left dodging a strong right hook. Then Rey connected with an uppercut in the chin. His hand throbbed, but he followed with a left hook, then a right jab to the nose. The large man bled. Again Rey flew around the ring again, celebrating. He looked at Cutler and shouted, "You own my soul, I'd think you'd know enough not to bet against it."

"Just finish him off, Rey."

Rey attacked the man again; he blocked his nose with both hands, to avoid any further damage. Rey delivered a dozen more body shots until he fell on his knees.

Rey ran to the ropes, stood on the corner, and shouted into the microphone, "And now, the greatest fight in history, Edwin James Riley against Shanahan."

The crowd erupted. Despite Rey's entertainment, their money and stomachs came to see two champions battle. Rey put his pants back on and collected his cash from Cutler. He gave L.J. the money and sat to watch the battle.

"What the hell is this?" L.J. asked.

"It's for you. I figured you could use it."

"I forgave that debt. Remember, we were friends."

"We still are, but take the money. I don't need it. It's Cutler's, God knows you deserve it."

The greatest fight in history wasn't much of a fight at all. It was much less exciting than Rey's fight. When Shanahan lay on the ground unable to move, the crowd announced that yes, Edwin Riley, the Genius of the Ring was the greatest fighter in history. Rey had bet on the Genius Brigade member. He always bet on his friends. But Sidney Cutler, the manager of the boxing legend, threw his hat in fury. Cutler's eyes never strayed from Riley's starry glare that slowly scanned the twenty thousand adoring fans. Riley never looked at Cutler. He only circled the ring with his hands extended waist high as if to simultaneously say he would fight anyone and he would receive everyone's praise. Riley had finally realized that all of Madison Square Garden was there for him, not Cutler nor Rey, nor the robots.

I could say more about Riley, but there are other books

dedicated to that.

The blond woman on Cutler's left stroked his silver hair. He did not respond to her.

Rey, drunk on his own vanity, shouted at Cutler, "What's wrong Sid, you bet against two of your prodigies tonight? I'd bet you can afford it." Cutler glared at the poet who continued his mania. "I feel like dancing. You mind if I borrow one of your girls, Sid?" The brunette giggled and looked at her boss as if to ask permission, but Rey said, "Don't worry sweetheart, he owns me too. Any mingling our souls do tonight, is bought and paid for by the Cutler Corporation."

Rey held her hand and walked her to the ring. She was gorgeous. "One dance, Rey," she said, "One dance."

Rey slipped under the first rope and into the boxing ring. Before the woman could slide under the ropes, Cutler grabbed her by the wrist.

"What the hell, Sid? Let the girl dance. God knows you're not going to do anything with her."

Then she added, "It's just a dance, Sidney." He pulled her close to his enormous frame and slapped her in the face.

"What the hell, Sid? You're hitting women now. I ought to beat you like that other guy."

Rey charged out of the ring, but was held back by two men in white suits. Cutler warned him, "Don't mistake my contract with you to think that we are equals, Rey. I used you. I now own you. That is the end of the story. I buy low and sell high."

"Why don't you say that without having your goons hold me back, you fat bastard?"

"Let him go."

Rey was a bull leaving the gates. He knew a body blow would have no effect on the enormous man. He had to hit him hard in the face. He had to move fast. He faked with the left, and before he could begin to move his right arm, Cutler had knocked him clean on the ground.

Rey regained consciousness to see the Cannonball walking up the stairs to the exit gate with the two beautiful women. When Cutler reached the top of the 100 level seats, he turned and looked at the fallen hero, "Rey, listen to me. Get your act together. Take a week off. Then my office will send your new touring schedule. You are more famous than you can imagine now. Don't forget why. Enjoy yourself, and if you ever cross me again, I will take what I let you keep last night."

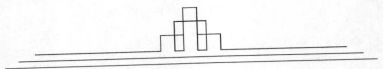

THREE KINGS

CH 32

JANUARY 6, 2010

Momentarily distracted by his reflection in a brass cage, Rey missed the red sun's reemergence from the ocean. He fiddled with the birdcage until it finally popped open. Placing his hand in the cage palm up as if he was begging for alms, the black creature hopped from its resting place to his gentle grasp. His beak searched for food, but nothing other than potential freedom was offered that January morning.

Rey positioned his left hand over the back of the bird and slowly removed the fowl from the brass cage. He looked at its two eyes, not that different from his, and spoke, "Brother, you haven't aged, have you? Unless you are simply a newer model." He laughed and sat with his feet dangling over the second story balcony. He was already weary of holding the bird, but he didn't think the cage was necessary. With his right hand he held its feet, and with his left he tried to untie a lace from his brown leather shoes. Once the lace was free, he attempted to tie it on the impatient creature. Wings twitched, beaks whistled, and then from behind Rey's back, came the familiar sound of a car beeping at a garbage truck that bounced through a city street.

Both creatures were startled by the horn. The bird took flight. "Damn!" Rey yelled and watched it fly into the air. Nervous at the prospect of having to explain to a near stranger that he climbed her balcony and let her bird fly away, all he could to do was lie down and sleep until she awoke.

166

She did, and he was still lying half-awake, when the barrage of curses flew from the woman's mouth. But Rey just lay on his back and looked upward listening to the cadence of a lost memory.

"What are you doing here?" she asked, finally getting the dreamer's attention.

"I'm sorry. I didn't mean to let him go."

"What the hell are you doing here?"

"I came because … well, I just … I guess it's hard to say. I thought the bird could use some company."

She looked at the sunrise to the far right then at the water, painted a stunning red. "So you came for a bird? You met me thirteen years ago in a bar and wrote a book about me being some symbolic quest and now come back to see my bird?"

"I don't think so."

"What do you mean?"

"I didn't come to see your bird."

"So why are you really here?"

"I had a week off. It's cold up north. I don't know. I didn't know where else to go."

Rey must have been as surprised by his honesty as she was. She quietly sat down in the other chair on the balcony. They watched the bands of sunlight turn from red to yellow on the ocean.

"Sorry about the bird," Rey repeated.

"He'll fly back. Just use the front door next time. Or call. That might be better."

"OK, I'll call next time. Hey, let's go to the beach."

"It's still early."

"Then take your time getting ready, and then we'll go."

"All right, why not?"

Aldonza got dressed as Rey explored the bookcases lining the walls of her apartment. She had a whole shelf of first edition Spanish novels. He thought about swiping Borges' *The Book of Imaginary Beings*, mostly as a joke, but decided it would be rude either way. Amid the photographs on the bookcases, he found no sign of a husband or boyfriend, just pictures of family, children— presumably nephews and nieces scattered throughout the bookcases. He wondered what it would be like to be in an image in an apartment like that—to matter to a person in that specific way.

When she was ready, they made breakfast and packed it for the beach. Rey carried it pretending to be a traditional man in a traditional world. He even told me he imagined helping with the dishes when they came home, though I have trouble believing it. They ate in silence watching the sun rise into its yellow fruition, then Rey took off his shirt and closed his eyes. "Sing to me," he said. I want to hear your voice.

"I'm not going to sing to you." She laughed.

"Then tell me a story. Tell me about your job. Weren't you a graduate student? I know that you were."

"I was. Now I teach and write literary criticism."

"So you struck it rich too? You ever teach my books?"

"I try to avoid them. I know that no one would ever figure it out, but I still don't want people thinking that I am Aldonza."

"You are Aldonza."

"I know." She stared at the grotesque scar on his chest.

"Did your heart malfunction? I've never seen an RHC scar like that."

"Me neither."

"It's still red. It looks fresh."

"I know. I've seen it, and I was there when it happened," he said as she touched the outline of the C carved into his chest.

"What happened?"

"The devil sliced me open to kill me if I didn't sell my soul to him. I think he messed with my heart while it was open. Hard to tell, I was pretty high."

"Are you capable of speaking literally?"

"That is all I believe in. I've made a career of it."

She looked at Rey and then at the ocean and people who were starting to arrive for the festivities. She laughed to herself.

"My friends will never believe this."

"So you'll tell your friends? Looks like I'm gaining ground."

"What is that supposed to mean?"

"I honestly don't know. I just say these things."

They watched the waves for a while without speaking.

Finally she asked, "Why me? Am I some sort of muse? Or do you have rounds of women that you visit to please you? Because I don't want you to think me going to the beach is a sign that my apartment is open for you to stay."

"That's not why I'm here. Honestly, for once in my life, I'm not looking for sex. And no, you are not my muse. I have a muse. She is not as beautiful, but she has this amazing voice."

"You really are a strange man."

"I don't often fit on the normal curve."

"I mean it, Rey. Why are you here?"

"I guess I am trying to relive a moment, that moment in life, in a relationship, before everything goes to shit. Like I want to walk into a photograph. In the flash of light from the camera, I mean. I want to feel that excitement that something good might last, that love might last. But instead, it is just a moment in time, an image like a flashbulb on an old camera. The image captures something beautiful that can only exist in that moment."

"So you are trying to recapture love at first sight."

"I guess so. I guess that is what it was about you. I loved you partly because you said you didn't believe in love. I mean think about the absurdity of it. I'm this 19-year-old guy, and I pledged my life to you and you say you don't believe in love. I had never heard anyone say that before."

"Well, I really don't believe in your type of love, your courtly romance, chivalric, patriarchal..."

"I don't think I do anymore either. I guess I'm just nostalgic. It seemed so simple ten years ago. I knew exactly who I was going to be and why."

"That's how it is with everyone, Rey."

"I guess so. Did you ever want me to come back?"

"Well, I'll be honest and say that up until a few years ago, I secretly wished you would come back."

"Here I am. I'm back, kind of. Well, a new version of me is."

"So you have changed?"

"Absolutely."

"How so?"

"Well, it's hard to describe, I guess."

For a long time, they listened to the waves and children

shouting, "Mira, mira, mami."

"Here is the change. When I met you before I really believed in love at first sight. And now I only love the images of a moment, if that makes sense, which it probably doesn't."

"No."

"I love images, snapshots of the past."

"You love memories?"

"Kind of. Like the moment that I chased you from the casino. That moment has changed. Now it is an entirely different moment connected somewhere outside of time to this moment now. The thing is, I don't believe that time is like a line or a long piece of string. I only believe in moments. We have new cells, new thoughts, new clothing, new skin. All that remains is the fiction of memory. The memory of you to me and me to you. And even that memory is informed by a series of poems and stories written thirteen years ago, and then changed a hundred times by editors and my imagination. How can that reality have anything to do with this? How can love transcend moments? I only love the passing glimpse, a glance at the sunset."

"So, you do not want me, but rather moments with me in the past."

"No that's not it. It's this, you are the moment that I want."

Rey knew that was a line to woo a woman, plain and simple. And if Rey Pescador, the Chitown Cassinova, had a line to say to a woman he couldn't resist.

The sun continued to beat on her skin. Aldonza, already conditioned to the eternal energy of the sun in the Caribbean, remained the same, as he slowly changed to another hue. She rolled up the bottom of her pants and took off her shoes. Then she turned on her side in the sand and looked at Rey who lay with his eyes closed. His face hadn't changed after all of those years. She wondered if fame was simply that easy on people. She touched the fresh scar on his chest and wondered where his RHC scar was. If this scar was new, there must be another scar hidden beneath. She leaned over his body, holding her long, brown hair on one side and kissed his forehead. The crucifix she wore dangled against his face. He opened his eyes to Christ on the cross and her neckline. He propped himself on one shoulder and touched her crucifix.

"Are you religious?" he asked.

"Not at all. Are you?"

"A little. Or, at least, I was." His eyes wandered beyond the image to the woman behind it, then back to Christ. He was not in pain but rather appeared to be standing with his arms held in strength over creation.

"I used to be super religious. My problem was that in moments like this, I always ignored the hanging crucifix and focused on the woman's neck, her chest, the place where her skin touches her shirt." He tried to demonstrate, but she pushed his hand away.

"Well, you are a man. God can't blame you for that. He made you that way."

"I don't know. I've broken every rule in the book, so that can't be good for my chances."

"Chances for what?"

"To avoid hell."

"I don't believe God would send people to hell."

"I do."

"That's such an archaic notion, Rey. People are bad because of how they are raised. I don't think that people are truly evil, deep down."

"What about Hitler, Stalin, those who have killed millions?"

"Well, maybe they're in hell. But not normal people like you, Rey."

"I've never been called normal, and you would damn me too if you were God."

"Come on, Rey."

"It's just that I was raised by monks, like a character from a stupid medieval romance. I spent every morning in the chapel or the sanctuary for at least an hour. Sometimes I doodled in the hymnals that no one ever used or slept, but the rest of the time I stared at the image of Christ. He was tormented. And I feel like all of my life has been under the weight of that image."

She removed the crucifix from her neck.

He sat up, and she placed it around his. "I want you to have it."

"Why?"

"Because it might help you change the image of torment in your mind. Isn't Christ supposed to be about love? The ultimate sign of self-sacrificial love."

"I think so. But you said you didn't believe in love."

"I said I didn't believe in the type of love Rey Pescador raps about. But they say Christ was God and man, so under that viewpoint, the rules of selfishness might not apply to him. Maybe he can love."

"I guess."

They stopped talking for a while. Lost in the chant of hypnotic tide, they fell asleep as crowds flooded the beach for the celebration. When Rey awoke, he saw fireworks and families. Aldonza was gone. He was alone on the sand in the heart of the Caribbean. He could no longer hear the waves. A band played just west of him. Rey laughed. He thought about hell. He thought about heaven. Then, he thought of hell again. He decided that the only heaven he would know was in that moment on earth. He searched the crowd for Aldonza. Then he shouted. She was nowhere to be found.

HOMECOMING

JANUARY 28, 2010

Rey remained in Puerto Rico writing poetry and playing dominoes with guys who drove IROCs and had rattails. In the nights he would search for relatives, but we always knew our Mexican relatives more than our Puerto Rican side. The Puerto Rican relatives that I was close to were on my dad's side, so they weren't related to Rey at all. Either way, Rey found families that would invite him to stay at their house in the mountains as a surrogate nephew or cousin, and he would drink beer or moonshine with them late into the night, telling stories and listening to the coquis and their eternal chant.

During those weeks, I braved the Chicago cold and spent my mornings at mass and afternoons in the library. My bishop cast the vision for the year during a series of incredibly boring meetings at the cathedral. During the long discussions with collared men I tried to write poetry, but found that I had no skill. Life was ordinary, and I started to loathe it.

I lost myself in fantasy. I planned my future, how I would overthrow the RHC. I walked the streets thinking about the beauty of the city. I became more obsessed with you than ever.

The morning of January 28th was the same as any other morning that I wasn't working. I watched myself carefully in the storefronts as I walked to the diner that morning. Waiting for you to take my order, I drank ice water and listened to the patrons, especially a family of five that almost shouted about the elections, then music, then art. When referencing the Genius Brigade, the

173

teenage son motioned in my direction. I feigned focus on my book, but purposefully brushed my hair out of my face and then looked out the window like a wanderer who sensed home is just past those mountains. Sometimes I wondered if I was as vain as Rey, just not as good at it.

When you greeted me, you handed me the newest *Time* that named Rey as the man of the year again. I was mentioned briefly in the article, and you were thrilled. Thanks for that. It was a deviation of their normal article, since Rey had done almost nothing of note the year before. The article described Rey as the man of the future, the man of art and passion in a world of circuits. It chronicled his past journeys and his promise that this year would be devoted to a search for a window in time with L.J. Brovault. It was a farce. L.J. was an animal with a super-human brain. And Rey, Rey had sold his soul. In the article Rey quoted Kierkagaard and Hegel. He pontificated about the soul's desire to move not throughout space but throughout time. He said that poetry moved the soul throughout time and slowed the aging process. He claimed that studies show that true lovers of poetry have no neurological responses when it is read. He claimed that that was proof that the soul was moving.

It was off-the-cuff pseudo-psychological bullshit that had made him so valuable. Cutler could never have created that. Rey still had one of the best creative minds in the world, yet he was soulless.

I found out about his loss of soul from a letter that he wrote me from Puerto Rico that explained quite simply that he had sold his soul to Sid Cutler. Rey said that he "signed in blood and everything," and that he would be in Chicago soon to figure out how to get it back.

What was it like to sell the soul? I wondered that day in the diner.

Did he feel it? Of course he did. Could I just forgive him if he confessed? I wasn't even sure if I could absolve that if I wanted. It seemed above my pay grade. Most of the literature on selling souls was archaic and apocryphal. The precedents weren't exactly like dealing with an alcoholic or something. The old legends involved something fantastic, something otherworldly.

Rey knew the legends better than anyone, including me, and he would never settle for any solution that was less than legendary. Either way, I figured that I would let him in my house if he ever got back. I could do that much.

Delighted by the hum of the fan and the orange of the sunlight scattering through the windows, I kicked Rey's problems out of my brain. I still hated him, but not as much as before. I finished writing a lecture. You had left the restaurant for lunch not long after I came in, but I stayed for a while. It was calm in a way to be there without you, without the possibility to consider the "what if."

When I returned home Rey sat outside my door, his knuckles were dry and his hair was as oily as usual. He still wore it long. A child in a duplex down the street saw Rey walking toward my house. He ran out of his house toward the celebrity holding his favorite Christmas gift from this year, Pescador's *Poems for the Niños* DVD, and a Sharpee marker. I opened the door as Rey signed the child's book. The air was warmer than I thought. Rey smiled at the kid and patted his head and told him to follow his dreams or something. Then he turned and looked at me, still smiling from the interaction with the kid.

Rey looked at me as if nothing happened. His face was still young and tan. It seemed darker than ever juxtaposed against the thick gray clouds in the foreground. The South Side waited for the snow to cover everything as the forecast promised. I greeted him on the porch. He had sold his soul. He knew I hated him, or had hated him, yet he still was able to smile and give me a half hug like he was an excited teenager visiting me at UNC again. His hair had started to gray: that salt and pepper look that I also had inherited from our uncle Gabriel oddly framed his youthful face.

"Well cousin, I'm back."

"Are you?"

"I guess so. Thanks for opening the door this time." Rey lit a cigarette.

"I read about you today," I said and sat next to him on the porch, "about you and L.J. experimenting in time travel. That's good fiction."

"Brovault thinks it might be possible."

"Yeah, I guess, I don't know anything about it."

"Brovault thinks it's impossible to know at this point if it can get my soul back, if it even exists, which is also impossible to know at this point. Something about space-time gaps and last year's harvest moon, but I guess... I mean, what am I supposed to do?" We watched the snow for a while. Then it slowly turned to rain.

Inside I poured two glasses of wine. We drank, and Rey opened a flask. He smelled it briefly and poured it into the wine.

"What's that?"

"It's Sid's own personal stock of Lilac Whiskey; it tastes good as hell with anything."

I reached to the table, grabbed the whiskey, opened the window to the alley and threw it out. I heard it land on the pavement and shatter. Then I grabbed Rey with my left arm on the lapel of his suit and pushed him against the wall with my right hand.

"If you want to go to hell, then go. Don't you dare drag me down with you!" My actions hardly fazed him. He dumped out the corrupt wine and poured himself a traditional glass. The cool air still moved through the room from the open window.

"Don't be so melodramatic, David," Rey said. "Melodrama is my job. It doesn't really fit you."

"Shut up."

"So what should I do?" He asked as he crossed his legs and closed his eyes.

"What did you do after you met with Sid that night?"

"Well, I fell for ten seconds, landed softly, and the next thing I knew I was in the gutter on 7th Avenue holding the Lilac Whiskey like a teddy bear. I spent most of the morning dreaming some crazy ass, beautiful, frightening dreams. At least one new Pulitzer's worth. Then there was the fight that night. After that I flew to Puerto Rico to find this girl, Aldonza."

"Well, I'd say you're off to a hell of a start. The greatest wordsmith in four hundred years dreaming 'crazy ass, beautiful dreams' high as a kite on an especially strong vintage."

"At least my priest will speak with me now."

"How about this, you just stop being an idiot, and I will try to figure out how to get us both into heaven."

"That's the best offer anyone's given me in years."

"I know."

We each finished our wine and listened to the rain that should've been snow.

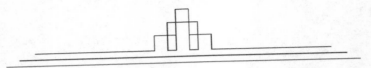

DOCTOR SOLOMON BIRAM

34

FEBRUARY 3, 2010

In February Rey was leafing through old journals and found a business card for a Chicago psychiatrist, Dr. Solomon Biram. A few years earlier Cutler said that Biram would give Rey whatever pills he needed. At the time Rey had no interest in psychiatry, even if it could lead to prescription pills, but now Rey thought a doctor of the brain could find his lost soul and return it to him. If that didn't work, he'd at least get a good conversation out of the deal.

Biram greeted Rey in the waiting room, walked him into the office, and explained that he would be taking notes and not to think he isn't listening if he is looking at the paper. The office walls were a faint green and covered with semi-motivational calendar art. The king of the arts nearly cringed as he noticed a painting of a lighthouse over Biram's desk. The seasoned therapist asked the basic questions and tried to pull from Rey's mind the forgotten memories of the night Rey sold his soul.

Rey said, "I need to confess a most grievous sin against God and myself."

Biran replied, "I don't believe in sin. At least not in the way you are saying it."

Rey thought he was joking and laughed. Then he recounted the evening, "There was a woman. I remember that much. The singer was there, her red hair rested on my shoulder, after I drank way too much whisky. I guess we both did. She tried to save me."

"And that's it. You got drunk and sold your soul."

"They beat me first. I sold my soul to save my body, and I

wasn't drunk, I was intoxicated on Lilac Whiskey. I don't think its alcohol. It's made of nepenthe, at least the real stuff that Sid drinks. The commercial stuff is pretty much the same as booze. Anyway, I was a little drunk on Scotch, but the real high was on the Lilac Whiskey."

"All right, and Sid Cutler gives you this Whiskey often?"

"You know what, brother, I need to leave."

"Why do you want to go?"

"Solomon, you seem like a pretty decent guy. But you work for Sid too, or at least you used to. I didn't think about it until that last question. But I can't trust people who work for that guy."

"Rey, I am a medical doctor who specializes in behavioral and developmental issues. I'm not concerned with the status of a legal document that says that Sidney Cutler, who originally referred you to me, owns your eternal soul. What the hell does that even mean, Rey? I'm more concerned with how that affects you. You are a poet, and Sid is an executive. This whole thing is ridiculous; think about it for a minute, Rey. Now, I don't deal with melodrama in the same way you do; it's not really my field, unless Shakespeare was right in suggesting that we are all actors in a play. If so, that would make me another literary critic—though I sadly don't get paid like one. Either way, for this particular situation, to better understand you, I need to examine the 'literary elements' for lack of a better term."

"So you want me to tell you a story?"

"Exactly. Actually, I might have a better idea. How about you write a poem? Say it. Close your eyes and tell me what happens. Do whatever it is you do when you write that poetry. Don't worry about plot and all of the constraints of a story. Just tell me what you are thinking, unfiltered."

"You really want to know?"

"Yes, I certainly do."

"Does doctor-patient confidentiality apply to this?"

"It does."

"Does Cutler see your notes?"

"Never."

"What are you writing?"

"Rey, let's focus."

"Well, I'll try. But I can't promise anything. The poetry isn't up to me."

"Who is it up to?"

"The muse."

Biram laughed, then realized that Rey's face was not laughing with him. "I'm sorry, Rey. I thought you were joking. Tell me about her. Seriously, I want to know."

"I'm not going to talk about the muse, but I'll try to freestyle a bit."

"All right."

"I really doubt I can compose with you in the room. Unless. How about this? Hide behind your desk over there. That way it's like I'm by myself."

"Sure." At this point Rey was simply teasing Biram, to get back at him for laughing at the muse. Rey stood in the middle of the room. "One last thing, I really would rather you not look at me during the process."

"All right."

On top of the unsteady surface of a couch, Rey unbuttoned his shirt. He took off his glasses and removed his sandals. He breathed deeply.

He shook the room as he cried, "Muse!"

Biram would have laughed if not for the tremendous force of Rey's voice. It shook his stomach. Rey started this thing as a joke, but once he started going, it was pure theater. He lived for it.

"Muse!" he bellowed again. The receptionists down the hall crowded around the closed door and listened. A final time he sang in a deep, carnal baritone, "Muse! Sing, flood my neurons with ambrosia. Massage my heart, my human heart until the blood it beats and pours through my veins and into the streets and rivers and towns. Let this poem be. Let this poem be mine."

Silence, for a while.

Rey began to weep.

"That's all you're giving me. I can work with it, but for now, it seems, well, OK."

White, fresh blubber of a whale,
With two lips,

Two eyes, and a butcher knife, cuts the sternum.
This Cannonball Man, his fuse is in my hand, laughs.

Immobilized again, he drinks as she buttons my shirt,
she with pumpkin hair who sang to me once,
on a yacht. Who called me, the last man
without proper ceremony. She- whose call, I answered.
The bated hook bobbed on fresh water.
The cosmic line enticed for ten years, until Pluto reeled
The last man onto his concrete shore.

Body and soul separated. They cut open my chest,
The crescent scar left as proof
That MAN is etched in the mockery
Of a human heart still beating.

Does the soul remain if contract blood dries
While a room spins, if the mind forgets
Under the ancient art of nepenthe?
If the devil holds the ultimate soul,
If the devil holds my eternal soul,
If the devil holds their dying hearts,
Can hope remain in the suffering Christ?

Biram's phone rang. He swore under his breath, "Continue, Rey. Please continue, I think you had something there."

"No, I was finished."

"You really can continue. That was absolutely fascinating."

"The muse was done. She had nothing else, and truth be told, she doesn't like cell phones."

"I apologize for my phone. Do you always compose poems like that?"

"Usually, at least first drafts. Well, I don't really spend too much time on drafting. So, yeah they change very little."

"Interesting." He scribbled several lines about the poet.

"What are you writing? What is your professional opinion?"

"Well, I've only talked with you for one session."

"Tell me."

"All right, it seems like you see yourself as a representative of the human race, an everyman whose failure jeopardizes all of us."

"So far so good. What else you got? Let's get to the real issue."

"Would you consider yourself a perfectionist, Rey?"

"Listen, Doc. I respect you, but I've sold my soul. This is a big deal, my perfectionism is not. But to answer your question, no I am not a perfectionist, except with my fame. I am an attention hog, and I care very little about how I get it. There is an aspect of perfectionism in that, but I think I have bigger things to deal with. I'm surprisingly reflective, and I can fill out your chart if you want. Narcissistic Personality Disorder, check. Attention/Hyperactivity Deficit Disorder, check. Attachment Disorder, bingo. BiPolar disorder, etcetera, ad nauseam. But there is one more thing that brought me here. I sold my eternal soul. It's kind of a big freakin' deal, Doc."

"Well, that depends upon you view of God and the afterlife, which I would like to discuss."

"I know there is a God. I've heard him. More importantly, I believe in hell, I stepped foot in it and saw what the big fuss was about. Even if I hadn't, you shrinks care about how people are raised, right?"

"Of course."

"Then get ready to go deep, Doc, cause I'm about to throw you a bomb. As an infant my mom gave me to brothers at Holy Cross Monastery to raise me. I don't think I mentioned that to you, but I was raised by monks. I spent every moment of my developing years searching beauty and truth. And these guys were saints. I was shitty to them in high school and beyond, but what you need to know is that I need to save my soul. If you can help me deal with this problem, that is great, but if not, I'm wasting my time."

"I think I can help you, Rey. I'm not a rabbi or a priest, but I can help you."

"Can you tell me about your parents or the monks that raised you?"

"I can. I know nothing about my father. Though I met him once in a dream. He had amazing hair and was taller than me.

My mother saw me on holidays, well for a while, but always denied I was her son. I'd rather not say anything more than that. She hit the kill switch. He drowned or something. That's all that needs to be said, and it's all I really know."

"Good, I think we are getting somewhere. Can you come back next week?"

"Sure. Why not?"

Biram stood up to shake Rey's hand then said, "Listen, Rey. If you feel down, give me a call on my cell. I think I kind of know what you are going through. I won't charge you."

"I appreciate that."

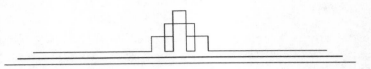

THE WOUNDED KING

CH 35

1981

Rey wasn't lying to Biram about his parents. He knew nothing about his father, Francisco Sifuentes, who had not drowned. In fact, I found him a few years ago, while I was researching Rey's legends. Anita Rodriguez Rosario was my aunt and Rey's mother, though her role in his origin was equally difficult to ascertain.

It's important for you to know about Rey's parents, so you can tell Christian if I never get the chance. He should know who his paternal grandparents are. Most of this account comes from Anita and Francisco or other eye witnesses, but there is some speculation here. Although, I guess there are speculative elements in all of these tales, but the rest Rey swore were all true.

Rey's father, Francisco, was a tall, Mexican man with long, brown hair that most people would think is black. He had a ridged nose: it prominently announced his entrance more than the smell of liquor or the click of his boot heels. His family owned a successful farm in Baja. As the proliferation of robotic farm hands increased, he was no longer needed for the local harvest. His parents, who had his best intentions in mind, suggested that he "do better" than farming and got him a visa to study in the United States. When his college job heating food at athletic concessionaires became a full-time position, and his grades started to slip, he changed his visa status and began to work exclusively. Within a year, he managed concessions at horse tracks from Tijuana to Sacramento.

Anita was a senior at Visalia High School. In January she received her acceptance letter to the University of California

Berkeley to study medieval literature; in February she turned eighteen. Her friends took her to Fresno to celebrate at the casino.

Francisco had the evening off and was sitting in a park across the street from the casino downtown on Van Ness Avenue. Francisco played music from his truck. He wore cowboy boots, a plaid shirt, and jeans.

Anita jumped off the bus onto the sterile concrete of downtown Fresno. She was from the slightly more aesthetic suburbs, but this gray city sang to her. It sang all winter leading to her birthday. It told her that from its desolation, beauty must emerge. On its sterile concrete, life must be celebrated; legends must be born.

All of the girls spun and looked at the wounded city. Francisco sat at a picnic table chewing sunflower seeds and drinking his second beer of the evening. Anita was beautiful. He noticed that immediately. But he was not Rey Pescador. He would not woo her. He just sat and spit seeds and sipped beer. Hearing the music from his truck and smelling beer, the girls approached him. They laughed and flirted.

They asked for beer. Francisco was only a few years older, handsome, and gladly gave them beer. They convinced him to go to the casino. They lost their money, so they found a club where they line danced. Francisco refused to go to a disco, at first, but Anita was quite convincing.

"Of course, I'm 21," she said again at the disco. "Just buy me one more drink."

He bought her drink after drink.

He shouldn't have gone driving with her. Her friends were already asleep. She should have slept, but the sunrise was so close. She had to see it paint blue and pink across the sky.

It was the perfect Central Valley night.

They drove east to catch the sun early. Outside of Clovis they parked, and lay on a blanket on a parkway next to a large almond farm.

It was still dark, though the sun promised to rise soon.

She had no thoughts of taking off her clothes. She had never thought of taking off his clothes, but the tequila's spirit lied to her: it made the stars shoot across the sky; it changed the inhuman hum of the fruit harvesters into a princess' serenade; it spoke to her nerves and explained that touch was all that mattered, that loneliness could forever end. She asked if he had protection because that's what she thought you were supposed to ask.

He explained that he had chemotherapy as a child. He was sterile. He thought it was true. He was a cancer survivor.

The sun rose.

A month later Anita was back in Fresno. She sat in her brand new 1980 Honda Civic outside a Planned Parenthood. The Civic was a graduation present from her father, who did not understand why she wanted an imported car. "America has the best machinery in the world, Anita," he had said, but he wanted to make her happy.

It was early morning. She had left that morning as if she was going to school. She hadn't realized that it was too early for the clinic to be open. She watched every car that drove down the street in her rear view mirror. She was certain her parents would find her somehow.

Our Lady of Guadalupe rested on the rosary that hung from her rear-view mirror. She was semi-religious and fully-tormented by the Virgin's gaze. She decided that if she was willing to go through with this, she should be willing to destroy the guilt of the Virgin's blank stare. She pulled the rosary down: the beads sprinkled the ground like any number of prayers.

She cried. A woman walking toward the building saw her and knocked on the window of her car. "Are you all right?" she asked.

Anita waived the stranger away.

The woman gave a consoling smile and unlocked the building. She flipped the closed sign around. Open.

Anita surveyed the beads again and decided that there might be another way. After all, the timing could have been worse. If she deferred for one semester, she could have the child. She could even travel to her sister's house in Chicago, so her parents would never know. Better yet, she could stage a post-graduation trip at the end of the summer. They would never know anything.

That's it. She thought. The plan was complex, but possible.

She'd tell her parents she was invited to backpack Europe with Stacey or Sarah. Stacey or Sarah's family was wealthy enough, Stacey had even invited her to Disney a few years ago all expenses paid. Anita's parents might agree to the free trip, and if they did, they wouldn't follow up. She was 18, and her father never liked talking with the rich gringos.

But even a summer trip wasn't enough. She had to think. All right, she had it. She would forge a document from the college that would inform them that she was awarded a scholarship for the incoming freshman summer program followed by a semester of study abroad. There were such programs that she couldn't afford. The fake scholarship would keep them out of her life for a few months. All she needed was to leave Visalia and have some time to think.

Francisco walked around the College of the Sequoias daily for nearly two weeks. Each day he purchased flowers and searched for Trini: that was the name that Anita gave him. She said she was in her final year of a nursing program, specializing in artificial heart surgeries. Everyone was in those days. All infants were required to have the new hearts, and all adults needed to receive the machine by January of 1982. Trini never arrived to College of the Sequoias. Trini, the college girl, never existed, and Francisco never had a chance to tell her that he loved her.

After a month of searching the college for her and waiting at the same table of the casino bar each night, he ran out of money, and had to return home. He left a note on the college message board and in the newspaper.

But Francisco would not give up. He was a true romantic and was smitten by Trini. After one night he planned to marry her. He had one last plan.

By that time, he recorded a local radio ad that he was certain she would hear, but she had already taken the winding road up the mountains to the National Parks and forests where she decided to spend the summer waiting tables near the Giant Forest. She had to escape the valley.

The forest welcomed her as did her coworkers who all were escaping something. She brought only a few books, but the ex-hippies who lived and worked in the back country would come back to the lodge every week or two and trade books with her. At nights she rested from waiting tables by sitting near, and eventually in a creek carved in the granite of the Sierra Nevada batholith. When the moon was near full the rocks were especially bright and beautiful she would read by moonlight. When there was no moon she risked her life hiking through the forest alone.

There in the darkness of the woods she made no plans for the child or herself. She no longer prayed to the Virgin. She simply assumed the Virgin prayed for her.

After working nearly twelve hours on Labor Day, she made a plan. She would hike a trail lighted only by the full moon fourteen miles to a place called Twin Lakes. Then she planned to go up and out into the backcountry. Her goal was to have her child there, with only the Virgin to protect her.

She made it to Twin Lakes. She slept. The next day she hiked further into the wilderness. Nine miles past the trail to the lakes the contractions began, but Anita refused to slow down. She hated herself, her body, and the pain that the child brought.

She stumbled forward slowly and screamed to the trees, the marmots, and the rising sun. When the contractions overtook her, she crawled to a granite creek. Closer to the snowy peaks, the rapids were stronger here.

She could hardly walk; she surely could not cross the creek. For a moment she thought of diving into the creek to end her life more quickly. But the child seemed so near. She couldn't imagine not seeing his face. She hated him. She hated his pain. She hated his father. She hated the rushing water. She hated the people who judged her as she waited their tables instead of studying *Sir Gawain and the Green Knight* at Berkeley.

Anita lay on the forest floor and let the Virgin pray for her. Anita screamed in pain.

A backcountry ranger heard shouting while he was having his morning smoke. He assumed an over-zealous tourist had lost her way to Twin Lakes and now screamed at the face of a harmless black bear. He thought that though she sounded terrified, her strings of Spanish in between were fiery (that is what white people always say about Latina women) and beautiful. Half-stoned: he carefully placed his joint on the ground.

He had a dilemma. He did not want to ruin the weed in case she was interested in smoking some after he scared the bear away and asserted his dominance. He also did not want to burn down the forest, so he sat watching for a bit to make sure it wouldn't cause damage.

During the delivery Anita never saw the ranger. She only saw the Our Lady of Guadalupe in the sky. She cried out to her. She prayed for her son. When the baby crowned, Anita seemed nearly dead to the ranger. He tried to remember his EMT training, but all he could do was close his eyes, hold out his hands, and pray.

The child was born. He was alive, but Anita had lost a lot of blood.

The ranger carried Anita, and Anita carried her child back to the tent. It took the better part of a day. She slept in the stranger's arms. When they reached the tent, he cleaned her and the child again. He dressed her wounds, as well as he could and watched mother and child sleep.

When she woke, he said to her, "You and your baby are healthy, but you need to rest here while I get help."

She refused to let him leave. She was incredibly convincing. She asked if he had anything for pain. He said that he only had cannabis, so they smoked together.

The moon visited them again cooling the late summer air. As they smoked, he asked her dozens of questions, "What will you name the little guy?"

"Rey."

"Why Rey?"

"After his father."

"Is he your boyfriend?"

"No."

"Does he live in the valley?"

"I don't know. I only met him once."

"What is his last name?"

"Who, Rey or his father?"

"Both, I guess."

"I don't know his father's name, first or last, but his name will be Rey Pescador."

"Maybe I've smoked too much, but I thought you said you didn't know the father's name."

"Have you ever read the legend of the Fisher King?"

"No."

"Well, the Fisher King is the wounded king. He is sterile in most stories, and the whole kingdom suffers from his wound. The whole kingdom is unable to grow crops. Well, the thing about this sterile king is that he has a son. Rey's father told me he was sterile on the back of a Ford truck eight months ago."

"So he lied to you?"

"I guess so. Though part of me thinks he believed it, but that is probably naïve."

"So what is your plan now?"

"Well, you and I will raise him together."

"Um, oh. Well, the thing is."

"I'm just joking. I swore to the Virgin that if I lived, I would give him to the Holy Cross Monastery in Chicago. My sister knows them and lives nearby. I just can't let my parents know."

"They don't want you to give the baby up?"

"They don't know I was pregnant. I'm supposed to be a freshman at Berkeley right now. So I never told them about my pregnancy and hid away in the lodge all summer."

"Wow, that is intense."

"Yeah, my dad is old-fashioned and self-made. He worked hard to be able to afford my college education. I don't want him to be disappointed in me."

"I bet he would forgive you."

"That's none of your business."

They both fell asleep.

The ranger tried to sneak out that night to find help. His tent was relatively secure, and he left her with a gun and a note. He thought that he would be able to get back within a few hours with help. Before he reached the door, she grabbed his leg, "If you leave, I will find you, and I will kill you." She was immobile, not much more than five feet tall, and the most beautiful face he had ever seen, yet she terrified him. He waited for almost a week hoping a search party would come, but the employees just assumed she went down the mountain to have the baby.

After a few weeks in the tent, Anita told the ranger he could find help. She said she was mobile enough to be on her own. She made him show her a map of where they were and where he would go. She charted another course. As soon as he had gone; she and Rey journeyed off trail back to civilization and a 1980 Honda Civic. She did not want the search party to come. She would not go home. She would not have an artificial heart installed in her son.

While I collected leaves for a school project, she drove to Chicago to change all of our lives.

A HUMANITARIAN AT HEART

APRIL 2010

Rey journeyed from those mountains to Chicago and below.

Anita requested that the monks hide the secret of his heart. Of course, urban monks tend to be countercultural. They hid that secret, as did his family members who knew.

Rey was never as cautious as we were with the secret of his heart. He alluded to it dozens of times in his poetry, but the secret of Rey's heart officially ended in April of the Year of Lilac Whiskey on *NBC Nightly News*. Rey described why he had spent all of his energy and cash on humanitarian efforts during the first quarter of the year of Lilac Whiskey. He said, "This world is full of people who have nothing—some have no food, no water. Others have no dreams and no hearts. Now here's my secret. I have a human heart. It's kind of a big deal, one of two operating models by my count. I will give it to all of you. First, I write your dreams then climb into your bloodstream. I pound on your tin hearts until they beat. By the time you realize that you need something, that your world is in pain, I'm there on the ground with whatever you need from food to medicine. Our field team is incredible and we are reaching people who truly need help all around the world."

Rey had revealed his biggest secret and survived. No RHC agents found him in the middle of the night to install a pump in him. Perhaps it was Sid Cutler. Perhaps it was because virtually everyone thought he was using another archaic metaphor to describe his philanthropic work. There were fans or fringe groups, like my own, or the Organic Heart Society, that took the poet literally, but no one cared what the OHS had to say, and I certainly wasn't going to say anything.

While Rey tried to save himself by saving the world, I fell in love with you, Rebecca.

Forgive me for the exposition, but I think it's time to let you know that I have a hidden motive with all of this. By this point you can probably tell, and now that I've reached 2010 in this story, it is going to become clearer, so I might as well say that I hope that by reading this you are able to forgive me. I know that you are probably rolling your eyes. Maybe you already forgave me. Or you might even be pissed that you are even reading all of this but have kept sustaining these sections because of Rey. If you are still mad at me for the stuff from this spring, know that I am sorry and will explain soon.

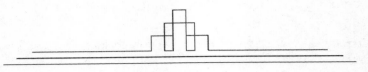

DAVID "THE LEECH" ROSARIO

CH 37 •

APRIL 2010

How well do you remember the night I fell in love with you? The day started simply: coffee and cinnamon rolls delivered by you as usual. Only things were different with you. You sat down next to me and cried at my booth. You said your cousin James had died. "Fr. Rosario, please come to the funeral."

I couldn't, of course, you remember that. I had my public lecture that evening.

I made the crying worse when I started talking about the lecture and how I would miss not having you there.

That lecture at the UIC Pavilion was the high point of my academic career. Every college in the city sent buses to hear Rev. Dr. David E. Rosario speak on "The Infinite Death of a Robotic World." I was a rock star without the help of Sid or Rey. I paced; I shouted; I informed; I entertained. I was good. I was sure of it. I was also sure that I would change the world, cripple the RHC and bring back organic hearts and death for all humans.

After the lecture, I opened the floor for questions. I'm sure you remember the moment that I lost it. That abnormally tall guy wearing a golf cap coughed right into the microphone then said it before saying, "Dr. Rosario. Can you tell us about Rey Pescador as a kid?"

The crowd erupted. *Rey, Rey, Rey, Rey.*

I erupted.

"Part of the problem of the contemporary world, part of your problem, sir, is a lack of intellectual desire. Rey Pescador's success shows that we have a desire for the beautiful, the mystical, and the unseen. I applaud you for that, but I fear that it is mostly for an attractive, charismatic man. Your question, sir, shows me that you neither listened to my critique of society's view of the Genius Brigade, nor understand how to ask a legitimate question. It also shows that you will not understand this answer. Next question, please."

I defended the honor of the intellect.

After the lecture, I walked into the rain. It had been raining all month. I considered getting a cab, but I had my umbrella and the rain was warm, so I walked toward the bus stop to the Hyde Park home. I was ready to celebrate. I could already taste the bottle of wine waiting on my kitchen table.

Less than a block into my journey, you were there. I couldn't believe you came to the lecture with the funeral and all. You touched my shoulder and asked to share my umbrella. You still called me Father Rosario then. You had never called me David, yet you stood close. Your shoulders touched mine. I could smell your hair. I moved into the rain. I offered you the umbrella. You refused and insisted that we walk together under the umbrella. We couldn't find a cab, so we took a bus, which meant more blocks of walking together under the small plastic shield before we reached your destination.

Here I was a man in his mid-30s, a Ph. D., a celebrity, and a priest, and I was absolutely taken aback by your confidence and touch, even the touch of your shoulder with mine. It was embarrassing, so I tried to say something witty. You probably don't remember, but I said something about how Spanish for the cool refreshing air is fresco, which is similar to refresco, the word for pop, how I always thought that the cold, carbonated reality of the spring was best understood in the rain. You didn't seem too impressed. Maybe you realized that I was just trying to sound exotic and bilingual. Maybe you just thought the air was warmer than my description. I don't know. Either way, we kept walking through the city during that cruelest of months talking about everything but the funeral.

Feeling confident I said something like, "Can you believe that idiot who asked about Rey?" Your response was characteristic of you, but I'll never forget it. You said I was way too hard on that guy. You used the word ungracious. I said something about leeches feeding off of Rey's life for entertainment and not understanding that there is more out there, and that these theological concerns regarding the RHC are significant.

Then you asked, "And you think that you aren't a leech yourself?"

I didn't know what to say. Here you are this twenty-something grad school dropout who I thought was at least impressed by my CV if not a little attracted to my confidence and hair, and you called me a leech. It was absolutely true, of course. I was the biggest leech in the city. I was the one who filled a stadium with Rey's fans to make some extra cash and assert my claim as the ultimate scholar in Chicago. But still, it shocked me. It was the best thing I had ever heard you say.

We reached the front of Brazel's Bar. "This is where I'm going," you said. "This is James' funeral." You pulled me out of the rain for a moment. There under the overhang I hoped you would kiss me. I loved your eyes, your face red from the rain, your voice with its loud Chicago cadence. I loved your curly hair, your body: your height too tall, lips too small, your teeth too crooked, your legs too long. I loved your soul.

You told me to come in with you for the funeral. I said no. I muttered something about early mass, but really I didn't want death to damper my mood. You told me that you needed me. You asked me to pray for James. You cried and hugged me right there under the overhang for a long time. Then you turned and thanked me.

I followed you into the bar with my eyes and eventually my legs.

FUNERAL

CH 38

APRIL 2010

I didn't expect that the corpse would be right there on a table in the middle of the room. At first I avoided him. I avoided his shell, rather. Maybe I should have known from old Irish movies that he'd be there. You said it was the funeral, but I kept thinking it was the reception. I thought it would be just a bunch of sad drunken people.

I lost you immediately in the crowd. I stared at the open casket for what may have been a long time. I saw his stark white face. What was it like to touch the discarded shell of a human soul? I wondered what it would be like to be in a box like that, to look down from heaven and laugh at all the moments worrying about such a fragile shell that was now not different from a snake's skin. Maybe that isn't how it works. But that was what I thought, at least.

Music played. Everyone drank and waited as if someone was going to say some magic word and he would rise again. Body and soul would reconnect. Resurrection would happen. Or maybe they were waiting for their own deaths. They just wanted to enjoy a few moments before death. That's how I felt, at least.

A tall middle-aged woman wouldn't stop looking at me. Still high on my fame, I figured that she was a fan. I smiled. I don't think I winked, but that was the way I looked at her. She turned to her husband who was facing the interior of the bar, and said more loudly than she realized, "He's here. I can't believe the priest came."

I didn't get it. One of the few things I knew about funerals,

197

was that priests weren't exactly rare. Other Mexicans were in the room, so it couldn't be a race thing. I was no Rey Pescador, but virtually everyone in the Southwest Side knew me, or at least of me. I couldn't figure it out. I didn't really care to. I wanted to console you and let you know that I loved you, though I knew that one of those things was certainly not going to happen.

So I sat there and drank a beer and stared at the casket thinking that it should have been my shell in that box. God, two years earlier, I was almost that man surrounded by people drinking beer and whiskey with no idea what the hell to do.

When I found you, my mind raced through the possible scenarios that could lead to me and you together. I had never felt so awkward or alone. Let me make this clear, I had traveled with the most famous men in the world, and it was not until I put a collar on and realized that you were sitting at a high-top table with an unbearable blond guy, that I ever felt such envy.

Your eyes betrayed that you were a few drinks in already and a few drinks from the end of the journey, and this spiky-haired, blonde dude, who looked like the biggest tool I had ever met, stared at your legs that were hard to ignore. Laughing at his own joke, he put his arm around you while you and I tried to add something intelligent to his diatribe, but he dismissed it for something he "just had to say" about his stock portfolio and the latest Bears game. The two topics were addressed seamlessly. Then another intolerable joke followed by him placing his unnaturally large hand on your intoxicating thigh, the smooth part above the knee, just where the dress stopped.

Shit, I had to intervene. "Hey Rebecca, can you walk with me for a minute, I have a quick question."

Do you remember what I said when I acted as father, and warned you about the blonde guy? I do. But I'm embarrassed to repeat it.

I'm also still embarrassed that you slapped me in front of 150 people at a funeral.

Who slaps a priest in a funeral? Seriously, Rebecca, I still think that would have been awesome to see if it was some other priest.

Then realizing you had made a scene, you lowered your voice

and said that just because I was a priest didn't mean you were a nun—even though I'm sure you were as annoyed with the blonde dude as I was. Sorry about all that. I still can't believe I did that. Seriously, it is embarrassing to think about.

You returned to your serenade of stock tips. Reeling from my idiocy, I tried to leave, but the tall, middle-aged woman who saw me when I first entered took advantage of my vulnerability, she asked me, "Father, please, will you pray for his soul?"

"Of course, I will."

"Will you say last rites?"

"Hasn't someone already done that? When did he die?" I looked at you, and you informed me that he didn't get hit by a car like you had said. He killed himself. Some holier-than-thou priest must have refused the final sacrament because it was a suicide.

What did that mean? Was he in hell? Damn, I think I am the one who is supposed to know, but seriously, I'm not God. I know I don't plan on ever killing myself, though I guess I've tried twice now. I just don't ever want to wager on my belief that that is not the unforgivable sin. His casket had oak walls that were ornate with carvings: a cross, a chi-rho, and a lamb each adorned the visible side. Inside that beautiful box, he lay there. By this point a crowd had gathered. I wondered what to do. I grabbed you by the arm and pulled you close to me. The onlookers looked away but strained to listen. "Why did you lie?"

"I wanted you to perform last rites, David."

"How did he do it?" You were silent. I looked to the crowd. "How did he die?"

"Father," an old man said. "He was simply following you."

I climbed the table upon which the ornate box lay. Other than the sound of people taking sips of beer, the bar was silent. I looked at his body: it was completely pale. I touched his hand and his forehead.

"What do you mean he was following me?" I asked.

The old man stared at me then replied, "He left a note. He was in your class and you said that the artificial heart was a sin. You said that it was the work of the devil." He paused as I climbed on top of the table. I reached into the casket. I unbuttoned his suit and shirt until I could see his pure white chest. Where the robotic heart once reigned was a crossed shaped scar sown over a recess. "Dear God, he cut his heart out."

I was no longer the hero in the bar who represented salvation. In fact, I only ever was in my imagination. I was the man who had been slapped by the bereaved and had sent James to hell.

I closed my eyes.

I stood on the table over the body.

I should be drinking wine right now, I thought.

I thought of you in the rain.

I thought of Rey, of the kill switch, of my lectures, of the dilemma of the RHC. I opened my eyes and looked at the crowd. "Has it been longer than three days?" The curly-haired woman replied, "No, it was two days ago."

"Then, I will do what I can, but ultimately, I'm not the decision-maker on this particular issue. Then I realized that I had no idea how to perform last rites. Dealing with death wasn't exactly the most common thing for a priest these days.

"Almighty and ever-living God" I shouted with my hands raised to cloak my extemporaneous prayer in confidence. "We are unworthy. Ashes, we are. Dust, we are. We are nothing more than earth in the end," I felt the audience slipping away. "But we know that even the deceased are more than robots, more than metal, more than programming. And we ask that you, who gave us will, would bend your will to the deceased in our midst. Restore him to you in paradise everlasting, and restore the hearts of those who have died within—those who have died through tying themselves to darkness. In the name of the Father, and the Son, and the Holy Spirit. Amen. Amen. Amen."

I jumped down from the table inebriated by a certain type of sacramental ecstasy. I was the hero. That surely wasn't a sin. You hugged me in front of all those people. While you hugged me, I closed my eyes imagining that you loved me. Then I locked eyes with the spikey-haired man and without a word explained that I was the dominant man here.

That, I fear, was a sin.

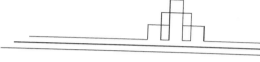

THE THIRD HEAVEN

39

SPRING 2010

That spring, I found my rhythm of life. I wrote. I lectured. I drank coffee with you in the mornings. I ate dinner with you during your evening shifts. We became friends. Rey came home in the middle of May and lived in the guest room. L.J., wandered in one day asking for a place for him and Doctor Knapps, his cat, to stay. L.J. bought a mattress and dragged it into my attic. I'm certain no one has ever had wealthier boarders live in their 2,000 square foot home without offering to pay rent.

Despite our decade-long acquaintance, L.J. still acted like we were strangers. He only referred to me as "that guy" and "you, over there." He had asked me at least five times over the years, "Who are you, and why are you in my light?" After I was ordained he was puzzled, "Where did you get that shirt? What the hell are you wearing around your neck?"

I don't think it was a joke.

Since his arrogant youth, L.J. had slipped from a coherent if not articulate little bastard to a glassy-eyed man who once put his shoes on the wrong foot and didn't notice or take them off for three days.

But now things were changing with L.J., Rey, and me. It was finally May. The sunlight and warmth returned. Rey spent over a month at the Hyde Park house without touring. He prayed at St. Ambrose's each morning.

The three of us would sit on the porch all afternoon and drink wine and talk about the multiverse and the meaning of beauty. L.J. claimed to have proof that there was a universe almost exactly like ours except literature was not big business, and no one had robotic hearts. Of course, that is absurd. He said that Cutler had been alive, but in 1906 a Methodist priest received a vision that he should kill Cutler. L.J. swore on his eternal soul that his friend had been there, to this other universe.

"Listen to me, Rey, I'm serious. The only difference is that Cutler lived in our universe. This pansy Methodist minister did nothing."

"How is he a pansy if he killed Cutler in a different dimension?" Rey asked.

"In that universe he wasn't a pansy, but in ours he was." L.J.'s tone had not shifted yet from informative to condescending, which I suspected it would.

"Is there a universe where I'm a pansy? No that's impossible. Wait, shit, is there a universe where I have bad skin?" Rey asked.

"No, Rey there isn't, and you are being ridiculous."

Usually, I avoided these conversations, but this one was gold.

"Hey L.J.," I said. "Is there a universe where you've gone on a date?"

"I go on more dates than you, David. Everyone does. And anyway, that isn't how multiverses work. Everyone knows that. You guys are retards. I'm going home." L.J walked toward the front door back into my house.

"Sorry man," Rey said. "Stay out here. I seriously didn't get it. I didn't know, but you scared me for a minute with all the bad skin talk."

"All right, I'll stay, but listen, this is the truth. Sid Cutler isn't alive there, but he is coming back. You can't actually kill him. He just comes back after 109 years. I have all of the equations. I have proof."

While L.J. ranted, Rey smoked a pipe and thumbed a leather journal. I don't remember him writing very much that spring. And he certainly didn't keep any of his writing. When I went through his journals before starting this project there was almost nothing from that year. Still he never left home without pen and paper in case the muse felt especially benevolent that day. That was also when I started compiling Rey's stories. I wanted to find a way to save his soul. I wanted to learn how and why he fell so far from grace.

When L.J. finished his tales of interdimensional travel, he sat on the railing and stared down the street. Then he jumped the railing into my hostas. "What the hell, L.J.?" I yelled, but he was already out of the plants and staring up at the sun.

L.J. shouted, "What day is it?"

"It's Thursday," Rey said.

"No it's not. It's Friday," I corrected.

"Shit, man," Rey said, "I need to make some changes. I really thought it was Thursday."

"No, I'm asking, what is the date?" L.J. said.

"That sounds like your department, David. I'm pretty sure it's spring."

"What is wrong with you? How do you make it to your tours and book signings?" I asked.

"A car picks me up," Rey said.

"Are you going to answer me?" L.J asked.

"It's May 14th, and I'm buying both of you calendars."

"Listen, David," L.J. said. It might have been the first time he called me by my name. "Or should I call you Father Rosario?"

"David is fine."

"All right Father David, let's get a drink. It's my birthday."

Rey responded before I could, "Hell yeah. Happy b-day buddy. Let's go to Brazel's. I'm buying."

The bar was almost empty until the first literate Chicagoan saw us through the window. It didn't take long for anyone who cared to know that the Genius Brigade was at Brazel's. Of all the fans, L.J.'s were unsurprisingly the most bizarre: a group of three started measuring the bar so they could stand at the corners of an equilateral triangle around L.J. Members of Brovault's former fan-club turned cult, the Synoptics, had sworn to follow L.J. in everything, except for his expressed wish that he repeated every time he say them, "Drop dead and leave me alone."

Rey and L.J. threw darts. I ignored the guys for a while and looked at the perfect sunlight illuminating the street hoping you would walk by. Rey snapped me from my meditation when he shouted at L.J, "What the hell did you just say? Don't you ever joke about that again."

L.J. apparently didn't take the warning seriously. He was still smiling, drunk no doubt. "Why not? I'm sick of these morons!" He screamed at Rey.

"Just go for it, then!" Rey cried back at him.

"What did you say?" I asked L.J. But he just laughed some more and kind of drummed on his thighs in excitement. The bartender poured another round. The festivities were beginning and people began dancing around Rey who ordered a bottle of whisky for the crowd. I took the opportunity to ask the bartender, "What did he say? The little, creepy guy?"

"Listen, it's none of my business. But he said to one of those guys drawing triangles to get him a gun or suicide kit because it was his final day. Or something like that."

Something in me snapped. I picked up L.J. and held him to the wall. I took my stole and put it in front of his face. "Listen Brovault, I don't know where you've been or what you've done, but I like you. We need you around. Rey needs you. I hardly know you, and I need you. I've already dove into the depths of hell for that one over there. I sunk into the muck and awoke a new man with purpose. If you ever take your life…if you kill yourself, I will crawl into hell itself and beat the living shit out of you, then do my best to pull you back out."

I lowered him. He gave me a hug. Then he walked toward the door.

"Where are you going?" I asked.

"Back to my shed. There is nothing beautiful here."

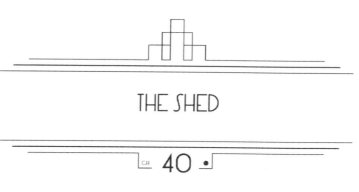

THE SHED

MAY 14, 2010

It could hardly be called a shed. Brovault spent a fortune to transmogrify the guesthouse of an Oak Park mansion into a robot fighting arena. The rest of his savings—which was quite extensive—he invested on research and development for fighting robots and parts for a new "science machine" dealing with time. It was all very weird and very illegal.

Since the Madison Square Garden fight, underground robot fighting grew in popularity and was now reaching frenzy. Some fans were deranged: attaching human organs into the machines, but the majority of society enjoyed robot fighting to simply see the greatest scientists and engineers battle each other in a sporting event.

L.J. had gutted the entire building. It was now one large room, about 1200 square feet with a twenty foot ceiling. It would look like a relatively normal boxing arena if it wasn't for the standard robot cage with its eight corner, triple-reinforced, titanium fence. I guess the aesthetic choices were strange too, especially the massive stained-glass window of a robot being sacrificed by L.J. on an altar on the southern wall. Light passed through the robot sacrifice onto the titanium fence as well as the chrome exterior walls.

After a minute of silence, Rey said, "What the hell is this place?"

"It's my shed."

"What do you do in here?" Rey asked.

"Seems pretty obvious, right?" I said.

205

"Sorry, I'm just shocked. So those kennels in the back yard are for robots?"

"I call them hotels. But yes."

"Where's the bar?" Rey asked.

"I don't have one. It would distract from the artistry."

"You need a bar if you're going to make any money," Rey added.

"I'll make plenty off the gambling."

"You need a bar."

Rey made a few phone calls, and before we knew it, the room was fully stocked with alcohol. Still dumbfounded by the bizarre residence, I finally spoke, "I need to go L.J. This is really strange."

Rey interjected, "Come on David, it's not like you've never been to a robot fight before. If I remember correctly, you tried to fight yourself."

"That was you?" L.J. said, "I remember that. I had good money on the robot. We were in Brazil, right?"

"Yeah, no. It was South Africa. But this is just strange. Stained glass windows? Seriously?"

"I thought you would like that part. It's satirical, right?"

"It seems like it should be, but what is it satirizing? I don't know what any of this is. All of this is just strange. We have other things to focus on."

"But it's fun."

"Since when did you like fun? And the other thing that gets me, L.J. is that you've been living in my attic and building this thing for months, right?" I asked.

"Yeah."

"Wouldn't you rather have your own place or something? I thought you were out of cash?"

"I have tons of cash. I just liked hanging out. Do you want me to leave?"

"No. I like having you there. I was just wondering." I laughed. "You're a strange dude, L.J. But seriously, I'm a priest, and this is totally illegal. You know we'll get caught."

Rey stopped measuring the proposed bar area and joined back into the conversation, "Listen cousin. You spend all your time arguing that robotic hearts are inhumane that they keep us from eternal life and give the devil power over all of humanity, and now, you have the opportunity to take part in something that challenges the humanity of machines, something that is growing throughout the country, something that could give your theology teeth."

The soulless wonder had a point.

The robots fought at midnight.

I wore my collar. I had nothing to hide.

After all two cyborgs ripping off each other's skin, arms, and legs was nothing more than a microwave falling from its mount and landing on a toaster. Metal destroying metal cannot be inhumane.

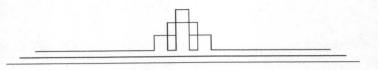

THE GENIUS BRIGADE II OR THE SPACE LION

SUMMER 2010

Gambling on robot fights, drinking coffee with you, and administering sacraments dominated the first half of my summer.

The GB was still on top, maybe even more than 2008.

On Rey's Lilac Whiskey Tour, he crusaded as a humanitarian activist and poet. One hundred trucks carried the equipment of the dozens of poets and musicians that traveled. He synthesized sports and art. He read one poem while the Los Angeles Philharmonic played Wagner and three professional fencers fought on strings. He rapped while two volunteers from the crowd drew mustaches on priceless works of art with markers. It

was excessive, exhausting, and expensive.

Riley, however, did not find the year of Lilac Whiskey to be as forgiving as Rey. Shortly after the Madison Square Garden fight Riley's back was broken by men with baseball bats. A federal investigation ensued, but no one was charged. Riley healed quickly with the help of two state of the art robotic spines. Within months, his golf game improved to a world-class level, as did his boxing, but nearly all professional sports banned him because of his "performance enhancing robotic parts." He slipped into depression. Things worsened when the anti-robot lobby almost convinced the U.N. to cast him into outer space. The argument was that the spine was the center of the soul, and he was an obscene half-bred monster who must be made into a cautionary image visible by anyone who looks into the night sky. That, however, is a whole other story.

In July, federal agents stormed Brovaults robotic fighting ring. Part of Brovault's problem was that he published a series of public interviews and articles implicating Riley as a robot. In fact, he pushed for Riley to be cast into space more than any. If a human could become a robot—which L.J. argued ironically—the implications of robots fighting to the death were disturbing.

The New York Times Op-Ed of December 15th read: *Brovault's, Oak Park robot fighting ring finally reveals his true motivation in proclaiming that Edwin Riley is a robotic life form: he merely wants to see him ripped to pieces to the entertainment of his savage guests. Brovault lives in the violent modern world that we have spent trillions of dollars as a nation and global community to overcome. The only solution is to give Brovault what he wants for others, to be locked in a room with oil-thirsty robots. I wonder who he'd bet on in that scenario.*

Brovault responded in a letter to the editor stating *I often lock myself in the ring with oil-thirsty robots. Fortunately, unlike Riley, I have no oil for them to sense. If I did, I would congratulate them as they tore me to shreds. The fittest must survive.*

I flew to Europe with Rey in August. It was two months of old-fashioned Genius Brigade hijinks. We drank vodka with Russian bureaucrats and wine with Greek mystics. While Rey performed, I usually waited at cafes or hotel bars researching the life of Rey Pescador. I figured I could be his official biographer and find a way to save his soul. It was my calling, my mission, and I obsessed over it. I studied the stories of his life to determine what and where and when he sinned and what he needed to receive absolution. Of course, there were so many stories to hear, so many that I have not mentioned in these letters. There were horse races on Michigan Avenue, and bar fights in Prague, and bull fights in Brussels.

On August 20th, in the South of France, Rey sat next to me in a café. The server brought him a letter. Assuming it was from an adoring fan, Rey opened it hastily. He still loved adoration.

"David, you got to read this, man."

"Another love letter?"

It was a love letter of sorts. Only it was from the President of the United States. He wrote, among other things, *"In the wake of our global experiment with infinity, beauty must coincide with technological strength again. I believe that your composition of a series of poems performed and read from space will act as a hope for an apathetic people who are slaves to their own fears of eternity. We ask that you travel to space in a rocket ship for the betterment of the United States, the United Nations, and the world."*

"Wow, man. This is big time."

"You know what this means? You do, don't you?" He stood up, threw a few hundred dollars on the table, and ran out of the café, saying, "David, I'll meet you at the hotel tonight."

By the time I saw him that evening he had paid one million dollars to the top Parisian designer, François le Moyne to design a space-suit for him that was both "form-fitting and obviously phallic." He called *Time* magazine and the *New Yorker* to sell the story. His initial cover titles were, "Space Lion" or "The King of the Cosmos." I vetoed the second for potential blasphemy—not that I would normally care, but when you've sold your soul, you shouldn't take any more chances. Rey apologized immediately. I think he liked Space Lion more anyway.

A couple of weeks later, the President grounded the moon mission to receive more votes on an agriculture bill. Rey always hated agriculture bills.

Although we wrote letters during the trip, I missed you. Traveling with Rey was dangerous to my reputation as a holy man. Women chased me more than ever. I'd like to say that virtue kept me from them, but really it was thinking about you.

Other priests confronted me as pictures of me with Rey began to flood the tabloids. My vanity grew when *People* called me "Rey's Sexy Priest." I even watched celebrity news in hotels hoping to see myself. It was in September of that year. On Rey's birthday, we had a costume party in Turkey. Rey wore his designer space suit, and I, as usual, wore my collar. The gossip pundits said that the priest thing was simply an act. Others said that I was Rey's bodyguard. In some ways I was, but I'm sure that's not what they meant.

The strangest thing about 2010 was that Sid Cutler was nowhere to be found. We certainly didn't miss him. I searched for him in articles and magazines and the news, but it was if he never existed. The Genius Brigade was no longer Cutler's, at least according to public perception.

On September 15th, the Lilac Whiskey Tour was over, so we flew back to Chicago's rain soaked streets. Nothing had changed. I still had mass and fall lectures. You were still beautiful. And Rey Pescador was still damned.

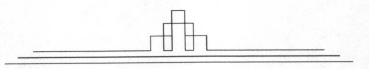

TIME TRAVELING

CH 42

AUTUMN 2010 - WINTER 2011

The fall was littered with court dates, rain, and as always, beautiful, dead leaves. It is the most academic season, so I researched classic Catholic poetry that explored any topic relating to the human heart. But I was distracted by the flood of electrons from CNN and PBS that both determined that L.J.'s robot fights, Riley's potential robotic soul, and Rey's role as chief GB member were worthy of nonstop coverage.

Somehow, L.J. was found innocent of running a robot fighting syndicate. He had no lawyer and defended himself arrogantly and semi-incoherently. I think he was just so brilliant that no jury could synthesize his claims enough to understand that he had actually, kind of, confessed. At least, that's my reading of his closing statements.

That December, a week after the trial and semester ended in, Rey ran into my office screaming, "David, wake up man! L.J. is gone. He just freaking disappeared."

"He does that all the time."

"No, David, you're not listening to me. He didn't get up and leave. He vanished. Look at me I'm L.J. POOF, I'm GONE, out of thin air."

"All right Rey, I don't have time for this crap."

"I promise. I was in the attic, I lit a cigarette. He was writing with chalk on the floor. I heard the chalk drop, and he was gone."

"That's impossible, Rey."

"Nothing is impossible."

212

How do you respond to that? We searched the attic without luck.

"Are you sure you were smoking a cigarette?" I asked.

"Really funny."

"I don't know what to say other than I think he'll be back soon."

Of course, I knew Rey was exaggerating. It was one of his classic lies. The problem is I also knew that most of his lies were true. This one could not have been true. People don't vanish into the air.

On December 21ˢᵗ, L.J. reappeared. He walked down from the attic and asked us why we were in his house. That was it.

L.J. was back.

On the first day of 2011, L.J. reached an epiphany. It was 7:30 in the morning. Evidently the fan clicking from the ceiling of the attic, the stale Chinese food in a carton on his mattress, and the spectrum of colors on the window all sparked L.J.'s imagination. None of this would interest me except that he climbed out of the attic with his sleeping bag and pillow and "set up camp" on the floor of my room.

That New Year's Day began as dozens of days with L.J. eventually would. He was standing over me smiling. He shouted, "David! You salty son of a bitch, wake up!"

I opened my eyes and heard him screaming in the other room.

"Citius, citius, citius."

My room was scattered with books of theology. Theophilus, Aquinas, and Saint Cervantes lined the walls and the floor. I looked around for the clothes that I wore the night before. L.J. had already run out of the room and was laughing with joy somewhere in the house.

"What the hell, Brovault?"

"Get in here! It's in my room!" He ran up to the attic. By the time I got up there, he was hanging from the ceiling fan.

"Citius! Citius! It means higher."

"I know what it means, you idiot. What is wrong with you?"

"The sunlight in the prism... The colors on the window..."

I looked at the window. It was not sunlight or condensation, but rather the brilliant bouquet of grease.

L.J. continued his nonsensical theorizing, "It is the light and the sun and when they are triangulated in the same spot...We've solved it you crooked saint. We can triangulate it after all. We can save Rey's soul. We may not need to time travel. But we certainly should use it at some point."

I punched him in the back of the knee, and he fell off of the fan. He couldn't have weighed more than 110 pounds at this point. L.J. believed that humans were wild beasts, and that wild beasts only need to feed themselves three times a week. The problem was he never remembered when the three times were, so most weeks he ate no more than twice.

"Listen priest man, all we need to do is get Rey into a prism, and he will be, you know, healed. It's the triangulation, dammit."

"I need to go to sleep," I said. But Rey walked into the room before I could escape.

"What's going on here?" Rey asked.

"We are going to get your soul back," L.J. said.

"All right, that's cool," Rey said.

If you've never heard a car explode, you wouldn't believe how loud it is. I never had until that early morning. The lights in the attic turned off. Then the house shook. We looked out the west window in the pale morning light. Rey's Cutlass, which was parked in the driveway off the alley in back, was on fire. Rey lurched toward the window to jump after it, but we held him back and convinced him to use the stairs.

No neighbors were investigating. Maybe they were hiding in their basements. Maybe they were plugging into their RHC safe suits. Maybe they just were more hung over than we were.

But there were people outside. There were at least a dozen men, all in white suits and white fedoras scattered throughout the yard. Three black Cadillacs crept down the alleyway and stopped by the burning car. The men in white fedoras boarded Cadillacs that slowly drove away.

Rey was terrified. L.J. was confused. I was certain that our time on earth was coming to an end.

"What the hell was that?" I asked Rey.

He lit a cigarette. "That, cousin, is Sid Cutler informing me that my soul will always belong to him."

"Should we leave the house? Where should we go?"

"David, if he was going to kill us tonight, we'd be dead. I think he's proven that he can do that."

"Let's get some coffee and make a plan."

L.J. was obviously less affected by Sid's statement than we were. He spoke at length about ways that he could erase Sid Cutler from the world. Most involved traveling in space or time.

"One other thing, if I could fix my time-space vehicle, I could go to the Ming dynasty and finally get some high-quality opium."

"I thought your space time machine was 'spinning like a top,'" I said, referencing a comment he made a day or two earlier.

"Well, the thing is that you don't quite understand how this all works, David."

"Shut up, L.J. It's 7:30 AM on New Year's, and we just almost died," I said.

"Don't shut up L.J.," Rey countered. "But let's get serious. I really want to know how I can defeat this demon."

The conversation circled around three possible solutions from L.J., Rey, and me respectively:

1: Time travel

2: Blackmail

3: Penance

Rey wanted to explore time travel first.

PART 3

RESURRECTIONS

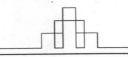

ORDINARY TIME

CH 43 •

MAY 10, 2037

So we've reached the point where I should probably address what I've been putting off since the first page. I need to tell you what happened this spring when you walked into the attic and saw me lying there almost dead. Originally, that was all this letter was going to be, an apology for that and all the other shitty things I've put you through: a confession of sorts. But how can I show you why I was prone to such a foolish, grand action without showing the silliness and childish faith of the Genius Brigade?

I mean, Rey and L.J. really believed that they would master time travel and right all of the wrongs in the world. After living through a decade of those types of amazing and absurd delusions, then two decades of the mundane, then writing and rewriting their stories, how could I not be driven to one final fantastic feat? That doesn't excuse what I did. It was inexcusable. Or at least, I've heard that it's unforgiveable.

The years of Rey's fame—Genius Brigade decade—were saturated with fantasy and fiction and, the third alliterative term, faith—sorry, I've written too many homilies. I can't really help myself sometimes. Even the material elements I encountered signified something fantastic: bread, wine, robes, stoles, robots, hearts, and all the other physical items whose elements we infused with meaning. Then, after almost fifteen years dreaming of changing the world, I climbed down to an ordinary life of diapers and tears, of paper and PTA meetings and trips to the hardware store on Monday afternoons when everyone else was at work. For a few years, I delighted in it: the idea of creating something sustainable that mattered so much to a few people. I decided I would be the greatest rector and foster father ever to live. I decided that was my true calling and was a calling worthy of a great man (which I so desperately have wanted to be). The physical became sacred. The sacred became physical and then normal and then sublime again. Any single day could be euphoric or drudgery, but in the drudgery I determined to believe in the beauty of the ordinary.

That was my life with you for the last twenty-five years. Beautiful and ordinary. I have written far too little about us in those stories. To think that five or ten pages could fill all the drama of our relationship and that everything else was just us sitting around discussing books or cooking dinner would be insulting to both of us. But I'm not going to write about those years, not at any more length than I already have: not because they don't contain the beauty or mystery that justifies prose, but because you were there. You know those stories as well as I do.

But there is one other reason. I guess I think that telling the fantastic stories of Rey and L.J. and Riley says why the monotony of everyday life—warming milk for an infant or caulking loose shower panels—matters as much as if I spent two hundred pages on those seemingly ordinary experiences. I'm not sure what all those stories say. Either way, those ordinary days ended for me when you moved out, and I miss them, though I'm not sure I will never experience them again.

All right, now I'm just procrastinating. It's easier to go on and on reflecting about the ordinary than get to the point. So here goes nothing.

The day you found me this spring trying to take my own life began as ordinarily as any.

I woke with the sunlight. Lying in my bed, I fixated the very center of the ceiling fan, wondering how much it would cost to replace it with something more contemporary, and if I could do the work myself. I figured I could, but I might accidentally turn off the wrong fuse and kill myself. I should invest in one of those little pens that check to see if a current is running through the wires. I lay like that for a while. Around 9:00 AM, I finally got out of bed because the call of coffee was stronger than the siren song of my sheets. You were visiting Christian in California, so I was alone.

I filled the coffee press with grounds I had purchased the day before. I remember that specifically. I opened the bag and wanted to drink the whole pound while it was still only a day old. The roaster promised it had just been flown in from Bolivia. I imagined the men with hats shielding themselves from the sun picking the beans up and down rolling hills, or whatever the hell they do. Just a few days later me unfolding the top of the bag and opening it as the beans overtook my olfactory sense. The kettle whistled that the water was ready. The water enveloped the grounds. Four minutes later I pushed the grounds to the bottom and was ready to drink.

I drank on the front porch. It was one of those first—and few—nearly perfect spring days that sparks the whole city into moving like it hasn't in months. Then everyone realizes that though it has reached the 60s and the sun is out and it might hit 70, the wind is so strong that the kites are struggling and the rollerblading trip north was much easier than the trip back home. While nine million people emerged from their houses, I listened to the benevolent, southerly wind rip through the neighborhood.

Motorcycles roared back to life, and every dog that hadn't had a decent walk since October panted as his overzealous owner decided that he would walk an extra mile or two.

I filled the coffee press again, boiled water, I pushed and drank. The mail came from the concrete up four steps to my hand. Kids played in the street. I leafed through the restaurant and air-duct cleaners' coupons before seeing a letter from the RHC Clinic of Chicagoland.

In characteristically stark font the yearly health report that had been freshly uploaded from my heart informed me that most of my body was healthy. The reports were almost always the same. The heart had filtered plenty of cholesterol to ensure health. It had leveled the sugar in the blood. I would never be obese or diabetic or suffer any number of ancient diseases. Then below all of the usual jargon and numbers four words shook me:

PANCREATIC CANCER CELLS ELIMINATED

The notification burned in bright off the page and into my

retinas. I was relieved. Cancer eliminated. I am sixty-three and would be dead within the year of a painful disease if it wasn't for the RHC. With this miraculous appliance ticking under my sternum, I would probably live another hundred years before some catastrophic accident finally wiped me out.

Somehow reading that was the most ordinary thing I had experienced last year. Cancer eliminated. Huh. Who would have thought it would feel like that? Under the red text was a toll free number to the RHC clinic. I dialed and spoke with a doctor in India who explained to me that I should say an extra prayer of thanks for the robotic heart tonight.

I agreed with him on the phone. I even went to the attic to pray. But who was I praying to? That was the question that got me thinking. Who saved me from cancer? Sid Cutler or the Trinitarian God I had spent my life seeking. God, my God, never designed that tin box in my chest that kept people from faith or hope or joy. So (as foolish and immature as it may have been) I reverted to my old hatred of that spherical Satan. I could not let him save my life.

Even now, after all the pain it has brought me, it's hard for me to think of another conclusion to the news that he had kept me from eternal life. What would you expect me to do but kill myself?

As far as I could tell, God wanted me dead. Sid Cutler wanted me alive.

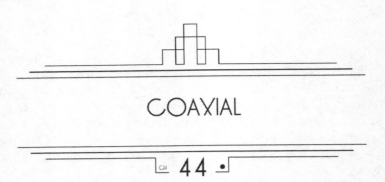

COAXIAL

MAY 10, 2037

But I had a dilemma. God wanted me to stop my heart, but I couldn't commit suicide. I searched the Internet for answers.

The Anti-RHC forums catalogued plenty of ways to stop a ticking heart. Common solutions rose to the top of the screen: gun, blade, pills, and of course, the kill switch. All seemed tantamount to suicide. I didn't want to test fate. The kill switch was a decent option, but it was a two person job. Plenty of people would help. There was a whole community around undoing the RHC one death at a time, but I couldn't make someone a murderer any more than I could murder myself.

Finally, there was a creative solution. Being an early adopter, I still had the original ROBOTIC HEART DELUXE. It had plenty of upgrades, but the software was still within the average man's programming ability. Evidently, the early models had a problem where it would remove necessary cells from the bodies. Cutler's engineers created an ingenious solution for the time, which allowed doctors to target a specific cell that the RHC Deluxe had terminated and reverse the steps of removal and replace all of the deleted cells. If it had targeted and removed your healthy thyroid cells, you could simply recreate them. I don't know the details, and don't care anymore than what I've already written here. All I know was that if I could find or recreate the machine that doctor's used, I could reverse the deletion of cancerous pancreas cells. I could expedite the process. I could simply replace my original cells that may or may not kill me (but certainly would kill me quickly without a miracle). I could let God

222

decide whether I lived or died.

I wrote you a note and gathered the first versions of these stories about Rey and me, which I left on my desk. I hadn't finished them all, but as I said I had been scribbling notes about Rey for decades. I placed the note on the table in the attic where I decided I would end my life. I'm sure you remember my brief prose:

Dearest Rebecca:

L.J. once told me of a universe where we could live at peace in love and die together, where the RHC never existed, and where Sid Cutler was killed a century ago. There is neither robot fighting nor need for it. The church is thriving. In my dreams, we are there. We are all happier.

It would take a book to explain why I did this, but trust that I had to take my life to ruin Sid Cutler.

I will wait for you in eternity. Read the stories on my bedside table. They are unfinished but true.

I love you,
Fr. David Ezekiel Rosario

I gathered the materials: steel wool, 25 ft. of coaxial, a twelve volt battery, three metal dog bowls (or cat, but most experts recommend dog bowls), and the Macintosh 512 that cost me a fortune at some electronic nostalgia shop. I pieced it together and studied the programming code for a while. Cutler insisted that the first generation's programming was based on Latin, which helped. When L.J. returned from one of his disappearances, he had the idea of a language of only 0s and 1s. It never caught on. I told him that Latin made the most sense; after all, there were more classics majors than anything. Why would someone base a computer language on numbers? Sorry for the digression.

When the steel wool was properly secured to my feet and the coaxial, that I just unscrewed from the wall and my T.V., I remembered the bottle of Lilac Whiskey. The forums all agreed that the process could be painful. By my estimations, I would be pumping my body so full of pancreatic cancer that my eyes would bleed. If ever there was a time for Lilac Whiskey, it was this. It also served as a final way to piss off Sid Cutler. I hesitated again. I rechecked that the letter was on the desk where someone would find it. The coaxial insert was less-than pleasant, and the whole idea of dying was obviously terrifying, so I ran through the list again and again:

Macintosh, battery, coaxial, steel wool, lemon juice (did I mention that), dog bowls. I ran over it all in my mind one final time before deciding to take a nap, to pray about it. So I slept there on the couch in my den shrouded in a fog of self-hate and mortality.

I dreamt of other worlds, of L.J.'s prophecies, of the mountain, of you.

You screamed.

You were home.

I was alone no longer. I hoped you hadn't read the letter. I would just pretend I was doing a science experiment. But from your tone not only had you read the letter, but the pain you were about to inflict on me would make me wish that I had chosen a different exit strategy.

The Macintosh 512 burst through the second floor window. You threw the dog bowl filled with liquid in my face. If you wonder why I never looked at you, why I only cried while you went over an exhaustive and pathetic list of my idiocy, it was because the lemon juice was in my eyes. Either way, you were probably right. I never thought about you during my whole plan to smote Sid Cutler by killing myself. Not until the lemon juice ate away at my conjunctivas did I consider your reaction.

I'll never forget the final thing you shouted, "I wish you did live in another multiverse, or dimension, or whatever the hell you are talking about in this letter. Then maybe we'd both be happy."

Maybe subconsciously I expected you to catch me. Perhaps I should have taken a different tone in the suicide note. I thought you would be sad for me. I'm sure you would have been if I was depressed. But I wasn't. I was just arrogant.

When I calculated your response, I had this fantasy version

of you that wanted me to be like Rey and overcome the devil in some grand way, rather than simply living with you here in Chicago in an old house in the minutia of seasons and years.

Hours later in the soundless house it hit me, what you must have felt, what I would have felt if you killed yourself: I would have thought that you never loved me. So the secret's out, Rebecca. I know that you love me. I never thought I deserved it. I still don't, but I believe I have it.

When I realized all of this that night staring at the corked bottle full of Lilac Whiskey, I cried without the aid of lemon juice.

I guess what I'm trying to say here is that I am sorry.

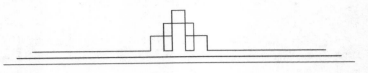

HOCKEY PRACTICE

JANUARY – FEBRUARY 2011

It feels good to get that off my chest. I've been thinking about it a lot out here, about how much I want to live, especially in the mornings before I write. I think about you as I watch the sunrise from my tent and look for the signs that were revealed to L.J. in our cell at the monastery. Hopefully, you will forgive me and join me and we can laugh about how stupid I was and study the sky together and walk into eternity.

But first, I will finish the story of Rey Pescador, so you know what I'm talking about.

As 2011 commenced, Rey and L.J. researched and developed Brovault's Time/Space Vehicle. Rey dubbed himself Chief Engineer and argued that poetry was the key to time travel. His syllogism was rock solid: "Poetry has power and power is needed for time travel; ergo, poetry is needed for time travel." L.J., who had been skeptical moments before, celebrated shouting, "That's just illogical enough to work." So Rey penned one million lines, while L.J. did whatever it is L.J. does when he is creating pseudo-scientific machines that promise to do the supernatural.

Those were the moments that the GB was its best: hanging out at the house plotting ways to change history or save Rey's soul or revive Jerry Garcia for a tour with Rey Pescador. Rey swore Jerry was his cousin on his dad's side, but of course he had no idea who his father was. Come to think of it, for a while it seemed like every badass celebrity with a Spanish surname was Rey's cousin.

I hoped that with the New Year we could forget all of the

robot fighting nonsense. I hoped the public would forget about L.J.'s stupidity. It did, but the Vatican tends to move more slowly than public opinion. During the past few months while Rey toured and L.J. defended himself, I was linked by satellites and cameras to television screens where I debated with other priests or "religious professionals" regarding robot fighting and scientific developments. I became the voice of the old guard, the conservative group that believed technology was destroying us.

Ironically, I fought for an ancient life against technology with Sid Cutler's RHC cash, while being a member of the group that defined the avant-garde in the arts.

On February 19th, the Vatican requested that I answer questions about robot fighting and time travel. In Chicago, this was news: GB PRIEST TO VISIT VATICAN. On February 20th, as Rey took his daily siesta, and L.J. skinned a rabbit in the attic, I read alone on the porch and watched kids play street hockey in full Blackhawks garb.

In the bright cold of winter, you emerged from the flashes of red and shouts of "GOAL!" and "CAR" up all four of the stairs to my porch. I stood to greet you. You called me David. We were closer than my comfort, maybe a foot away. I could smell the cold sweat of your journey from the diner. The late winter air, the afternoon sun, and the children playing hockey on the street all disappeared in the proximity of your soul to mine.

I never expected you to congratulate me for my trip to the Vatican. After all, the trip would almost certainly lead to my defrocking. Honestly, that was what I wanted. That was my big plan. We could be together. But your frustration was well beyond what I expected. You called me immature, and spiritually abusive. You asked how someone as passionate for faith and theology as me could jeopardize his ministry for something as silly, as absurd as robot fighting. You ended with something like, "David, I thought you cared," which mixed with the emotions of the argument and the scent of perfume and cold sweat catalyzed a biological imperative to prove my care in the most visceral way possible.

I pulled your body to mine and kissed you.

Of course, you remember your response to my gross

misunderstanding of the sentiment. You punched me in the stomach just as Rey opened the door.

Free from the fear of all these things, the children continued to play hockey down the street.

As you walked back down the steps, Rey said, "Pretty feisty girlfriend you've got there," which led to another assault: this time it was me pushing Rey through the front window into the pale yellow front room.

He lay in broken glass and said, "David, what the hell, man?"

The kids playing hockey finally stopped and saw me turn to you and say, "I'm sorry, Rebecca."

You never turned your head. You just raised your right forearm perpendicular to the ground with your hand just higher than your head and your longest finger protruding upward while the other digits remained balled in a clenched fist.

46

MARCH 1, 2011

A week or so later, I was on the aircraft to Rome searching *Summa Theologica* for a home-run argument against the existence of artificially intelligent machines. I fell asleep. The plane dropped to the ground. I boarded a train. I'm embarrassed to say that I didn't even look at Rome until I arrived at my room, and even then all I noticed were a few drugstores and cable television. It had been so long since I had a TV in my house, at least one with any significant number of channels that I spent the majority of the day before the tribunal watching international news. I decided that I needed to lose some weight. It was about 8:00 AM when I arrived. I worked out in the hotel recreation center; then I fell asleep. I slept for almost four hours.

I awoke to the knock on my door. Cardinal Theodore O'Toole, the ancient man, could still somehow knock on a door. He was from Scotland and was possibly the only clergy member outside the Pope to have more articles written about him over the last decade than me. He was nearly 120 years old, but looked no younger than 200. He had an icon of Christ that transmitted everything he heard to an ancient code. The code was sent wirelessly to an inner ear receiver. It sent electrical impulses and chemicals to his brain for him to perceive reality. Without the icon, he was blind and deaf.

I traced his gait and followed him to the street where a car was waiting. He walked, as if he was forty years younger. His back was hunched, but his legs moved accurately and confidently, even down the stairs. The car stopped just outside the Big Man's place.

I hadn't been there since before I was ordained, just before the Africa trip. I can't tell you how proud and insignificant I felt wearing that collar in that place: it was one of the happiest moments in my life, despite my inevitable censure. Tens of thousands held banners and chanted. Some kneeled and wept. Most of the signs were in unfamiliar languages, but the roots of the newer words were clear: ROBOT, ROBOT, ROBOT, ROBOT. I read an English sign that said, "Baptize robots." Another sign read, "Kill Edwin!" It kind of killed the proverbial buzz, if you know what I mean.

The Pope sat in the inquisitor's room with about thirty other members of the church. Needless to say it wasn't how I hoped to meet the Holy Father. Most of the crowd appeared to be lay people, security, or priests like myself. A few others were being interrogated by Cardinal O'Toole. As far as I could tell, however, I was the only one to enjoy his presence on the cab ride to the Vatican. The room was free of the ornament of the rest of the city. It was drywall painted white with several photographs of popes littered throughout. It was, for all intents and purposes, a modern conference room. *It is still sacred*, I thought. It had to be sacred.

Though I secretly hoped to be defrocked, so I could marry you, I don't want you to think I was resigned to the fact that I'd lose my collar. In fact, I had some reasons to be confident that I would defeat O'Toole in a flourish of classic oratorical zeal. I had read the Pope's writing on the artificial heart, and veiled as it was, he appeared to disapprove. He seemed concerned with some of the implications that I saw. Cardinal O'Toole, the breathing Radio Shack himself, did not share my zeal. And his role as inquisitor did not bode well for my chances. Cardinal O'Toole had the ego of one hundred men: and why not, God had killed him one hundred times over, and his heart kept clicking, clicking, clicking, clicking.

Cardinal O'Toole began the interrogation, "Fr. Rosario, do you consider yourself to be a member of the Genius Brigade?"

"I consider myself to be a member of the Catholic Church."

"What then is your relationship to the Genius Brigade?" he continued.

"I am cousins with Rey Pescador, and I deeply care for the soul of each member of my flock. They live in my parish."

"So you consider the Genius Brigade to be your parishioners?"

"I do."

Then O'Toole asked me something that shocked me, "What is your relationship with Mr. Sidney Alfonse Cutler?"

I paused for a bit wondering what angle O'Toole was playing. Then answered, "He is a corporate mogul who owns imprints that have published my books."

"Is that the extent of your relationship? If not, please detail it more fully."

"His management of my cousin's literary career has led me to making acquaintance with him in several social situations. I have also met with him in two business meetings."

"Could you chronicle those meetings?"

"Cardinal, with all respect, I have met Mr. Cutler several times. To chronicle each meeting would be exhausting. Could you give me something more specific to answer?"

"Is it true that you have attended his birthday parties and golf outings where sins unto death were committed?"

"I witnessed no such sins."

"Is it true that Rey Pescador has sold his soul to Mr. Cutler?"

Never in my wild imagination did I expect him to ask this question.

I was angry. Perhaps I showed it too much, "The acts of my parishioners are not public record. I am insulted that you would ask such a question. On another note, the suggestion also seems far-fetched, sir; this is reality not some medieval legend."

"Recently the Genius Brigade published articles and statements regarding an inhumane robot fighting syndicate. You have also publicly stated 'although these battles represent a financial loss to me personally, I do not believe that robot fighting is a sin.' The church has been outspoken in its effort to stop robot fighting especially amongst humanoids. This tribunal asks you to recant or explain this quotation and your role in the robot battle rings."

"I will not recant. The issue of robot fights is personally and theologically important to me."

"Are you implying that you will not follow the church's mandate on this issue?"

"Cardinal O'Toole, do not try to scare me with smoke and no fire. I understand my role, and I understand the history of the church's teaching regarding the humanity of robots. Although many within the church have spoken publicly on this issue, no official dogma has been created. Also, I am currently publishing a treatise of my own on this issue. You may read it when I am finished. It will be titled *Robot Oil*. Several bishops in the American church agree with my teachings on the sinfulness of robotic creatures. The church must desperately fight for the lives of human beings born and unborn; however, classifying robots as humans is a dangerous step."

At that point I realized that the Pope would not step in and support the cardinal. Maybe he allowed this whole thing to have me challenge the cardinal. It was impossible to tell, but I figured I would test the waters a bit. I began my offensive, "Cardinal, why is it that sin is in the world? Did God create it?"

"Of course not, sin is a result of our own choices and depravity. I don't see why you are asking such a basic theological question."

"Why would God create a being that would choose sin over holiness?"

"I suppose because he wanted us to praise him out of our own choices. He did not want us to be..."

"Finish the sentence, Cardinal."

"He did not want us to be programmed to follow him."

"In short, he did not want us to be robots." There was an audible response in the room until the Pope looked at the whispering crowd with the unsaid command to continue in peace. I continued my argument, "God did not want robots to exist, and science has created these unholy beings. If I confess anything it is that I have allowed robots to assist me too much in life. I will confess that I have personally watched them annihilate their own kind, but I will never consider it a sin. Robots are unnatural, and I for one take pleasure in seeing them demolish each other. Any other questions?"

"Fr. Rosario, are you implying that robotic hearts and other mechanical limbs and organs are sinful?"

"I am."

"Fr. Rosario, you may not be aware, but I am nearly one hundred and twenty one years old. I would not be alive without the help of my artificial heart. The most recent download of my heart's activity showed that it had killed several cancerous cells. These cells were targeted by machines in the hospital and eliminated. Is that sinful, Father? Do you wish I had let the cells run their course?"

"Cancer is a bad way to go. If I were you I would have left the heart out and died naturally thirty years ago."

"To wish our own death is to reject God's greatest gift."

"I didn't wish my death."

"But you wished mine, Mr. Rosario?"

"It is Reverend Doctor Rosario, and for both of our sakes I wish nature had taken its course already."

The room roared with commotion. The Holy Father looked at me with deep eyes. His face was pure white, as was his hair. His chin angled to a point that drew the eyes to the crucifix around his neck. Even amidst the vacuum of contemporary architecture, he exuded the spirit of the golden era of Christendom. Immediately, I apologized to Cardinal O'Toole for my disrespect. I added that I only wanted to the best for the Church and for my parish. The Cardinal ceased questioning me. I stood to leave, then stopped. I looked at the Holy Father and addressed him personally.

"Your Holiness, may I ask you a question off the record?"

"Yes, my child."

"If a baptized Christian had sold his soul, how might he regain it, and how would he know when he had?"

"David, it is not our sins, but our faith that determine salvation."

"What acts of faith could overcome such a grave sin?"

"We all have grave sins that would keep us from grace. That is why we repent. I would recommend that the person whose soul has been lost speak to a priest who cares. Together they will walk the path to heaven."

"Thank you, your Holiness."

"David, on another note, tell my child, Rey Pescador, to keep writing. You know that when I met him last year, he called me, 'Most Swaggy Father.' I have not laughed so hard since they gave me this pointy hat."

"Well, if you ever need a Vatican jester, you know where to find him."

I returned to my hotel. The next morning I received a letter from my Bishop requesting me to assist in research in a Spanish monastery. It was as if I was being grounded, but I didn't mind. I can imagine worse things for someone like me than studying in a Spanish monastery. I took a train. Part of me was happy for the outcome of the tribunal. But I also wish they kicked me out of the priesthood and into your arms. I went to Spain. I wrote you an apology.

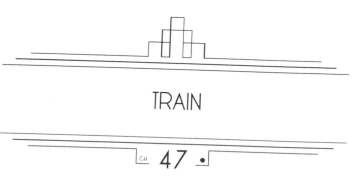

TRAIN

CH 47 •⌐

On the way to the monastery, I switched trains in Madrid. I had a two-hour layover, so I walked the streets until a Romanesque church rose from the strip malls and cafés and pulled me inside. Void of vitality and faith, the building had become a museum filled with people searching for artifacts and mysteries of an ancient culture. There I was in my collar, another relic of a time past. I thought I might deliver a homily or make holy water from a tourist's canteen before dousing the crowd and declaring them witness to a new era for the Church, but those sorts of grand announcements never worked for me as well as Rey. Instead, I reverently crossed myself and kneeled and hoped that something supernatural would happen here and now. Nothing did, so I walked back to the train station, boarded my new train, ordered a glass of wine and read a newspaper.

The rows of trains arriving and departing drew my attention. This part of the station was underground and there were about twenty tracks where trains were coming and going. As far as I knew trains almost never crashed despite being on the same rails and moving so quickly. It seemed like an administrative nightmare. I'm glad that it isn't my job. I'd probably send a dozen careening together in a week or two.

The standard announcement informed us that, yes, the train was moving, and yes we would arrive at our destination in the south of Spain. I read a book and drank my wine, trying to ignore the passengers rushing to their seats. Then a bumbling man sat across from me with such force that my wine spilled a little over the top. I didn't look up until he said my name.

It was L.J. Brovault; he had actually gained weight in the last month. He carried a rucksack with a Canadian flag on it and explained that Europeans treat Canadians better than Americans. I asked how the plan works if people know the American because he is a famous person. He didn't get my point. We ate a light lunch. He attempted small talk. He still spoke with his chin high and his eyes darted above my head as if he had been coached to make eye contact, but couldn't quite let gravity drag his glare to the ground.

With L.J., I've rarely been surprised when he shows up at strange places, but even I was surprised that he would be on the same train in Madrid. I asked him how he found me. He said, "I talked with Rey, and he said that you were in the Vatican."

"But I'm in in Madrid now."

"Oh yeah, that. Well, I called the Pope to find your hotel, and he informed me that you were leaving for Spain."

"How did you get the right train? Wait, forget the train. You didn't call the Pope. You can't just call the Pope, and he wouldn't know where I am."

"David, this doesn't matter. I'm here, man. I wanted to talk."

"All right, let's talk."

"Sid Cutler is waiting for you."

"In Spain?"

"No. Well, I don't know."

"What do you mean, he is waiting for me?" I was still high on the thrill of debating O'Toole in the Vatican, and I half believed I could defeat Sid Cutler once and for all. I half believed he would kill me within the week.

"It's hard to explain. I saw him last week. Maybe two weeks ago. This wrap is amazing, the steak in it is actually rare. You say rare, but they usually make it medium rare."

He paused to chew. I was almost tired of him already. L.J. continued, "The thing is, I saw him with you. I saw a vision of you and Sid together. The triangulator, well I've made some modifications. It's hard to describe. I dreamt that you and my girlfriend were with Sidney Cutler at dinner. Rebecca was there, but she was older. She walked in while you were eating with him, and she looked pissed. All I know is there was a contract. You had a pen. Sidney's hair was black. That's the thing I don't understand. At first I thought it was the past because of his hair, but it couldn't be, so it must be the future."

"L.J., thanks for the warning. But it was just a dream. I will never again sign a contract with Sid Cutler."

"I hope you're right."

"L.J., can I ask you something?" He just kept eating. "I hope this isn't rude, but it surprised me that you would come and tell me this. I mean, you flew across the ocean to warn me about a dream. You could have called me."

"I was in Europe already."

He was quiet for a long time. The train rapidly crawled through a river basin. The speed made our silence more pronounced, but harder to end.

"The thing is, Father. I guess I need to make up for being an asshole my whole life."

We were quiet again for a minute or two. I started reading.

"There's another thing that I can't get over, Father. Something I need to confess to you."

"What is it?"

"I told Rey there was no soul. Then he signed that deal."

"I thought you believed that."

"Does it matter if I do or not?"

"I guess it doesn't."

"You're right. It doesn't matter at all."

Before long, we reached the monastery. Within a few hours, I started to wonder if L.J. would ever leave the monastery. I certainly understood the appeal: it rested on a cliff overlooking the Mediterranean in Southern Spain. Silence and books and serenity suited him. We shared a cell. The brothers welcomed him, but over the stay, his ascetic nature made even them uncomfortable. He fasted the three days we were there and spent most of his time in silence. While I met with the brothers regarding theology in a post-human creation, Brovault read the Old Testament. When I returned the final night he was weeping. It was after compline, so we didn't talk. He wept until I fell asleep and maybe after.

At dawn we awoke for prayer, the brothers and me.

The light invaded the cell orange and yellow and white.

Brovault had left during the night. He left only his jacket, several crumpled pages from the Old Testament and a few gum wrappers.

The cell's northern wall, across from my small cot was covered with a chalky substance. In the night, L.J. ripped out several pages of Exodus and Genesis and plastered them against the wall with bubble gum. He drew a diagram of a large triangular mountain. At the top in what appeared to be the smoke and ash of a volcano he wrote the words: THE MOUNTAIN OF GOD. A dotted triangular line surrounded the mountain. The attempted perspective of the illustration suggested that the mountain was the center of the three points. The angles of the larger triangle featured the illustrations of a serpent, a woman, and a man. In the ashes of the volcano under the words THE MOUNTAIN OF GOD was a four-legged creature with sharp teeth. I believe it was a lion, but it was a stick figure, and the mane may have simply been more ash. A bird with a significant crest was near the top of the mountain next to a circle that may have been lava or water or nonsense. It may have all been nonsense. On the ground of the cell he had outlined a man as if a murder had happened there.

Within the human was a heart and the formula: S=ori.sin (XP + [CR]). The most readable passage bubble-gummed to the wall was from Exodus:

> Then went up Moses, and Aaron, Nadab, and Abihu, and seventy of the elders of Israel:
> And they saw the God of Israel: and there was under his feet as it were a paved work of a sapphire stone, and as it were the body of heaven in his clearness. And upon the nobles of the children of Israel he laid not his hand: also they saw God, and did eat and drink.

Over the mountain, Brovault drew a horizontal line resting on the tip. Above that he wrote: heaven. He signed his name BROTHER L.J. at the bottom. Then he left.

Astonished at the vision before me, I stayed in the room instead of going to prayers and jotted down Brovault's illustration in my journal. An hour later a few of the brothers arrived at my room assuming I had slept through Morning Prayer. When they saw the pages of the Bible pasted to the wall, they were astonished. Immediately, I left that morning, but I stayed in Europe and searched the ancient Catholic libraries for answers.

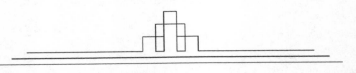

THE MARIOKALYPSE

APRIL - MAY 2011

While I researched in Spain, Rey decided to thwart Sid Cutler by making him believe that he was still obedient to him. He published his final and most nonsensical book, *The Mariokalypse*. Later, it would be seen as Rey's worst book. But in early 2011, it was hailed as an "incoherent triumph" by *The New York Times*. Rey dazzled readers with the 5,000 line dramatic monologue of the Nintendo pop-culture icon. It was nearly unreadable, but critics praised Rey for hiding the meaning "under layers and layers of bile and subtext, reminding us that there is beauty and truth in the shit of the world."

Yale University's *Walt Whitman Chair of Poetry*, J. Karl Svensson, described the poem as "subterraneanly esoteric...the best English work of its kind... it is best read in a state of opium-induced sublimity. Pescador reminds us that fun can also be part of the epic." The only thing that created more bizarre modifiers than Rey's epic was the body of criticism surrounding it.

Despite its veiled and absurd vernacular, Rey's *Mariokalypse Tour* was a commercial success. Filled with martial arts and music, Rey danced around the stage for the majority of the four hour show. The ending climaxed as the poem did, with Rey conjuring the spirit of the first "mans" of the first Mario Brothers game. Deceased for many and many lives, Rey curses and consumes him. He donned his clothing and danced on strings across the spectators on the ground floor. He shouted classical Greek phrases and Black English Vernacular mixed with literary jargon until he finally defeats the King of the Koopahs and launches

240

himself into space.

The day after the first performance, the *Washington Post* editorial read, "He puts the verb in verbose."

I'm not sure where L.J. went during the tour. After he left the monastery, I tried to contact him dozens of times unsuccessfully. I wanted to let him know that he should check out the New Testament.

I missed you while I was in Spain, or I would have never left. I could have stayed in that ancient country forever. I could have lived an ancient life. The wine, the cafés the churches, the silence at night, the mysticism all appealed to me, but eventually the concrete and metal of Chicago called me back to you. So when I finished my research in late May, I took a plane back.

Maybe I should have stayed in Spain. Maybe you would have been better off. It's hard to tell.

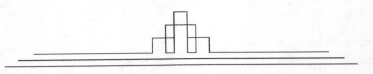

CONFESSIONAL

⌐ CH 49 •⌐

JUNE 12, 2011

I saw you again at my first mass since seeing the Pope.

When the organ stopped, it reminded us that our metal world was filled with bus exhaust and car stereos. The gloria ended after preparing the small congregation for the mass. It was my first week back. When you opened the door, the noise resonated through the sanctuary's open door as it had with the hum of the brass pipes. We heard rain fall on concrete and through metal grates. Men and machines—harried while creating new technology, to remain viable, competitive, orderly— walked past the open door of the church. You must have heard the organ walking up the concrete steps, though it stopped just as you stepped onto the marble narthex floor. You must have heard the pipes bounce ancient harmonies across the lanes of traffic. If only a moment of synesthesia could show me the colors of the waves of sound that bounced like so many drops of rain. The nave, consumed the world's poisons and gurgled them, spinning and moving and mixing the sound until all that remained was white noise that drowned the constant click of my soul.

You lingered in the door for a moment before holy water and Latin syllables ushered you into the congregation. My original homily was going to be on textual criticism surrounding the inter-Corinthian epistle. The topic was too academic, too boring for the day that you walked back into my church. I never thought you would see me as your priest again, so I changed it to a reflection on the role of Mary as the second Eve, cosmically. Then in the midst of my rambling, I paused. I was preaching about you. Your eyes, blue; your alto voice that cut the trains of the city; your body that touched me once; I had elevated you to perfection, even your crooked teeth became in their own right, an idol.

I took the pieces of you in my mind and built my own robot. You became an idol of perfection, a pre-lapsarian Eve destined to fall. I forgot the story, of course. I forgot the inherent will of humanity, the inevitable choice.

The service continued.

You received neither the bread nor the wine that I had turned into God.

At the end of mass, you ignored me and the others. You walked to the confessional and sat silently waiting for me to shake hands with the handful of parishioners who cared to shake hands.

When I finally sat in my box, you said you had sinned. Conflicted and curious, I had to hear your confession.

Then you paused for what seemed to be a long time. You waited and looked at the room, and started to cry. "I'll confess someday, but not to you, at least, not now, and not like this."

"What do you mean?"

"I should've kept calling you Father. I'm sorry, David."

You left. The church was empty. I drank the remaining communion wine. I had made far too much that morning. Sitting at the altar under the crucifix, I drank a glass or two and meditated on the stained glass around me.

Nothing changed. Nothing ever really changed in my mind. So I sat for a long time wishing the organ hadn't stopped and wondering if the city ever became mute.

The door opened again welcoming the scent of June: the aroma of late spring hidden under the cool rain. It felt like it should be summer already. I hoped it would be you. Of course it wasn't. Rey walked the aisle to where I was lying just in front of the altar. He did not look me in the eye. He knelt before the altar and began to cry.

"Father," he called me for the first time.

"Yes, Rey."

"Father, I sense too much," he said. He said he felt too much. He said he smelled too much and tasted and thought and heard and wanted.

"I saw too much, too much in her alabaster skin, too much of her thigh at the table, enough to see that there was more to see. God forgive me, there's always more to see. Take my eyes and my senses. Take whatever part of the brain processes stimuli, and let me lie, like a plant, free from the fruit of sin."

I told him to calm down. I told him there was forgiveness. He became more animated. He stood and paced. If it was anyone else, I would have thought he was performing, but performing was his only way to be sincere.

He continued, "Father, she laughed and moved her head down and her hair fell forward. I saw the first inch of cleavage. What was I to do? She was drinking, not drunk, but happy. She thought I was someone else at first. But when I sat down she called me *Mr. Pescador*. Shit, of all the things she could say. Of all the things to hear: *Mr. Pescador*. If she called me Rey, I would have been pure. If she called me the Poet or the King or El Rey, or even the freaking Bard from the Barrio, we'd be all right. We may have gotten drunk, but that, that's different. Her voice dropped in tone when she said it; I think she even said *good evening, Mr. Pescador*. What was I supposed to do? My eyes are weak. You know that, but my ears are weak too. You know I've worn glasses since I was a boy. How can such a weak organ be the door to my soul? Dammit! I'll just leave."

"Rey, calm down. Just ask for forgiveness. It's not the first time you've sinned. There is forgiveness, Rey. I can tell you feel bad."

"I believe God could forgive, but not you."

"Of course I will, Rey."

"I'm not an animal. I can control myself. It's just everything added together. I think it was the air, that summer air that ages the city. You know what I mean. In the winter, you love the women in their boots and their hats. You wonder what's underneath the long black coats, but it's nothing like the summer.

"I guess I'm trying to say, the city is new—it's modern—the moonlight and streetlights shine off the windows, but there is no history. At least that's what it seems like, right? Everything with life is dormant, and you get a drink or tell a story and go to sleep until the snow thaws. But in the summer, David, I mean Father, in the summer you can smell it: you can smell the blood under the dirt, under the cobblestone, under the layers and layers of pavement. You can smell the water in the air. You can smell bread trucks, and liquor from any number of bars. And each aroma triggers my heart. It triggers my memory. It triggers my damned heart and tells it to beat. Before I saw her, I could smell the summer, the weight of a thousand summers. I could smell the sunlight that rested in the pavement and begged to be released. I could smell the wind remind me that the world will end with or without my pleasure. Then my heart beat and beat and beat and beat until it beat the scar off my chest, and it beat the crucifix off my neck, and it beat the still-soft voice from my brain. It beat until it could no longer beat alone, until I needed to share its rhythm, its voice, its story.

"When she called me Mr. Pescador, with that alto voice descending through the syllables; when she asked me to dance and seemed so perfect and innocent and different from the women in New York or Paris or Tokyo, I fell. I decided I loved her. I even told her I'd marry her. David, I meant it. David, I meant to. The courthouse was closed. I sinned, and then she disappeared until she walked up to the front porch last week like when she yelled at you a couple of months ago and told me the news. David, forgive me: Rebecca is pregnant."

I said nothing for a long time. We sat and listened to the city remind us of all the things we wanted to forget. I meant to forgive him or kill him. I did neither. I was not a man of action, like Rey. A little while after Rey had gone, I left in the newly fallen rain and walked home then to the attic. It was quiet and the remnants of L.J.'s stay were scattered across the ground. In the corner I found my old chest. I opened it and stared at the bottle of Cutler's Lilac Whiskey. I read the note for the first time. I read, "David, you cannot forgive him, but you can forget." I held the bottle and lay down on the ground. I did not want to forget. I did not want to forget.

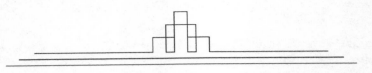

FIRST BREATHS

⌐ CH 50 ¬

MAY 1, 2011

Later, when we were in the backcountry Rey told me about how he fell in love with you. He described it fantastically as we climbed up and up and up: how you healed him; how you brought vision to a dead man.

When Rey first saw you, he was deaf and blind to beauty. Only through the artificial lens of Lilac Whiskey did his eyes perceive stimuli that revealed the Creator's mind. His last sober vision of beauty was the singer just before he signed his name. The last image was her silhouette against the darkness.

He trudged the city that first day in May. Perhaps he was inundated with requests for autographs, perhaps he looked like another damned body looking for something to distract his mind. Out of soul, out of consciousness, and out of love he searched for one of the three. He imagined his soul near the Chicago River, coins over the eyes. He visualized it climbing back into him through a graceful breath of wind. If he could just get breath back into his body, he could finally feel something again.

But Rey Pescador's soul was not on the banks of the Chicago River.

He searched longer and farther, but his body did not find his soul, so he sought more temporary cures: sex, adoration, substances. He assured himself that it would be the last time that he sought beauty this way.

White Sox Park rose from the outskirts of Bronzeville and Bridgeport. Rey saw the glow of the stadium like a child, waking in the middle of the night, sees a fire through the deep blue of a tent. Rey always used the player's entrance. Today was no different. He was a mascot of sorts for his hometown team. The players greeted him.

"You playing for us tonight. Rey?" the manager asked.

"I'm feeling limber."

"You still got that speed. We could use a pinch runner."

"Always, but I don't want to make Guitierez look slow."

He drank some Gatorade, but wanted a beer. After the first inning, he scanned the crowd for beauty but was distracted by his face on the jumbotron. He smiled and stared into the night until he saw, at the top of the stadium, at the pinnacle of the empty nosebleed-section, the silhouette of a woman etched against the yellow and white backdrop of the Chicago skyline.

It was who he had been looking for his whole life.

So Rey Pescador, the South Side Superman, climbed the steps of White Sox Park to the very top, where the light of the city burned like the hot red coals of a campfire. He climbed toward the singer. He hoped she would devour his body and throw it from the top of the stadium into the urban embers. His empty body would find his soul in some merciful afterlife.

At the top of the first section, he considered climbing one of the pillars to the 500 level like a great saint scaling a castle. But instead he walked through the concourse to the ramp that hung on the concrete skeleton of the massive structure.

At the 500 level sections, above the skybox seats, he had to look up again. He had to make sure that something was there, that some vision beyond veil of a tent would be waiting for him. He wanted salvation, but not now. Now he wanted to feel, and he prayed that prayer would escape him now. He prayed to sin once and for all and be free from the body forever after that. He prayed that he would enter into an orgasm of light and touch and smell and heat. He wanted to feel one last time, to think one last time before losing consciousness forever.

He took off his cap, held it over his face and looked through two of the four holes on the top. The silhouette was still there, hair moving in the wind, light burning behind. It was the middle of the seventh, the crowd was standing and singing when Rey starting running.

You snapped a few photos of him. Then fearful of the maniac running directly at you, you dropped the camera and turned in terror. Rey reached your body before he had composed a course of action. So he grabbed you around your waist, and pressed his body against your back. He smelled your hair and hoped that for a moment he would feel the way he had before he lost his soul. You turned, which relocated his unwanted hands to your back. He realized that you were not who he thought you were. You punched him on the left cheek. His glasses fell down the steep grade. His hat popped off.

Then you saw that it was the excarnate poet who had kissed you. "Rey?"

"Rebecca. Shit. I thought you were someone else."

"Well, I'm sorry to disappoint."

He placed his broken glasses on his face and sat down to watch the game. You sat too, evidently. He said you didn't say a word for a minute as he began analyzing the White Sox season.

"Rey," you began.

"Yeah."

"Why are you up here?"

"What do you mean? I'm watching the game."

"You know what I mean. You climbed up here, basically assaulted me, said you thought I was someone else, then sat and talked for an inning about the hit and run."

"It is a powerful scoring method... I mean scoring runs."

Your camera was still on the ground where it had fallen. Rey picked it up and analyzed it. He apologized for it dropping and offered to buy a new one. Then he looked through the lens at the field and the city and you. He said, "I didn't realize you were a photographer."

"I'm not really."

"But you enjoy it?"

"I took a few classes in college. I guess it is a hobby now."

"All right. Then tell me what it is that you like about photography."

"I don't know."

"Yes you do. You studied it in college. You probably have written papers on the philosophy of photography or something. I can tell you have thought about it, but you don't want to say anything."

"Fine, I guess I just like the idea of capturing something that exists in a moment. Something that may not have been noticed otherwise."

"Hmm. I've never thought of it that way. I always saw it as a lesser art."

"Thanks."

"I mean, you have helped me see that it could be art."

You watched the game for another few minutes in silence. Then you asked Rey again why he was there.

"Well, the simple answer is that I was in the dugout mourning, looking for my damned soul when I saw the light radiate around you up here. Your silhouette was beautiful, and I thought that you could save me from hell for a moment."

"Wow, that is quite the line. No wonder you are famous with the ladies," you said sarcastically.

"Quite the line? You know what, I'm sick of people saying stuff like that to me. You stand on top of this mountain and call me to the top with your silhouette. I follow, and I'm giving you a line. Do you think me saying I'm damned is a line? I'm damned. Do you know that? A mortal sinner, and I found you beautiful. I really thought you could help me. I wish it was a line."

"Sorry, Rey, but I'm confused."

"Don't worry about it."

"I wasn't apologizing. And don't talk to me like that."

"I'm sorry."

Rey said the rest of the inning was small talk. He talked about how you laughed at his jokes and anecdotes. How he listened to you and really cared. How he looked into your eyes and never even thought about sex or himself. He walked to the concourse for a few rounds of beer until they stopped serving it. Then the 8th inning, the White Sox scored two runs. He said it was the first time he didn't shout or jump for a run scored at a Sox game. He simply sat close to you and breathed in the air that you breathed out without you noticing. Then when he was fully distracted from any quixotic quest, he spoke, "Rebecca, can I ask you a question?"

"Sure, Rey."

"If we were young, I mean. Shoot, if I was young, and you were my age, and we had a whole life ahead of us, would you believe that I could do something amazing? Would you believe in me, that I could spin the world faster on its axis and contribute something beautiful to the earth? Do you think that I could love someone normal like you day in and day out?"

You thought for a while looking at the lonely poet. Then you said, "Rey, take off your glasses."

He took off his glasses.

"Rey, can you still see me?"

"Yes. I wear contacts too."

"Why?"

"I see better that way; the glasses are to look smart."

"Take out your contacts too." He took out his contacts. "Look at me," you said. He looked at you. You looked exactly the way that you always had to him: alabaster skin, noble cheekbones, blue eyes: pale and delicate. Then you spoke again, your voice low and rhythmic.

"Rey, take a deep breath." She held both of his hands. "Now look around and feel the air. Feel my hand. Now listen, Rey. It's spring; the world is still young and so are we. As for this bullshit about your lost soul that you and David try to hide but believe, your soul is right here under your shirt. I can feel it beat. You are the soul. You are a human. No one can take that from you. You can't give that away."

He loved you. You loved him, I assume.

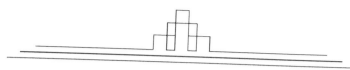

SAVE THE DATE

JUNE 1, 2011

Like a jealous teenager, I blamed Rey for taking you from me. I blamed him for you and Brenda and everything else in my life.

In late June, I walked home from mass. There in my front room, looking at the pale yellow wall was Sid Cutler. His gray hair gave the illusion of decay. He coughed, turned, then stared into my eyes and smiled.

My posture threatened him to leave, but I thought at the time that I could never intimidate him. He began to sweat, or perhaps continued; he was almost always sweating. His pink cheeks lifted to his eyes in glee before he spoke.

"When are you going to give up this farce that you are a priest, David?"

I refused to respond. I only stared into his eyes. He continued, "I know you, David. Remember how well I know you? You are not priest material."

I finally asked, "What do you want, Sid?"

"I want to call you off."

"From what?"

"From trying to save Rey Pescador. He is mine, not yours. He signed the contract. He belongs to me."

"You go back to hell."

He punched me in the face. I tried to fight back, but I could hardly stand. My mouth was bleeding. I finally reached my feet, and he threw me against the yellow wall. I slid to the ground. He sat on the couch across from me and rubbed his hand. He wiped the sweat off his forehead and spoke, "David, you think that Rey

251

marrying this girl is going to save him, but Rey will ruin her life. I need Rey as a playboy poet. He can't get married. And you must care enough for her to keep her from marrying someone like him."

"Married?" I asked. He laughed.

"You haven't heard? This is wonderful."

"What?"

"You are a damn fool, David. Rey and Rebecca are getting married in a week or so, in Ireland." He reached into his briefcase and handed me an invitation. "I'm sure yours just got lost in the mail."

The card-stock rested in my hands. Cutler laughed again and walked the four steps to the sidewalk and out of my vision. I sat on the top step of the porch, on the chipped green paint, like I had a hundred times before. All around me the city moved, each person a different cell in this massive body sustaining common life. There I was, motionless as always, sweating in my black clergy shirt. My head was pounding, so I lay down with my feet still on the step just below me. My knees were up, but my back was flat on the porch. I looked at the painted plywood above me. There were always cobwebs around the light in the middle of the porch. I guess I never really tried to clean it much. I closed my eyes and felt the sweat increase all over my body. It was so hot. I thought I might blackout from the pain in my head. I may have fallen asleep, or maybe I just daydreamed. I guess it wasn't really dreaming. There were no images, just the black and red of my eye sockets in the shade of the porch and the simple emotion of hate.

Then I thought about L.J.'s favorite universe, the one where an ageless Sid Cutler had died in the early 20th century. I imagined that Methodist minister in a bar in California 1906 writing a sermon on an old mahogany table bartop. The sermon must have been about the apocalyptic beast. The top right of the white paper is moist from the condensation of a Coca Cola. Then Sid Cutler eclipses the room with his tremendous girth. The minister thinks for a moment, and in that moment two realities split. In one he continues writing. Decades pass. Sid creates the RHC. I am born. Rey is born and 29-years-later, I want him dead. In the other, the minister jumps over the bar grabbing hold of the shotgun hidden on top of a case of Budweisers. He knows it's loaded. He aims and shoots buckshot into the stomach of the now charging globe of a man. Then he throws the gun to the ground and jumps back over the table. He crosses himself and stabs a knife into Sid Cutler's faintly beating heart. He leaves the knife but collects his sermon and Coca Cola.

That is how L.J. always told it. But he usually included the orange ripples of fat in Cutler's bleeding belly. I fantasized about that moment, the first time that I laid there on the porch. I always thought of myself as a pacifist, but if I had a gun and the shot and a knife, would I kill Sid Cutler?

I fell into a deep sleep after an hour or so. When I awoke, my head hurt even more. I resolved that I would finally become a man of action. I would win you as my wife regardless of the cost.

So I took a boat and got drunk every night on the Atlantic while dreaming of a different world.

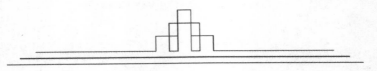

ANOTHER BOAT STORY

52

JULY 2-6, 2011

On the last night of my voyage, she emerged out of the velvet sky, illuminated by the boat's lights. I thumbed the bottle's cork with my left hand and my right rested on my chest feeling the dull click of my heart. I thought no one on the ship was awake but me. Some of the crew must be awake, but she was not part of the crew.

She wore a black dress that shone the fog light whenever it passed. Each glimpse was a new temptation. I was warm and drunk on north Atlantic air, revenge, and cabernet. She became the fourth intoxicant. In instances like this the truth may seem unbelievable. It may seem mythopoetic. It may seem too parallel with the past, but it is true. That is how these things work. He uses trends like waves to push and pull us where he wants.

She started to sing under her breath. She bent her leg at the knee lifting her foot, and then placed it back down on the ground. I watched her in the moments when the light of the boat shone on her. She did not know that I was there. I imagined that she would seduce me. I deserved it. I imagined taking off my collar and pretending I was someone normal. I imagined saying it was simply remnants of a private costume party.

I knew who she was. I had seen her in his sketches, his stories, his poems. This had to be the woman who seduced him on the boat. I wondered what it would be like to speak with her. To speak to her. To tell her that she is beautiful.

She stood so lightly on the ground. Her deep, auburn hair, the only color against the black and white of July clouds, remained in my occipital lobe even when I closed my eyes. I coughed. It was childish, but I coughed. I was afraid to speak with her. But a cough, of all the ways to get her attention, surrendered no part of my being.

She turned and looked at me. Her face, now apparent, was soft and distinct. Her eyes popped out from her face, slightly, just enough to hold my focus despite obvious trepidations.

"The clouds are amazing tonight," she said.

We paused and looked at them. She continued, "Look at that one. It looks like skate marks on the ice. Like God skated on the sea of heaven."

"It is beautiful. I've never seen anything quite like it."

"What is your name?"

"David."

"It's nice to meet you, David." She turned back around and looked at the sky a little longer. Now I couldn't hold my focus on her. I saw the stars lit behind the skate scars, and the crests of the northern Atlantic's waves. She leaned her head over the side of the ship and laughed. Singing under her breath, I almost stood; I almost walked to her; I almost stood behind her and touched her shoulders. I almost forgot everything I had learned. Then I thought of Rey's face. I thought of him standing in front of the altar a week earlier. The rain and the organ and the clouds and the waves and the black dress. The decision was simple. I would sit here and wait until she left. Then I would kill Rey Pescador.

"Don't you want to see the waves? You can't see them from there."

"Yes I can. I see them, a little farther out."

"That's no way to live watching the ocean through two rails of a ship."

"Come over here, David."

"I'm feeling a little dizzy. I think I should stay."

"You're drinking wine alone on a beautiful night? Let me have a drink."

"I don't have a glass, just the bottle." She walked to the chair and sat on the ottoman in front of me like a Buddha at the moment of enlightenment. Her dress rested just above her knees. Her legs were sublime. I took a long draught from the bottle and felt my mind swirl.

Then she took the bottle and drank. She looked at my face for a long time. I stared at her white and green eyes. I rested in that image for a moment until I said, "You're not who I thought you were."

"Who did you think I was?"

"Someone I heard a story of once. But she had brown hair, or blonde, I think. It's hard to keep it all straight. Your hair seems natural."

"It is. What was the story?"

"Well, you wouldn't believe it."

"Those are the best types of stories."

"All right, well, basically, my cousin told a story of a woman sent from the devil to seduce him on a yacht once. They dove in the water together, and when he came back to the surface he was lost in a search for her the rest of her life."

"That is unbelievable."

"Well, there's a lot more to it."

"So you thought I was sent here to seduce you?"

"No, that isn't what I'm saying."

"You think I am sent from the devil? Do you think that about all women, Father?"

"No, I'm not speaking metaphorically. This woman was sent by the devil. That was the story, at least."

"Maybe your cousin had it wrong. Maybe she was sent from God."

"Is there more wine?"

"A little."

"Let's finish it."

"OK."

"Who sent you here?"

"You tell me." She touched the white of my collar. "I never understood priests clothing. You wear black. Doesn't that represent sin, and then you have this tiny piece of white."

"Well, I'm learning that I'm mostly sinner, and a little saint."

"So if I pulled off this white collar, you would be like every other man."

"I guess I'd be unable to control myself."

"I shouldn't tease you. I should go. I didn't realize you were a priest when I first sat down. It's dark out."

She walked across the deck to the cabin. I stared at the clouds. Then back at her, but she seemed to have vanished into the Atlantic sky, into the clouds of ice. They were not scars. She was wrong about them. They were just clouds.

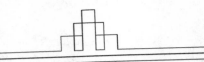

TO DIE IS GAIN

CH 53

JULY 7, 2011

The singer didn't visit me again on the boat as I traveled in a pocket of air across the Atlantic to southern France where it met another pocket and shifted, heating Ireland. It was unusual, as were its effects. The island boiled in a rare, blistering summer July. Record highs had swept across the Atlantic and now threatened the continent. Rey sensed the change nearly a week before and even suggested moving the reception indoors. He said that he could smell it in the air. The locals mocked him. It would never reach 35 degrees Celsius in Ireland. The day it finally did was the day of the ceremony. Rey dressed in his tuxedo early and walked the grounds of the church looking for something to distract his nerves.

The church was on a ten-acre plot of land. The building was small and white. There was a grassy field and a cemetery. The wind that pulled me to that island opened the clouds above the church. The sun shone and heated Sid Cutler's black Bentley parked just south of the church.

While Sid sat and I waited in a tiny European cab that bounced me through ancient streets to striking distance of Rey Pescador, Rey walked the grounds of the cemetery just beyond the rows of perfectly placed wooden chairs. I remember how white they were in contrast to the grass, the leaves, and the gravestones. As he walked, he saw the tombstone, which bore a worn Celtic cross. It was nearly two hundred years old. I visited it during the first year after Christian was born, when you refused to talk with me. I retraced a lot of my steps that year. The man buried there was named "Jon Keegan." Despite my best efforts I do not know much of his background, but I know his tombstone. Under the cross were the words: "mihi enim vivere Christus est et mori lucrum." Rey sat for a while sweating in the tuxedo. He untied his black bow tie. He hadn't studied Latin for that long, so he wasn't sure of the translation. His Spanish helped, but even that was rusty.

The parish priest was one of the first priests to receive the artificial heart. In 1976 he experienced an incredible pain in his chest. The doctors told him he suffered from heart disease. They told him it was the number one killer in the world. He never questioned the effects his decisions would have on his life, his soul; he simply fought to live. Receiving the artificial heart was not a conscious decision for him; it was merely instinct. After nearly twelve surgeries his "disease" was healed. He no longer had a human heart. He was free to live as long as he wanted.

The priest saw Rey in the graveyard from his office on the south end of church. When he arrived at the tombstone, Rey was sitting in the grass.

"Father what does this mean?" Rey asked.

"Well, that is one of my favorite verses. Rey, it says, "To live is Christ.""

"I got that much, but it says something else. Something about death. What is lucrum?"

"Oh, yes, you're right. To me to live is Christ; to die is to gain, to profit."

"So death is luckier than it seems?"

"There are pages of exegetical analysis on this passage, but they are for another time. Never think of death when the bride is near. Let's celebrate."

Rey stayed behind for a little while. He thought of composing a poem. He knew of no other way to process the weight of the moment. Perhaps he could read it at the ceremony in a few hours. He thought of his death. He thought of your death and determined there was nothing poetic about the death of a beautiful woman, but the death of a man, he thought, a certain type of death could have some poetry in it. A shovel rested against the fence. An empty plot stood ten meters away. He thought of digging his own grave there and then. His heart was sick. It was diseased. He knew he would die, and it had terrified him his whole life. Amidst a stream of thoughts, he began to breathe the words from the tomb. The experience was purely natural: no training from the monks, no words of encouragement from a homily could have taught him how to respond. He simply breathed in: to me to live is Christ. He felt the presence of the crucifix on his scar. He breathed out, "To die is gain. To die is gain." He thought of Aldonza on the beach: after she gave him the crucifix, she disappeared into the crowd of people celebrating the holy day. It was a day of epiphany, a day of light, and yet while he rested there he had seen nothing but the blurred images of the near-sighted fool whose glasses still rest on his bedside table.

The heat fell farther down on Rey. Amidst the freedom of epiphany, he felt the guilt of his sin creeping back into his mind. Guests were beginning to arrive, the men in their black and white and women in the colors of spring. The Bentley now waited fifty meters away on the small road just south of the church. The black in its metal radiated the heat. Rey saw it. He remembered his benefactor, his manager, his owner, and shuddered. He tried to speak out loud, "To me to live is..." He stuttered on the words.

It was time for the sacrament.

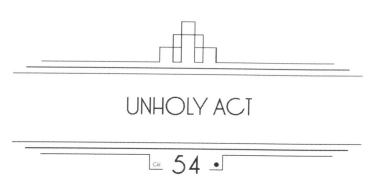

UNHOLY ACT

54 •

JULY 7, 2011

I don't think you saw me when the bells rang and the doors opened with the white and black flood of symbolic clothing. You stepped out of the church first, while Rey was holding your newly-ringed hand from behind. For that brief moment with the Poet in the shadows, I almost saw myself there with you in a little church in Ireland celebrating a commitment to live together in seemingly eternal joy. Then Rey emerged into the light; never before have I hated anyone so much.

To hate your neighbor is the same as to kill him; I never understood that until I saw Rey step from the shadows of that old church and kiss you. He smiled and kissed you again as the guests exited in the parabolic gravity of young love. Amidst all of my anger and self-righteousness, I never decided what I would do when and if I saw Rey married to you. I had imagined arriving to the ceremony early. I had imagined warning you of his lost soul. I imagined you slapping him and leaving. Then you'd seek my company to mend the loss that you felt.

The cab drive, the boat trip, the singer, the booze all hit me at once, as did the blinding light as I stepped from under the tree. I ran from the shadows of that tree. I heard the faint song of a bird. I heard the flashbulbs. I could almost taste the whiskey as half the crowd opened a bottle. I ran through the horseshoe of guests pushing past L.J. who hardly noticed me, and landed directly behind Rey as he kissed his bride. Surely you didn't expect me to hit him or you would have warned him. I punched him twice before he even knew what was happening. Then you, watching, unable to pull me from Rey, saw his face open and bleed.

The matter was worsened by Brovault's attempt to help. He grabbed my arm as it was cocked and ready to punch again, but he weighed so little that my attempted jab threw him over Rey and into the local sheriff. Until that point the sheriff was relieved to see the fight. For him, a simple fistfight of priest and groom was pure old-fashioned entertainment, until an emaciated genius fell into his newly poured glass of whiskey spilling it on his only good suit.

To tell you the truth, that is all I remember from the wedding. Rey later told me that I yelled some Latin. He said that I fell like a ton of bricks when the sheriff hit me with his baton.

In the cell that evening, I heard the sheriff say that he wished he had a gun like they had in the states so he could end the "commotion once and for all." Either way, I had served my purpose to some extent. Rey spent his wedding night with me and L.J. Brovault in a 12 by 12 jail cell rather than with his bride. I tried to contact the priest about annulling the marriage on the grounds that Rey was actually soulless, and therefore dead, but the fact that you were pregnant with his child and I had just attacked the magnanimous groom didn't help my argument.

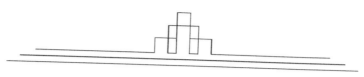

PRISON BREAK

CH 55

JULY 8, 2011

In the triangular void between L.J. Brovault, Rey Pescador's soulless body, and me rested the entire expanse of life and death, damnation and salvation, love and hate, or at least that is how it felt. No one spoke, save Brovault who simply muttered every so often to himself. I calculated the distance between Rey and me. I estimated that it was about seven feet. I thought of the size of the room as the perfect isosceles triangle. I thought of the angles, the significance of distance and possibility of mathematics. I've ignored it much of my life, but in that moment the time and space and physics seemed to matter more than anything. I thought of the movement it would take to reach Rey, to bash his head into the cement and to watch him die.

Brovault chanted and shook. He cried at one point. I focused solely on the fact that Rey Pescador's soul was disembodied and already roasting in hell while this abandoned shell mocked the image of God. Why shouldn't I, who gave him grace so many times, be the one to recycle his shell? I had the power to bind on earth and in heaven. Why shouldn't I kill Rey Pescador's soulless flesh?

Rey shifted in his sleep. He still wore his white tie under his tuxedo. He hadn't wiped any of the blood off his face, which had begun to swell and bruise. His hands rested behind his head with none of the significance of a Steinbeck character at rest. In another world he might be sucking on a long piece of grass reveling in the satisfaction of work, but in this world he simply lay on that cold cement floor longing for his bride. Then he opened his eyes in what first appeared to be horror. He moved his hands from behind his head and spread perpendicular to his frame, not at all like a bird taking flight.

"Tell me, David," he finally spoke. "Why do you love her so much?"

I didn't respond.

"I know it's not that you hate me. I mean, you don't hate me enough for this. You might have tried to justify it theologically, as if you were protecting her from an unholy marriage or some shit like that, but I know that's not what it is. So you must love her. I wish you would have told me."

I still did not speak. I just looked at his tired eyes as he stared at the ceiling.

"Well, I suppose this is it for you and me, David, but there is some information that you may have never considered. First, you are a priest. You chose that, not me. You can't marry her. Second, I love her too. Do you really think I'm not capable of being a good husband? Maybe you do, but that isn't your call anymore. Third, well, you promised to help me find salvation. And I would appreciate if you still did."

I clenched my fist ready to murder him. The room was silent save the muttering of Brovault. He rocked and whispered and groaned. Each groan became louder until he started to shout. Well, it was more like a bark than a shout. His brain was becoming lost forever. He had searched the darkest recesses of the human experience for so long that his neural make up could no longer keep up with the visions that he saw. In a moment of lucidity he paused and looked at me, then Rey and shouted, "Stop fighting! You must save us!" Rey and I laughed. We couldn't help it. In the midst of Brovault's vanishing into nothingness, he shouted again at us like we were school children bickering in class, "Stop fighting!"

It worked. We both said that we would stop fighting. He told Rey again that Rey must save us all.

"How do you suppose I do that?" Rey asked.

"There is a mountain. Climb to heaven. We must climb, all of us."

"Where is it?"

"It is the one I triangulated when David and I were in Spain. It is in my notebook in the attic. You need to leave soon."

"We need to leave, you mean."

He began to weep and shouted something in Latin. Then, L.J. Brovault, the prophet of the absurd, vanished into thin air.

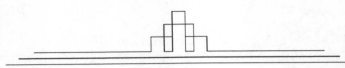

THE MOUNTAIN OF GOD

⌐ CH 56 ⌐

2037

Just west of the country's deepest valley is its tallest mountain: the mountain of God. Mt. Whitney rises out from Death Valley in the East and the world's largest living things in the West. It keeps heaven from falling on the earth, or at least that's what L.J. said.

I started climbing it again this morning, not the whole journey, just a day trip to Lone Pine Lake: holy water in the midst of a desert, 10,000 feet too high. I'll spend my day here finishing this story of the first part of my life. Then I'll walk back down to the base camp and imagine the water of the lakes and creeks that paint the backcountry in the colors of the sky.

I hope you see this soon. I hope you swim here with me.

I can show you where Rey told each story, where we got lost in the backcountry, and where we thought we saw L.J.'s spectral image. We thought he would come back that whole trip. But we never saw him again.

L.J.'s disappearance in the prison shook Rey more deeply than I expected. His response to L.J. and to you and me when we were released showed me that he wasn't my enemy. Rey Pescador was merely a corpse, decaying, lost. He was not a villain. In the prison, when he started to cry, I realized that there was more at stake than my revenge. I had to forgive him.

You know the next part. Rey kissing you goodbye the day after your wedding, and our journey to America. You know of the trains and boats and taxis. The plan was simple: find the mountain, climb it, wait for God to speak audibly to us, and ask God to make Sid give Rey's soul back. After that he would return

to his bride and child and live happily ever after.
It could not be simpler.

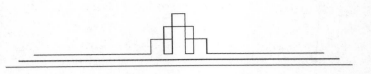

CHRISTIAN

57

2037

Last month, when I received the Bishop's letter, I didn't open it. I just put it on the empty desk where the white envelope juxtaposed my mahogany desk like a soon-to-be museum artifact. Christian was in town from California. We met for coffee and sandwiches. I knew the letter had to do with my post, but I wanted one more time to see your son with the status quo: as a parish priest and his spiritual father.

He had aged so much over the last year. He still had Rey's chin that narrowed and pointed to the ground, but his face had grown wider. His lifestyle, though exponentially healthier than his father's, is static, allowing fat and memories and money and love and education to hang on to his body in ways that Rey never knew. Facing the back of the restaurant I watched him through the reflection of a mirror. He ordered his coffee and sandwich. He smiled at the server and had Rey's charm, but he had none of Rey's ulterior motives. That is to say, if Christian thought of falling in love with all the women in the restaurant, neither they nor I expected.

He did not notice me at first. My hair has turned even more silver in the last few months. When he finally noticed my collar and the table filled with letters, he called out, "Father David," and embraced me.

"Christian, how are you?"

"I'm great. How are you, Father?"

"I am well."

"How is the church? I'm hoping to visit this weekend."

"It is good. It's dwindling, like everywhere. We still have a few faithful parishioners, and others float in everyday looking for something they've lost. Let's talk about something else. I want to hear of you and your youth."

"Well, I have a new job."

"Are you practicing law?"

"No, I am a consultant."

"Tell me about it."

"It's kind of boring."

"I don't mind. I embrace the boring parts of life."

"Well, I work in the enterprise content management and document management solutions. I deal primarily in litigious situations, offering legal counsel as well as document management solutions."

"Fascinating." I didn't understand a word of it.

"My office is great. I look out on the San Francisco business district. The metal and glass reflects the light differently all day long. The view is always changing."

"So there is beauty in a metal world."

"There always has been. You should know that as much as anyone."

We both ate silently and enjoyed each other's company. I asked, "Are you seeing anyone?"

"Yes, Father, that's one of the reasons for my visit. I am hoping to propose to her soon."

"Does she have a name?"

"Natalie."

"Natalie. Will she will take your name?"

"She will."

"Natalie Pescador. There will be another Pescador in the world."

"Father, would you be willing to perform the ceremony?"

"Of course, I will. Only God could keep me from being there. When?"

"We haven't set a date. But we have discussed next spring."

"This is the best news I've heard all year. Tell me about her."

"Well, she is beautiful and smart. She is a pediatric resident in a San Jose's children's hospital. She wants a large family."

"I didn't know that anyone wanted that anymore."

"She is quite an enigma, a true anachronism."

He spent some of our time looking at the phone in front of him. He read social media, checked the time, looked at stocks and scores and read the news. It wasn't rude. That's not my point. He shared with me what he was doing, and I wrote while he sat with me. We were as comfortable as we've always been. We talked about life for a while.

He seemed the same as Rey or I, though his whole life was foreign to me. Everything we did to raise him correctly ensured that he would never understand the world of my youth. He was out of some other world. I was pleased, but as I sat with him, I wondered if he would ever see beauty the way his father and I did, if he could ever summon the muse while advising CEOs where to place their make-believe documents stored hundreds of miles away in giant servers.

They say there are nine muses. Does one deal with workflow solutions?

A HUMAN HEART

58

AUGUST - SEPTEMBER 2011

In the mornings the sun watched us wake. Without agenda or alarms ringing we saw colors paint the ceiling of our earth.

I want to tell this part of the story now.

Never before have I wanted to. Never have I known how. When asked directly, I've ignored it, or lied. I even lied under oath. I have faced several problems with telling this section of our lives: the first is that Rey never told it to me. I never had the benefit of his muse. Everything else that I've written, he told me in detail. Some of the stories I had heard a dozen times. Others he told me during that month that we spent in the mountain. I've drawn from his style. The second problem is that, like much of this story, you will think that I have lost my mind, and this part I can't blame on Rey's imagination. This I know is true.

During the first week, Rey and I saw yellow and pink and white in the air. We said to each other, "It is beautiful out here." We said it as simply as that and soberly continued our morning. *It is beautiful.* The sun is beautiful. That is what men say, men who have seen robots fight, cars hit humans. That is what men whose hearts tick like antique clocks say when the sun gives color and energy throughout the ever-changing atmosphere.

We found a creek fueled by melt-water. We followed it. We lived from it and slept near it, and as we climbed higher and then lower and into the backcountry, we watched it become a snake with crystal scales when the sun set. Then Rey would lie on his back next to his blanket and tent right there in the hard earth and

271

sleep. During those moments, I would sit and smoke Rey's cigarettes. For Rey, it was a foolish time to smoke as the oxygen preferred the lower altitudes. I guess it was even more foolish for me. My heart struggled with the higher altitudes. It had not had time to adjust, and I certainly wasn't going to go to an RHC clinic and tell them I needed it recalibrated for high altitudes.

Lying there smoking with me, it's strange to think that Rey was only thirty. He had changed somehow, even since his wedding. But I guess that is the age for beginnings and endings.

His hair had ceased to gray, which it had a bit in the year after selling his soul. Eventually, he dyed it, but he carried a lot of gray hairs under the dye. Once we started hiking in the mountain, it was dark again without the artificial ink. He no longer had the pressure of striving, just the simple pleasure of being.

Primal, was the word that flooded my mind, partly because Rey always used it to describe himself. In Rey's third book, *This Primal Life*, he told a fable of a man who climbed a tree to avoid a serpent. In the tree was a monkey who taught him to laugh. I don't know why I thought of that, but everything around me was primal; it beat and beat and beat and beat.

One morning in the middle of August, I slept before the sun drifted out of view. Asleep, I saw the future: a white python crawled out of the stone where I rested watching the world turn black. It covered me and burrowed into the ground on the other side. Again and again it tied me to the solid rock until, the final time it emerged and, without looking me in the face or asking my name, it broke through my sternum without pain, it removed my heart. I heard its steady tick. I saw its red light. I felt my life slip away, and suddenly in a final moment of terror, it held a human heart in front of my face. It said *silence* as it planted the foreign organ in me.

Over a quarter century later, this year, it came true, though not literally, like the rest of these stories. The Sunday after Christian returned to you in San Francisco, that serpent, Sid Cutler, sent the woman from the boat, from several boats, to mass at my little church in the center of the city. It was to be my final mass. I still hadn't opened the letter that informed me I would no longer be a priest, but I knew its contents. I knew that the bishop was "freeing" us from our vows. There were other priests who needed posts. There were as many priests as parishioners and no one was dying to make way for the youth. They blamed the low attendance on us, so the solution was to let us go live normal lives after a full life of service. I would take the offer. I would take off my collar later that day and never put it back on, but I wanted one last mass.

I hope you forgive me for that. I loved being a priest, but I will follow the bishop. And you must have known that when you left I wasn't a very good priest anyway. You must have known that with you gone I would drink too much alone at night. You must have known that I would stumble late into the confessional and mumble during the mass, if left alone.

Rey's muse, the singer, was not the only one in the service, though I could not tell you who else was there. The others were simply a distraction from the singular focus that she drew. Her voice had force, momentum; it was unsteady and fleshy like Rey's. Stripped from the allure of our previous meeting, she wore black and never stood during the service, but she sang a few lines of a hymn and spoke during the peace. She said the Lord's Prayer; she may have said the creeds. By then, I was lost in a world of what ifs.

Then mass was over. I was in my office. She was in my office. It was the year 2037; everything in my life was normal except the fact that the mythical singer from my former life was sitting there in the office at my parish.

She sat there across from me. She was real, a relic of the past that was real and breathing here. By then, I had forgotten my dream on the mountain. I had forgotten the snake that replaced my heart. It was only a dream or maybe the result of the air shortening and my heart's mechanisms warning me that, despite the myriad upgrades, it required more steady oxygen. I never realized that I had been given a warning, a vision, a prophecy meant to save my eternal soul.

She had aged only slightly over the twenty-five years, but that was normal enough. Few people showed much age between 30 and 55-years-old. She looked at my desk. She saw the letter from the Bishop. She felt its airy weight. She touched it with her fingers. I saw her nails, polished purple. Between the freedom of that letter and her gymnast frame, she could have floated me out of the office into the sky above.

"David," she began.

"What do you need?" I said as coldly as I could muster though still moving closer to her without any self-control.

"Please do not be so harsh with me. I have never harmed you."

"I know who you work for."

"Do you? What do you really know about me? Let me guess, I am some creation of Rey Pescador's imagination, like any other number of women, some femme fatale. Do you even know my name?"

"No."

"Then what did Rey call me?"

"He usually calls you the singer, sometimes the siren."

"I'm not surprised, he would."

"What do you need?"

"I need your help, a business proposition. I am dying." The word struck me. I was deeply envious.

"How is that possible?"

"I'm dying of a heart defect. I need you to forgive my sins. Then I have an offer for you, something I think you've always wanted."

"That's impossible."

I walked closer to see her face. She was no older than sixty, maybe even younger: she still had the color of youth. There is no way she had a first generation robotic heart. Only the very first pilot model, before the RHC Deluxe (which was the first mass-market model) would have had any defects that could kill her.

"You cannot be old enough to die."

"David, you need to consider this proposition. If you don't believe my heart could fail, I will show you."

By then I was close enough to smell her breath. I could hear her breath more unsteadily, more deeply than anyone I had heard in a long time. She was wearing a black dress. She told me that she had something to give to me. She told me she had something for me to feel like I had never felt before. She told me she had what I had always wanted. She removed the two black straps of her dress, and pushed it slowly to the floor.

I put my arms around her back and pulled her to my body. She pushed me away, took my hand and held against her bare chest in the middle, just over her sternum. I did not move my hand to the right or to the left. I realized what she offered was more than sex. Her heart beat *lub dub, lub dub, lub dub, lub dub.*

My God, it was the most beautiful rhythm I had ever heard.

"David, if you grant Sid Cutler one request, he will give you a human heart."

"What is his request?"

"He wants you never to tell the story of Rey Pescador. He wants to meet you for dinner tomorrow to talk about it."

"Will you be there?"

"I will."

She put her dress back on and wrote the address for my meeting with Sid before leaving my office more hastily than I wished, though she sang on the way out; she gave me that much. I stood there for a long time looking out the window at the city. It was a quiet day.

Finally, I opened the Bishop's letter. It was more forceful than I thought. Not only did he want to promote a younger priest, but my fiasco with the Macintosh 512 earlier this year was enough to get me defrocked. I was no longer a priest in the one holy Catholic and apostolic church.

I drank some wine and decided that I must never see Sid Cutler again. Don't get me wrong, I wanted to meet with Sid. I intended to meet with him. I thought there was nothing I wanted more than a human heart, but then I thought about you. I had already ruined everything with you. I would give up that dream to have a chance with you. If I met with Sid, I would never have that chance.

Back at the house, I packed as little as possible. I took all of Rey's notebooks, some clothes, the bottle of Lilac Whiskey, my crucifix, and all the jeans and t-shirts I had. I brought letters and books, but not many. I decided I would write more than read from now on. I had read and lived a lifetime. I had plenty to say about it all.

I took a cab to Midway and almost bought tickets to Fresno before realizing that Sid Cutler might follow me. I'm not paranoid, but I figured if he cared enough about Rey's stories to offer me a heart, I should stay off the radar for a while. I withdrew all of my money from savings and bought a car in cash. Then I drove for the better part of two days, stopping only to eat and sleep before reaching, Lone Pine, California. I rented this room. I filled it with food and books. I've made it comfortable for the nights that I'm indoors.

My plan to stay off-the-radar hasn't worked too well. After all, Rey is a sort of god in this area, just off the mountain. It took about five minutes in town for a GB fan to spot me. But I like it. I have company regularly at the motel. Most of the guys are old, about my age, guys who can remember the tours and dreams of those years. Some are younger literature majors who wish that writing could regain its former swagger.

No matter whom I am with, we talk about the old days when the world was wild. At first I was scared to be around some of the old timers who have spent years on the mountain. I mean there are some who blamed me for what happened; or rather they blamed me for whatever conspiracy theory they had construed. Even you wouldn't talk with me after the wedding fiasco and the trip to the mountain. How long was it until you forgave me for all the stupid stuff I did that year? I think Christian was about eighteen months when I visited my parents, and you were there. Even though my parents were Christian's great aunt and uncle, it was gracious to go there and risk seeing me. I think you still hated me.

Luckily, none of these guys are into that conspiracy anymore. There are plenty of other conspiracies they believe, though. You wouldn't believe the people out here at the edge of civilization. There are still some fans who believe Rey is living somewhere out there under the canopy of heaven.

You will be the first to know what really happened, that is other than me.

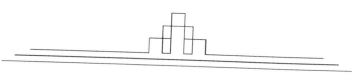

59

SEPTEMBER 2, 2011

It is evening. The sun is setting, and I am lying outside my tent. I hope that the desert keeps the rain away, tonight especially. A long time ago Sid Cutler gave me a bottle of Lilac Whiskey. I was always afraid to drink it. I feared it was akin to selling my soul, to making a deal. I am no longer afraid; after all, I am writing the story that he never wanted told.

I am writing it with that vintage in my blood.

26 years ago, I woke before Rey on that final morning. I saw the sunlight differently. It was grayer, some might say it was gray, but you and I both know that it is simply the palest blue, which became bluer and bluer and bluer until it merged into the pale pink of eternity.

We were near the top of the mountain around 12,000 feet. We had hiked, and soon we would have to climb. We had spent almost a week resting near Mirror Lake. Its water was undeniably pure. It is where I swore to the judge that Rey had vanished.

We left the lake while the pale blue was still pale and approached the summit. During those days no one climbed the mountain anymore. The metal hearts could hardly handle the fine air, and it wasn't until the most famous man on earth disappeared that climbing a mountain seemed cool again. Rey climbed faster than me, and while he waited for me to catch up, he prayed audibly. He believed, more than anything that God would speak to him from atop the mountain. He believed that he would be forgiven. He would return and fulfill his grand destiny. I told him that even without the audible word of God, this trek, this journey of faith was a sufficient pilgrimage, but now he was not content with salvation. He wanted to be a legend.

When we were just five hundred feet from the summit, I thought I was dying. I was dizzy. My mind tricked me. I remembered things I had long forgotten. I remembered things I hoped to forget. "Rey, I am finished here."

"You can make it, Cuz."

"You don't understand. I do not have the heart for it. It pumps the same, steady rate. My blood needs more oxygen. If we wait a week, it will recalibrate, but I can't make it today."

"David, your heart will continue. I promise. Men with artificial hearts have climbed mountains."

"Some have died."

"Since when have you feared death?"

It was nothing like I imagined. The landscape, rocks on rocks on rock, the result of billions of years of tectonic violence from far below the earth's surface. And yet, in the stillness of silence, I felt peace.

"I see the summit. David, let's move."

I crawled toward the top. My vision blurred. My lungs captured whatever they could and sent it to my blood. Then I saw the crystal water above me. It was an ocean with a floor. Over the valley hung what seemed like a giant piece of plexiglass aching with the eternal weight of heaven. The only cloud in the sky touched it and filled with water and began to leak and finally burst onto my head and arms and the rock. Rey was ahead of me, out of sight. Everything became hard and wet except for my skin. It was soft and slippery. The lightning that struck the mountain brightened the sky, and accompanied the thundering voice of God which echoed over the valleys. God was speaking to Rey and me, but it wasn't clear what he was saying.

I could still see some blue in the sky to the east and gray to the west, so I crawled more and watched electricity connect heaven and earth.

Then the cloud moved past the mountain and the colors returned. At any moment it could burst over the valley and make the forests oceans. The path was impassable. Now we had to climb. We had no ropes or experience. Rey was in sight now above me singing and chanting and rhyming. I could only guess the poems he composed during that hike, poems that the world had never known before. I would give my whole career to be able to recount the words that he said, but my brain only noticed the wet black rock and the ocean of heaven weighing ominously above our heads.

I stopped to catch what oxygen I could about fifty feet from the top. The accomplishment was good enough for me. "Let's head back," I shouted. I wanted to head back. But Rey was now a dozen feet or so away from me looking at the summit.

He took off his shoes.

He took off his clothes and fell to his knees.

The wind raced over the summit from the east into our faces. I covered my eyes and prayed that I could die. Then I prayed for the naked, soulless man in front of me.

Rey cried aloud, "God, forgive me! Christ, forgive me! God, forgive me!"

He stood and climbed carefully up the final ten feet. I thought of shouting to him to place his shoes back on his feet. He was killing himself; there was no way he would make it back without his feet infected. But I had no breath. I had no words. I only had eyes.

He reached the summit and jumped in celebration. His head hit something hard.

Lifting his arms with what must have been the last of his energy, he felt the strange texture of the plexiglass that I thought had only existed in my mind. It was hard; he knocked on it. I heard the sound. His eyes closed as he placed his hand through the barricade and water leaked through the strange glass-like film onto the mountain. It covered him and flooded down until it seeped into my clothing. Through the opening, light shone brightly amidst a million miles of crystal clear water.

L.J. had been right. It was the mountain of God, but God did not speak audibly. He simply opened the door to heaven. Then, like a gymnast reaching for the rings, Rey faced heaven. He faced upward with his hand directly above his body, and then pushed both of his hands back to earth. The force propelled him upward, above the pinnacle.

The water continued to flood the mountain from the sky. The light continued to bounce off each drenched rock. The wind continued to blow, and Rey Pescador's body met its soul on the bottom of the Crystal Sea.

He looked toward the earth shocked and confused. He stood on the floor of the water. His brown sinewy physique was not blurred by the water; rather, he seemed more himself than ever before. He walked toward me, surveyed the earth he loved, and smiled. I have translated that smile a thousand ways and still can't describe it to you. The closest I can come to showing you is that it is the way he smiled at you when he walked out of your wedding, just before I punched him in the face, but that seems too sentimental.

After smiling at me and his world, he faced upward and swam. I watched him for a while still trying my best to breathe. But soon Rey Pescador was forever out of my sight.

You may wonder why I didn't follow him. I tried. The door was not open to me yet. L.J. said it would be open that day. Or at least, L.J. gave us the signs that showed it was that day, but it didn't stay open long enough for me to make it. Or maybe I was deemed unfit. Somehow, I didn't regret it. I just climbed back down to the earth, to you and the normal life that I never knew I wanted.

I suppose I could say more about Rey or myself. I could definitely go deeper into some of his stories and your stories, but you know most of that. The rest, well, the rest is a series of myths and tall-tales as unbelievable as anything here. But as Rey often said, "You know they're all true." So after twenty-six years of remembering how the water of heaven saturated my clothes, I have returned here.

I hope you will join me.

I hope you will climb with me.

I hike up the mountain quite a bit, but I do not plan to climb to the summit for some time. I want to give you time to read this and find your way to me at the motel or Lone Pine Lake. I will promise to be at this address at the first of every month until I decide to leave for good.

But if you don't come this year, and the mountain promises

heaven, I will head for the backcountry. I will sleep next to my tent and watch the sunlight rise in the morning. I will climb to heaven and hope that it opens for me. If it does not I will climb to the bottom and try again.

If you join me, I hope you will marry me, and we will make love under the stars whenever you want. If you do not join me, I will wonder as I do now: is there sequence in eternity like the simple etchings on a timeline? Or do we move in heaven through time and space?

The resurrection is bodily, but could your body disperse into a million square miles to paint the sunrise in the fading eyes of an old priest? I believe that it was you that I saw that morning we climbed. It was you that locked the door for heaven to make me wait. It was your eternal soul in the sky, who made sure I would spend decades more on earth, so we could raise Christian together and live our lives together. This morning I saw you again in the sky: your body stretching miles and miles in the pale blue and pink. I saw you again send color to me.

I hope next month to hear a knock on my door and see you standing there. I hope to marry you. I hope not to be a bachelor for the rest of my life. I hope you forgive me and we walk this planet until our metal hearts rust or heaven opens in a rush of holy water. But either way the grayest blue of your eyes, the palest pink of your cheeks will refract the sun and wake me to each morning's mystery.

It was all true,
David E. Rosario

Made in the USA
Lexington, KY
01 November 2017